HOW TO
MOON A CAT

Center Point
Large Print

Also by Rebecca M. Hale
and available from Center Point Large Print:

How to Wash a Cat
Nine Lives Last Forever

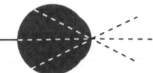

**This Large Print Book carries the
Seal of Approval of N.A.V.H.**

HOW TO MOON A CAT

REBECCA M. HALE

CENTER POINT PUBLISHING
THORNDIKE, MAINE

This Center Point Large Print edition is published in the year 2011 by arrangement with Berkley Books, a member of Penguin Group (USA) Inc.

The text of this Large Print edition is unabridged. In other aspects, this book may vary from the original edition. Printed in the United States of America on permanent paper. Set in 16-point Times New Roman type.

ISBN: 978-1-61173-231-3

Library of Congress Cataloging-in-Publication Data

Hale, Rebecca M.
  How to moon a cat : a cats and curios mystery / Rebecca M. Hale. — Center Point large print ed.
  p. cm.
  ISBN 978-1-61173-231-3 (library binding : alk. paper)
  1. Treasure troves—Fiction. 2. Cats—Fiction. 3. San Francisco (Calif.)—Fiction.
  4. Large type books. I. Title.
  PS3608.A54576H35 2011
  813'.6—dc23
                                                      2011032562

For the M's:
Morgan, Malcolm, and Miranda

Introduction

THE GLASSY BUBBLE of a full moon bobbed merrily up the California coast, its shining image rippling across the evening tide. Carefree and giddy, the bewitching orb frolicked above the shoreline's rocky outcroppings, skirted the east side of the Farallon Islands, and bounced softly through the looping lines of the Golden Gate Bridge.

Inside the bay, the moon's glowing marble rolled along the outer edge of San Francisco's waterfront, past a line of darkened and abandoned piers, until it reached a compact collection of apartment buildings fringing the financial district. The bulk of the glimmering mass hovered in place while a white shaft of light zoomed inland over the hard green surface of a tennis court to cut a twinkling path up through the empty streets of Jackson Square.

The beam stopped in the middle of a block of darkened storefronts and honed in on the red brick facade of an antique store. A spectral spotlight splashed across the front row of windowpanes, illuminating the green vase icon embedded into each section of glass. On a counter just inside the store, a cash register's burnished brass detailing flickered in the passing light.

Slowly, the focus of the moonbeam panned up

the side of the building toward the apartment located above the showroom. A slight spring breeze whispered through the night, fluttering the blinds hanging over the open window on the building's third floor, allowing a single sliver of light to maneuver stealthily through the narrow opening in the slats.

Inside the room, the luminous finger skimmed across the wooden floorboards to the bed pushed up against the far wall. Leaping nimbly onto the pile of sheets and blankets, the beam kinked to tickle the bottom of a cat's upturned foot, playfully tugging at the feathery white hairs that poked out between the plump pink padding of his toes.

Rupert's front incisors moved up and down. Dreamily, he licked his lips, but the peaceful rhythm of his snores continued unabated.

The warmth of the mischievous ray sidled up to the furry mound of Rupert's exposed belly and gave it a prodding poke—an action which elicited no more than a wheezing *snort*.

Momentarily stumped, the moon paused to reconsider its strategy. A more aggressive approach would be needed to wake *this* sleeping beast.

Narrowing to a pointed prick of light, the beam crept up to Rupert's chest and tapped the moist cushion of his nose. Rupert raised a paw over his face, trying to block the glare of the tiny spotlight.

Noting the movement, the beam branched out into an illuminated hand and reached behind Rupert's head to scratch the backside of his orange-tipped ears. As the corners of Rupert's mouth stretched into an appreciative smile, the beam gently teased the crook of Rupert's elbow until he dropped the shielding paw from his face. Sensing victory, the beam sneaked back up to the tightly shut juncture of Rupert's furry eyelids and softly pried them open.

With a wide yawn, Rupert awoke and glanced around the room.

It was an hour or two past midnight, dark and quiet inside the apartment above the Green Vase showroom. The other two occupants of the bed were still fast asleep: a second cat, his sister Isabella, and a woman with long brown hair who, in his opinion, was hogging the covers.

Rupert smacked his lips as the wild call of the moon worked its magic on his feline imagination. A shimmering figure danced across the bedroom, beckoning him to follow it into the hallway. Rupert blinked his eyes, trying to clear his vision as the trickling stream of moonlight tangoed teasingly toward the door, a tempting lure no cat could ignore.

With a muffled *thump,* Rupert hopped off the bed and followed the sparkling shape through the doorway. As he stepped outside the bedroom, the edge of the wall snuffed out the intruding angle of the moon, temporarily releasing him from its hypnotic hold.

Rupert set loose another mouth-stretching yawn and looked sleepily back toward the warm spot in the covers he had just vacated. The line of his body curved as his shoulders rotated to reverse course. But before he could complete the turn, a faint glow appeared on the floor at his feet, recapturing his attention.

Intrigued once more, Rupert proceeded down a trail of glittering moon dust to the second floor. He paused at the threshold of the kitchen and stared curiously inside, his head tilted upward, the orange tip of his fluffy tail pointed at the ceiling. A tiny lick of light lassoed the furry white cuff of his neck and led him forward.

Rupert ambled toward the kitchen table, the toenails on his chunky feet clicking against the uneven floor tiles. A rumble gurgled up from somewhere inside his pudgy round stomach, an instinctive biological response to the growing proximity of his food bowl.

The moon waited until Rupert reached the middle of the room; then it withdrew its influence and sat back to watch the rest of its mischief unfold.

Puzzled, Rupert plopped down beside the table, his tail twitching in bewilderment. His head rotated back and forth as his dazed eyes scanned the dark shadows that sank in around him.

What am I doing here? he wondered groggily.

He couldn't quite remember what urge or motivation had inspired him to leave the warmth of the blankets in the upstairs bedroom. His chin drooped as the weight of his furry eyelids sank down over his bleary blue eyes. The light drone of a snore began to ooze through his nasal passages. He was on the verge of collapsing into a comatose heap on the tile floor when his ears picked up on a sound coming from the far side of the room—the almost imperceptible patter of tiny feet.

With a surprised grunt, Rupert pivoted his round rump toward the back wall of the kitchen. The scampering footsteps came to a sudden halt, as if the perpetrator had sensed Rupert's presence.

Rupert listened intently for a long eerie moment, but the room was completely silent. *Perhaps it had all been a dream,* he thought drowsily.

Tiptoe. Tiptoe. Creeeeeeak.

Rupert's head jerked up, this time his senses fully alert. He slunk across the kitchen, tracking the tiptoe-er to a two-foot section of faded wallpaper. He sniffed warily along the floor next to the bottom edge of the curling fabric that covered the wall, his nose sucking up the foreign scent.

The white wires of Rupert's whiskers quivered as he analyzed the odor, trying to identify its source. The hair along his spine spiked with caution. You never knew what kind of critter might show up here in Uncle Oscar's old living quarters. He had learned to expect the unexpected since he and his family moved into the apartment above the Green Vase.

The intruder wasn't a frog. Of that, Rupert was certain. After their adventures last summer, he was now intimately familiar with an amphibian's peculiar fragrance. No, this smell was staler, fustier—the aroma of one of San Francisco's old rundown Victorian homes, laced with the slightest twist of cheese. He had come across this scent once or twice before . . .

Rupert suddenly puffed out an excited wheeze of recognition. He knew exactly what kind of animal was hiding behind that wall. After confirming his identification with a second snorkeling intake, he licked his lips, and his back end squirmed with excitement. It was a plain old vanilla house mouse. This was a creature even *he* could handle.

Rupert's energetic snuffling spooked the mouse, and a torrent of panicked footsteps raced across the rough boards that formed the wall's interior framing. Rupert followed the scurrying sound along the base of the wall, his own feet thundering heavily across the tiles of the kitchen floor until he skidded to a stop at the back corner of the room.

Another long pause descended upon the kitchen as the skittering sound again fell silent.

The mouse, Rupert deduced, was trapped. A

successful capture, he thought with elation, was mere seconds away.

Rupert threw his entire moon-crazed body into extracting the mouse from its hiding place. He rolled over onto his side and attacked the wall, frantically scraping his claws against the corner of the frayed wallpaper. He worked to hook the sharp curve of his toenails beneath the curling edge of the fabric until finally, with a loud *rip,* he pulled back a small section of the paper. Eagerly, he swung a paw inside the hole—and immediately retracted it.

Rupert hunched his body against the tile floor, his blue eyes crossing as his nose pulsed in confusion. He had been wrong; somehow he had miscalculated. This was no ordinary mouse.

Cautiously, Rupert backed away from the hole as a tiny creature peeked out the opening. Rupert stared at the mouse, shaking his head in disbelief.

The mouse was completely bald. Its wrinkled skin was the flushed shade of a newborn baby. The thin flaps of its round, oversized ears were nearly translucent.

Other than the trembling whiskers attached to the pointed tip of its face, there was not a single hair on its entire body.

Chapter 1

A MAN ON A BICYCLE

AS DAWN BROKE a few hours later, a white-haired man in a wrinkled linen suit pedaled a bicycle along the city's waterfront Embarcadero. The first edges of the rising sun stretched across the water, coloring the bay a brilliant blue, splashing light across the rolling green hills that framed the opposite shore.

There's nothing like a crisp spring morning in San Francisco, the man thought with an admiring glance at the surrounding city. Smiling, he tilted his head back and soaked up the wet ocean scent. "It's good to be back," he sighed contentedly.

A light breeze tufted the thin strands of hair combed across the man's balding crown. Two days' growth of salt-and-pepper stubble covered the lower half of his face. A bristly crag of wild flyaway eyebrows dominated the facial landscape in between.

The linen suit jacket hung loosely from the man's short round shoulders. The front buttons of the jacket were unfastened, exposing the frayed edges of a collared white shirt and the elderly paunch of his stomach.

An elastic strap secured around the man's lower right shin prevented the cuff of his pants from

14

being caught in the bike's spinning gears. The cinched-up fabric revealed an ankle-high lace-up boot, whose scuffed toe pedaled a slow circular motion in coordination with its mate to propel the bike forward.

Brief scenes of the bay flashed in the open spaces between the piers as the bike's wide tires squished against the pavement. Beyond the barrier of the once-bustling warehouses, squawking flocks of seagulls soared acrobatically through the sky, searching the shallow water for their next bite of breakfast. Farther out, the loaded platform of a container ship slid silently past the waking city, its hulking mass and thousand-foot length dwarfing the commuter ferries and sailboats that dotted the bay.

The man's boots dropped to the sidewalk as he braked the bike at a crosswalk and waited for a signal light to halt the mixture of taxi and commuter traffic that had begun to fill the Embarcadero's busy thoroughfare. He released his stubby fingers from one of the rubber grips fitted over the *U*-shaped handlebars and tapped the trigger of the center-mounted bell. The chipper *ring* startled a gull from its perch atop a nearby trash can.

The bike was a single-speed cruiser, painted the same simmering orange red as the Golden Gate Bridge. Sparkling reflectors had been threaded into the spokes of the wheels; a large wire basket hung beneath the bell. Designed to maximize comfort over speed, the bike's durable frame amply supported the rider's bulky figure. At his age, he thought as he pushed off from the curb to cross the intersection, he really couldn't do without the extra springs beneath the cushioned seat.

The man steered the bike, slowly but deliberately, along a sidewalk that tracked the outside perimeter of a tennis club's high green fence. He was headed toward his old familiar haunting grounds. He felt like a pigeon, his course predetermined by an innate homing instinct.

It had been almost a year since his departure from Jackson Square, and he still looked back longingly on that previous life. While it had been a tough decision to leave his home of over forty years, he'd felt he had no other choice.

He had tried, at first, to hide himself in a different part of town, but he'd abandoned that strategy after only a few weeks. Despite its international stature, San Francisco was a little city, its center spanning a meager five-by-five-mile area. Both the risk of detection and the temptation to make contact had been far too great.

And so, he had reluctantly waved good-bye to his beloved Bay Area. He'd spent the past year traveling the globe, hoping that, over time, his adversaries would move on to other intrigues, perhaps even forget about him. He'd gone south—

way, way south—eventually trekking to a rustic cabin in a Patagonian fishing village near the bottom tip of South America.

As the length of his absence neared a year, he'd started a slow migration home, gradually progressing north toward the bulge of the earth's equator. For the last three months, he'd been secluded on a remote tropical island, browning his once pasty white skin into a rosy-cheeked tan, finishing off the last preparations for this trip to San Francisco.

Now, at last, here he was, enjoying this fine glorious morning, the culmination of years of planning finally coming to fruition. Long before his inevitable exile, he'd begun plotting his return.

Tucked into one of the man's suit pockets was a deck of freshly printed business cards. He grinned to himself, thinking of how the gold lettering stood out against the dark green pieces of paper.

"Clement Samuels," he said softly, testing out his new alias. "Clem. Yes, Clem. I like the sound of that."

The bike rounded the last corner of the tennis courts and turned onto Jackson Street where the sun's early glint revealed the serene start of a typical Friday morning. Clem scanned the row of high-end antique shops as his bike passed beneath the neatly trimmed trees that lined the sidewalk. He noted one or two establishments that had changed ownership over the course of the last

17

year, but otherwise the scene looked almost exactly the same as the day he left it—the same, that is, until he reached the storefront of a three-story building in the middle of the block. Here, he thought, things were different.

Clem hopped off the bike and leaned it against the nearest tree. He rubbed a kink in his lower back as he stared at the exterior of the Green Vase antiques shop.

He'd been aware of the initial renovations the new occupant had made to the front of the building. The crumbling facade and cracked glass windows had been torn out, replaced with a wall of crisp red bricks that ran beneath a new row of windowpanes. Several of the glass panels were embedded with the image of a slender green vase.

Stroking his chin absentmindedly, Clem surveyed the glass door that hung in the entrance. Curling wrought iron strips complemented the gold script that announced the name of the store and its current proprietor.

A pleased smile crossed the stubbled surface of his face as he reflected on the woman now in charge of the antiques shop. A mop of dark brown hair hung down past her shoulders. The thick heavy locks often slipped forward over the plastic frames of her bifocal glasses, partially obscuring her face. A painfully shy soul in her mid-thirties who kept mostly to herself, the woman and her two cats had moved into the apartment above the store not long after his escape from Jackson Square.

"Little accountant," he murmured to himself as he shifted his attention to the interior of the Green Vase. "What have you been up to?"

Clem craned his neck, trying to see into the rear of the showroom. The once dusty space was now spotlessly clean. The wooden floorboards had been scrubbed, sanded, and refinished; the interior walls gleamed with a fresh coat of paint. The previously crowded collection of Gold Rush–era antiques had been winnowed down to a select few pieces, each one shined, polished, and laid out on a display table or bookcase for easy viewing.

Clem grunted and arched his scraggly eyebrows. The place looked almost respectable. A worried knot stitched through his abdomen. What had she done with the rest of the store's contents? He hoped she hadn't thrown anything away. Or worse, he thought with growing alarm, sold any important pieces.

Feeling somewhat discomforted, Clem turned away from the window and directed his gaze toward Jackson Street. He had brought himself up to date with the current configuration of the neighborhood. That was all well and good, but it wasn't what he'd come back for.

He had always been more interested in this area's past than its present. Squinting his eyes, he imagined away the street signs, the fancy cars—

all the modern-day trappings of luxury and convenience that San Francisco's current citizens took for granted. He created, instead, his own mental image of Jackson Square as it might have looked in the 1850s during the height of the California Gold Rush.

Despite the splendid spring sunshine, the street would have been a sea of mud, the soil still saturated from the torrential downpours of the winter months. Areas of recent landfill, like the place where he stood, were particularly treacherous, laced with sinkholes that were deep enough, according to some reports, to bury a horse neck-deep.

A weary line of recently arrived immigrants, all of them men, tromped across Clem's vision. The group wobbled and weaved on the slick wooden clapboards that bordered the muddy road, struggling to maintain their balance, their internal equilibrium thrown off from weeks of cramped ocean travel.

The men had met one another on the steamer they'd boarded on the west coast of Panama, a destination they'd reached after taking separate ships down from New York and crossing the jungle of the Isthmus on foot. After chugging through the Golden Gate for the approach to San Francisco, the men had disembarked several hundred yards offshore. That was as close as the large ship could maneuver to the city; a blockade of listing and half-capsized boats made it too dangerous to come closer. The captains and crews of these abandoned vessels had left behind the seafaring life for the goldfields of the Sierras.

A rowboat ferried the new arrivals to a network of elongated piers that stretched out over the water. After a long hike across the precarious wooden walkways, the men finally found their first solid footing on the streets of Jackson Square, known during the Gold Rush–era as the Barbary Coast.

Clem walked his imaginary characters past the entrance to the building that now housed the Green Vase. The stale scents of beer and whiskey emanated from its makeshift saloon. He watched with a chuckle as a female catcall drew the men's attention.

The youngest of the group blushed and quickly turned away, almost dropping the small worn satchel that contained the entirety of his earthly belongings. His fellow travelers, however, were unembarrassed to show their interest. A brutish fellow with a tobacco-stained beard stopped and leered through the doorway. His grubby hand reached into his pocket to dig out the last two coins that had survived the hazardous and expensive trip to California.

They were a sickly, haggard bunch, from youth to scoundrel. Their grimy faces were a pallid jaundiced yellow, the outward symptom of the

21

dysentery and malaria they had picked up during their voyage. That first night in San Francisco, they would search the sprawling, ramshackle city for a place to sleep or a shelter to crawl under, but they would find no vacancies. In this fast-growing boomtown, even the most basic commodities were in short supply.

But no amount of hardship could dampen the enthusiasm of these newly minted Californians. No temporary inconvenience could cool their fever. Each one felt certain that tomorrow, the next day, or surely the coming week would bring an upswing in fortune. Soon, their empty, threadbare pockets would be packed with nuggets of gold. They could survive any torture if it meant reaching that goal.

Clem strummed the unbuttoned front of his linen suit jacket and gummed his dentures thoughtfully. With a quick blink of his gray eyelashes, he dialed back the timeline of his vision, now picturing the area in the years before the madness of 1849.

The saloon and the ground beneath it fell away as the bricks and mortar that lined the street faded into a marshy wetland. The mounds of sand and rubble that made up the Gold Rush–era landfill disappeared, and the shoreline retreated a hundred or so yards into the distance.

In his mind, Clem walked down the swampy, uninhabited beach. The land that would later support some of the tallest office buildings in San Francisco's financial district was reduced to a blustery landscape of sand dunes, short scrubby trees, and tall whipping grasses. A quiet calm, unattainable in modern times, fell in around him as he hiked up a slight grade into the scruffy little village that was still known by its Mexican Territory moniker of Yerba Buena.

This was the Wild West in its infancy. The Mexican government, putative landlord to the scattered settlement, exerted little influence or control over the area's day-to-day activities. The Mexican grip on the broad expanse of its California Territory was tenuous at best, near-nonexistent on this northern frontier.

The residents of this remote outpost represented numerous nationalities, but American settlers were gradually becoming the majority. The inhabitants were, by most accounts, escapists— men with shady pasts who had slipped away to California's mythical, unknown lands to lose themselves in its lawless society and sparsely populated wilderness. In this dusty sand-blown inlet, it was every man for himself.

Clem strode up to a scattering of low-slung adobes that formed the middle of the settlement; then he turned in a circle as he surveyed the roughly constructed wooden buildings. One stood out among the rest, the only two-story structure in the group. His mental vision honed in on the property, sweeping around to the lavish garden that curved behind it.

This was the home of the tiny town's most prominent businessman, a shipping magnate who had moved to Yerba Buena from New Orleans. He was a tall, broad-shouldered man with a dusky complexion and thick muttonchop sideburns who had recently received the honorary appointment of American vice-consul. With the help of his beautiful Russian maid, he was the designated host for the area's most distinguished visitors: disgruntled Mexican military officials, steely-eyed ship captains who'd dropped anchor in the bay's protective cove, and the occasional renegade explorer determined to stir up the local American settlers into a rebellion.

It was this historical figure—the American vice-consul with the elaborate muttonchop sideburns—that Clem had been researching just prior to his abrupt departure from Jackson Square almost a year ago. That research had given him valuable insights into the local intrigues and political motivations of pre–Gold Rush Yerba Buena and had led to a breakthrough in his quest to unearth several hidden treasures from that time frame. The name of the man whose historical background had proven so useful was William Leidesdorff.

Clem turned back once more to face the Green Vase, letting the imagined scenes of Jackson

Square's past evaporate into the day's brilliant sunlight. As he peered in through the glass windows, he needed no creative assistance to picture the building's modern-day interior. He knew its layout like the back of his hand.

A narrow staircase in a darkened corner at the far end of the showroom led to an apartment that occupied the second and third floors. The wooden steps were worn slick from the tread of hundreds of years' worth of feet. A low-hanging beam over the sixth step, he cautioned himself with a wry grin, would nick your forehead if you forgot to duck beneath it.

The top of the stairs opened into a kitchen, an odd-shaped, heavily wallpapered room with a homey wooden table, an uneven tile floor, and a temperamental dishwasher that had rarely been used in the year since his departure.

Any minute now, Clem thought with anticipation, the woman with the bifocal glasses and the long brown hair would walk into this room. Today, she would discover something she'd been diligently searching for over the last several months. If Clem's little associate had done his part, Oscar's niece was about to discover a clue to one of her uncle's hidden treasures.

Clem reached into his jacket pocket and pulled out a large white mustache with bristly unkempt whiskers that matched the scruffy hair of his eyebrows. After thumbing off a protective strip from a square of adhesive backing, he stretched out the corners of his mouth to flatten the surface beneath his nose. His eyes crossed as he centered the hairpiece above his upper lip and affixed it to his skin. Checking his reflection in the storefront glass, he scrunched up his face to confirm that the mustache was securely attached.

"Perfect," he said with satisfaction.

His costume complete, Clem climbed back onto his bike and pedaled off down the street. He had a few more stops to make in the city before leaving for the next leg of his journey.

Chapter 2

BEHIND THE WALL

TWO WHITE CATS with orange-tipped ears and tails sat at the edge of the kitchen in the second floor apartment above the Green Vase showroom, watching as I bent down near the back wall to study what remained of the bottom corner's frayed wallpaper.

Sometime during the night, a creature with sharp scraping claws—that is, Rupert the cat—had ripped open a triangular hole, about six inches across at its base, from the lower section of wallpaper. A telltale clump of fluffy white hair had been left on the floor near the opening.

"All right," I said briskly, tapping the wall as I

stood up. With a quick nod to my cat audience, I turned toward the kitchen table and the home improvement book that lay open on its surface. "Let's go through this one more time."

My eyes skimmed over the paragraphs describing wallpaper removal.

"Gloves?" I asked in a stern professional voice.

I stretched my arms out in front of my chest and tugged, one at a time, at the cuffs of the thick rubber gloves encasing my hands.

"Check," I confirmed, glancing at the cats as I released the right cuff. The elastic rubber snapped back into place with a loud smacking *pop*.

"Coveralls?" I ticked off the list, lightly stamping my feet to flap the loose vinyl fabric of the orange jumpsuit that covered my T-shirt and blue jeans.

"Check."

"Goggles?" I asked, thumping the rubber thumb of my glove against the rim of the protective gear strapped around my head. It had been a tight fit, but I had managed to stretch the goggles over the plastic frames of my bifocal eyeglasses. An uncomfortable pressure was beginning to pinch at my ears. This project, I hoped, wasn't going to take very long to complete.

"Check."

"Face mask?" I slid the cup of a white cotton mask down over my nose and mouth and gave out a much more muffled "Check."

I turned to model my home improvement costume to my feline observers.

Isabella's sharp pixielike face carefully scrutinized my altered appearance. She raised her right paw in the air and made a series of intricate clicking noises with her mouth as if she were issuing instructions. There were few aspects of my life, in Isabella's opinion, that couldn't be improved by her modifications.

A slender cat with a proud, angular head and a silky white coat, Isabella had the color point pattern typical of a Siamese. But instead of brown or gray, the darker hair on her ears and tail was a peachy orange shade, probably inherited from a tabby ancestor. The orange and white fur of her coat paired with ice-blue eyes to make a stunning combination, a fact of which she was well aware.

Isabella carried herself with an elegant, regal poise, the self-appointed queen of all she surveyed. She was, for the most part, a benevolent ruler, although her patience was frequently tested by her lowly subjects: Rupert, who usually ignored her commands, and me, who rarely understood them.

After a long string of Isabella chatter and paw-waving, I nodded a pretended acknowledgment of her cat commentary and shifted my attention to her brother.

Even if he didn't match her in physique,

Rupert's chunky fluff of feathery hair matched his sister's in coloring. He had inherited the tabby forebear's more rounded figure, long-haired coat, and voracious appetite. He was content to play the sloppy joker, lolling about for hours on end in a sleepy, punch-drunk haze. Most days, the hunger pangs of an empty stomach were all that could wake Rupert from the pleasure of his daydreams.

Every so often, however, a short burst of insuppressible energy would sweep over him, and he would set off on a scrambling, high-speed sprint across the slick wooden floors of the Green Vase showroom, a furry white hazard to any antique—or human—that might cross his wild slinging path.

It was during these spontaneous moments of brief but frenetic activity that Rupert performed his most notable acts of destruction. His middle-of-the-night renovation to the kitchen wall was just the latest example of his handiwork.

Rupert had skittishly avoided the area all morning, as if he might implicate himself by proximity to the scene of his crime. He sat on the floor next to his sister, hunched forward as he nervously eyed my orange vinyl coveralls and goggled headgear.

"It's okay," I said shaking my head in puzzlement at this unusual display of contrition. Rupert had never been known to apologize for the messes he created. "You're not in trouble." I cleared my throat to emphasize the clarification. *"This* time."

I returned to the home improvement book to scan through the list once more.

"Check. Check. Check," I repeated to myself as I made another adjustment to my face mask and goggles. These last two items weren't actually cited in the how-to manual as required equipment, but given my late Uncle Oscar's eccentricities, I wasn't taking any chances. Who knew what might be lurking in the crawl spaces behind these walls? I slapped my gloved hands together optimistically—I knew what I was hoping to find.

For a pudgy cat with few cares in the world beyond scarfing down cat food and sedately soaking up the sun, Rupert had recently developed a unique and incredibly useful talent. Over the past couple of months, he had sniffed out several tightly wrapped bundles that my late Uncle Oscar had apparently hidden throughout the apartment prior to his death—bundles that contained wads of cash.

Rupert had found the first stash in the bedroom, stuffed inside the box springs beneath the mattress. During one of his early-morning episodes of high-octane exuberance, he had shredded a hole in the fibrous cloth that covered the open end of the box spring's wooden framing. Soon after he climbed inside to look around, his energy spurt petered out, and he settled in for a nap.

Despite Isabella's best efforts to guide me, it had taken the better part of an afternoon to find him. All that was visible from beneath the bed was a Rupert-sized bulge pressing down on the fabric cover of the box spring. After several sharp pokes from the bottom side of the fabric, I'd finally convinced him to leave his new hiding place. You can imagine my surprise when a packet of dollar bills followed a disgruntled Rupert out his improvised exit in the fabric covering of the box spring.

Since that first discovery, Rupert had ferreted out bundles of money from all sorts of nooks and crannies: in the false bottom of a cupboard drawer, taped inside the covering of a light fixture, and—in a situation that had required an extensive Rupert-extraction operation—in the six-inch crawl space behind the washer and dryer.

Oscar must have been squirreling away this cash for years; the bills spanned a wide range of serial numbers and print dates. The pieces of paper were wrinkled and worn from use, and each one carried a slightly greasy fragrance. This was, presumably, the scent that Rupert's olfactory glands had honed in on: It was that of his favorite dish, my Uncle Oscar's fried chicken.

I peered through my goggled glasses at the room around me. This was the kitchen where my uncle had spent countless hours cooking up his signature recipe. It had been almost a year since his death, but I could still picture him, standing over the stove, grumbling into his various pots and pans.

Oscar had been a crotchety old man with a wide stomach, thinning white hair, and a short stocky body that a long life had worn smooth around the edges. His regular wardrobe had rarely varied from a navy-blue collared shirt and pants, both of which were almost always dusted with flour and dotted with flecks of grease. His typically dour expression, however, had masked a warm, caring soul, albeit one that carried more than its fair share of eccentricities.

I chuckled softly into my mask. It was no surprise that Oscar had resorted to his own methods for ensuring the safekeeping of his money. He had been deeply skeptical of modern banking and financial institutions. The high-rise office towers of downtown San Francisco that shadowed Jackson Square had been the regular recipients of his scorn and derision.

"Stiff-suited . . . moneygrubbing *crooks* . . ." he would grumble under his breath with a dismissive shrug at the scrapered skyline that represented the physical embodiment of the city's thriving financial industry. "*Bah!* You can't trust 'em."

That I used to work as an accountant in one of these frequently cursed buildings had caused

Oscar no end of angst. He had, on more than one occasion, wondered aloud about the earthquake stability of the office building that housed my tiny cubicle.

I shook my head ruefully. I couldn't help but wonder what my uncle would have said about my current choice of occupation.

In the days following Oscar's death, I'd found myself unexpectedly unemployed, so the cats and I had moved into the apartment that occupied the two floors above the store. It had taken several months to clean up the place, but I was now the sole proprietor of the newly renovated Green Vase antiques shop.

The store looked altogether different from when my uncle had run it. Oscar had taken a rather unorthodox approach to his operation of the business. During his tenure, the showroom had been stacked from floor to ceiling with dusty piles of boxes and crates.

The containers had been filled with an odd assortment of my uncle's collected trinkets. There were broken lamps, splintered walking canes, rusted-out mining pans, a wide variety of gold teeth, and, inexplicably, a full-sized stuffed kangaroo. The place had looked more like a pawnshop than an antique store.

There had been, however, a method to Oscar's madness. What had appeared to the casual observer—and to me, quite frankly—to be a horrendous don't-touch-anything mess was actually a carefully organized outlay of historic relics that dated back to California's Gold Rush.

Oscar had been utterly obsessed with the time period. He had scoured the city searching for hidden remnants from that era, anything that might provide insight into the lives of those early residents. All of his findings, he'd brought back here to the Green Vase.

This section of the city had been at the heart of the Gold Rush's population influx, entertaining multitudes of hopeful miners in its numerous bars and brothels. Shadowed hints of that long-forgotten era could still be found in the neighborhood's historic red brick buildings—especially for someone who knew how and where to look. Uncle Oscar had been known throughout Jackson Square as just that type of "someone."

Oscar's fascination with the Gold Rush, however, had been more than just an intellectual curiosity. The decrepit appearance of the Green Vase showroom had dissuaded all but the most intrepid visitors, providing an effective cover for Oscar's true occupation. The elusive old man hermit-ed behind the cracked glass door of the inhospitable-looking antiques shop had been, in fact, a treasure hunter extraordinaire.

Rather than searching for high-end showpiece artifacts, Oscar had focused his efforts on discarded scraps and thrown-away remnants from the Gold Rush time period. In Oscar's expert hands, these leftover bits and pieces of lives lived long ago had revealed precious information about their long-dead owners. By delving into the mundane details of wealthy and influential figures from San Francisco's past, Oscar had uncovered lost treasures that no one even knew existed.

Unfortunately, Oscar had been extremely secretive about his research, and I still had no idea what hidden significance might lie behind most of the items in his collection. I had sorted through a small portion of it, cleaned up what I could, and stored the rest in the basement for later inspection.

Were he to stop by Jackson Square today, I thought with a grin, Oscar might have trouble recognizing the showroom downstairs. Months of cleaning, scrubbing, painting, and rearranging had changed its appearance into a place that actually resembled a functioning store. The antiques shop still rarely entertained customers, but at least the neighbors had stopped complaining about the mess.

After months of trying to lure in shoppers, I had finally given up trying to compete with the well-established boutiques up and down the street. The old image of the Green Vase was well ingrained in the collective memory of San Francisco's elite antique crowd. Despite the recent face-lift, it would never have the cachet or reputation that the other Jackson Square shops enjoyed. Almost a year after Oscar's death, the traditional sale of antiques had yet to provide a single penny of income.

With that avenue of revenue closed off, I had, instead, thrown myself into replicating Oscar's research. I'd read everything I could get my hands on about the early history of San Francisco and had started the daunting task of cataloging the bizarre and seemingly random items from Oscar's collection. I had no chance, I knew, of filling my late uncle's treasure-hunting shoes, but I hoped that I might be able to grab a small toehold of his success.

In the meantime, my monetary reserves were beginning to run low. It had been several weeks since Rupert's last cash discovery, and another wad of bills would sure come in handy.

I looked over at Rupert and Isabella, who were still watching me intently from the opposite side of the kitchen. Then, with one last adjustment to the goggles, I bent back down to the hole.

"Let's see what's behind this wall," I said eagerly.

Chapter 3

PEELING BACK THE LAYERS

I RAN A gloved hand across the lower half of the wall next to Rupert's hole. For some reason, this bottom corner had only been covered by a single layer of wallpaper. An interior framing board was visible at the edge of the triangular opening.

Not so the area above the hole. It, in contrast, was plastered by a haphazard mishmash of several different pieces of textured fabric. The sheets appeared to be randomly meshed together; some had been plastered vertically, some horizontally.

I shook my head, sighing at my uncle's craftsmanship. Oscar had been a do-it-yourself kind of guy, and he had not been one to follow the directions associated with any of the second-hand home improvement products he purchased. Still, I was intrigued by the odd transition between the lower and middle sections of the wallpaper. Perhaps this was something more than a random transition between building materials.

I breathed heavily into the mask, sucked in my lower lip, and picked up a metal hand-scraper from the collection of tools I'd spread out across the table. With the rubber tips of my gloved fingers, I ruffled the curled-up corner of the top layer of wallpaper, slid the edge of the scraper beneath it, and prepared to pull. It wasn't until my goggled glasses were mere inches from the surface of the wall that I noticed the faded image repeated in the dizzy floral pattern of the paper.

Much of the printing on the wallpaper had deteriorated into washed-out shadows, and it was difficult to make out the detail of the picture that repeated systematically across the surface, but my eyes latched on to one example that still retained some clarity. My pulse quickened as I studied the small painted blossom. Three tiny brushstrokes formed the petals of a purple tulip.

Tulips, I thought excitedly. That had to be significant.

Just prior to his sudden death last spring, Oscar had been researching a pair of gold cufflinks whose rodlike bars had been fashioned into the shape of a three-petaled tulip. The cufflinks had once been worn by a man named William Leidesdorff.

A charismatic figure with a secretive past, William Leidesdorff lived in San Francisco during its pre–Gold Rush–era, when it was still part of the Mexican Territory of California. A successful shipping magnate and entrepreneur who exerted a powerful political influence in the region, Leidesdorff famously succumbed to a mysterious illness days before the Gold Rush hit. He left behind a valuable estate that was tied up in the courts for years as multiple parties fought over its ownership.

Nearly twelve months earlier, right after I moved into the apartment above the Green Vase, Leidesdorff's tulip-shaped cufflinks had set me off on a trail of clues that eventually led to the decorative tulip-embossed handle on the front door of the showroom and the secret cavity mounted into the framing beneath. I smoothed my gloved hand over the faded tulip image printed on this top layer of wallpaper. I was now more certain than ever that Oscar had hidden something behind this wall.

Pushing the cotton mask up onto my forehead, I called back to my two feline observers, "I have a good feeling about this."

Isabella turned her head and made a sharp clicking sound with her mouth. After a short pause to puzzle over these instructions, I decided to interpret her remarks as encouragement.

With the slight flick of my wrist, the scraper slid beneath the top layer of tulip-decorated paper, and it fell easily away from the wall. The stiff, brittle texture crumbled as it hit the kitchen floor, sending a poof of dustlike particles up into the air.

Fighting the urge to sneeze, I quickly pulled the mask back down over my face. My eyes watered as I leaned in to study the sheet of wallpaper I'd just uncovered. The printing on this layer was clear and distinct: a design of dime-sized tulips with the same three-petal motif.

"Now we're getting somewhere," I shouted to my furry spectators, my voice muffled by the mask.

Isabella began walking across the kitchen toward me, her pert pink nose lifted up into the air. Rupert held back, warily eyeing the black hole in the bottom of the wall as his sister barked out a string of sharp, trilling—but to my ears, uninterpretable—comments. I knelt down to attack the second layer with the scraper.

After another dust-releasing tear, I found myself staring at a third fabric surface. This one was splashed with a blooming collage of even larger purple tulips. The image had expanded to such a size that you could see the individual bristle marks left by the paintbrush used to make the broad three-petaled strokes of the design.

When I wedged the scraper beneath the corner of this third layer of wallpaper, the tool hit a much more solid substance. I'd reached the two-by-four framing of the wall. Instead of attaching the wallpaper to drywall, my uncle had pasted this bottom layer directly onto the wood.

"Nice technique, Oscar," I muttered into the mask as I squinted at the white bead of Elmer's glue forming the seam between the wallpaper and the two-by-four.

"All right, Rupert," I said, eagerly anticipating

the sight of another bundle of cash. "Let's see what you've sniffed out this time."

I tapped the handle of the scraper with the palm of my hand, and the glued edge of the wallpaper gave way. Reaching for the loose corner of the third sheet of paper, I gripped its slick surface firmly between my gloved fingers. But just as my arm tensed to pull it back, I hesitated, my anticipation shaken by a sudden shudder of apprehension.

In the recent history of the Green Vase, I reflected, the tulip symbol had another, more menacing association. The multiple tulip references my Uncle Oscar left behind had also been a warning, one that I hadn't understood until it was too late to avoid the danger. The trail of Oscar's tulip-related research had led me right into the hands of his neighbor and former business partner, the nefarious Frank Napis.

Frank and Oscar had shared a mutual interest in Gold Rush history, particularly in regard to the historical figure of William Leidesdorff. They had both been searching for the obscure spider venom that induced the sleeplike coma that preceded Leidesdorff's death.

A cold tension clenched down on my shoulders. Unlike my uncle, Frank Napis had a vicious dark side, one made all the more intimidating by his mastery of disguises. In his efforts to unveil my uncle's secrets, Napis had threatened my life more than once.

Nearly a year ago, he had instructed his coconspirator, an ex-con named Ivan Batrachos, to slip me a dose of the Leidesdorff spider toxin. Thankfully, the effects had been reversed by the last-minute application of the antidote, a compound found in purple tulip petals. The poisoning attempt had sent Ivan back to prison; Frank Napis, however, remained at large.

Last summer, a secret group of my uncle's former colleagues had tried to lure Napis out into the open so that the police could enforce a warrant for his arrest. Calling themselves the Vigilance Committee, the group's efforts had triggered a massive frog infestation of San Francisco's City Hall—an event which had caused a great deal of mayhem in the Mayor's office—but, once more, Frank Napis had eluded capture.

Isabella sat down on the floor next to me. She gently nudged my elbow with the top of her head, and I straightened my shoulders defiantly. Napis hadn't been seen or heard from in months, I told myself firmly. There was no way *he* was standing behind these layers of tulip wallpapering. This improvised, slapped-together construction was clearly my uncle's work.

Pursing my lips together, I returned my attentions to the last layer of wallpaper. Once more gripping the loosened edge, I tugged at the tulip-covered fabric. There was a brief moment of resistance before the last bits of glue let go of the framing boards. Isabella jumped out of the way as the entire four-foot length peeled off with a loud renting *crack,* and I tumbled backwards onto the kitchen floor.

Isabella muttered under her breath as I dusted myself off, but she joined me at the wall when I crawled back to the expanded hole to look inside. I grabbed a flashlight and, with gloved-finger difficulty, slid the power switch to the *on* position. A dank moldy smell seeped up at me as the shaking beam of the flashlight panned the dark recess of the interior framing.

A dusty gray object sat on a ledge about a foot off the ground, next to a clump of chewed-up cardboard, a trail of tiny brown mouse pellets, and a nest of white cat hair. I rotated my head sideways, trying to position my goggle-shielded glasses to get a better look.

Isabella crowded beside me to get her own visual angle into the wall. Her nose snuffled in my right ear at the clammy scent wafting up from the crevice.

Gingerly, I reached a gloved hand into the wall space, wrapped my fingers around the object, and lifted it out. As the light from the kitchen hit the undulating sides of the translucent ceramic material, the gray-colored glass turned a dust-muted green.

"Hmm," I murmured, perplexed as I stared at the slender green vase. "Not what I was expecting."

Chapter 4

THE GREEN VASE

THE LOOSE FABRIC that formed the legs of my vinyl coveralls swished back and forth as I carried the vase to the kitchen table. My tennis shoes crunched on the layer of dust and debris now coating the ceramic floor tiles near the edge of the gaping hole in the wallpaper.

Isabella trotted circles around my feet, eager to inspect the vase. She hopped onto a chair by the table as I set the vase down in the center, just beyond the reach of her outstretched paw.

This certainly wasn't one of Oscar's hidden bundles of cash, I thought, feeling somewhat deflated by the results of the search.

I propped my elbows on the table's edge and shifted my glasses beneath the goggles to adjust the focus of the bifocals. The morning's efforts hadn't been a total bust, I thought and shrugged, as Isabella swatted the air, trying to get close enough to perform her own analysis.

The dusty vase was a grimy replica of one that had once been displayed on the cashier counter in the downstairs showroom. The victim, I suspected, of an inadvertent Rupert tail swish, the previous vase had shattered when it fell from the counter and hit the hardwood flooring below. I'd searched all over San Francisco for a replacement, including the flower shop in the financial district where it had been purchased, but I'd been unable to find anything that came close to the same shape and color—until now.

I straightened back to full height and pulled the mask and goggles up and over my glasses, perching them on top of my forehead. Still wearing the elbow-length rubber gloves, I lifted the vase from the table and held it up to the kitchen's central light fixture to inspect it more closely.

From the opposite side of the room, Rupert began a slow creeping approach toward the kitchen table. With each cautious step, his gaze swung between the vase in my hands and the enlarged hole in the wall behind me.

Isabella, meanwhile, balanced herself on her back feet so that she could reach up toward my chest with her front ones. I shifted the vase into my left hand, attempting to fend off Isabella's stabbing paws with the right. As the vase rotated, something inside it rolled against the glass.

"Mrr-ow," Isabella called out shrilly to ensure I hadn't missed this important development.

"Yes, thank you," I replied uneasily as I resumed my examination of the vase's dusty, translucent surface.

I aimed the top end of the container toward my face and squinted down into its narrow cylindrical opening. A hairy brown lump lay on the bottom of the vase.

"You don't want to see this, Issy," I tried to convince her. "I think some poor creature died in this thing."

Perturbed at my unwillingness to share my discovery, Isabella returned to the seat of her chair, but her eyes remained glued on the dark lumpy shadow inside the vase. I turned the vase on its side and gently began nursing the stiff object over the humps and valleys of the internal curvature.

I caught a whiff of a strange smell and assumed the worst. Wrinkling my nose, I swung the vase away from my face. A pointed edge connected to the furry mass scraped against the interior surface of the glass. I winced, imagining a gruesomely exposed bone.

The sound only heightened Isabella's curiosity. She chirped up at me encouragingly.

"You know, that might be reassuring," I replied sourly, "if you weren't a mouse-eating cat."

Isabella's voice warbled in confusion at my squeamishness. Her brother, however, appeared to share my apprehension. Rupert now sat on the floor near my feet, the furry orange tip of his tail tapping against the leg of Isabella's chair as he continued to stare nervously at the hole in the wall.

With a reluctant sigh, I gently jiggled the vase,

46

trying to coax the corpse out the top of the container, to no avail. The motionless lump appeared to be stuck midway through the vase's long slender neck.

"Mrao," Isabella urged as I turned the vase upside-down and secured my grip on its rounded base. Desperately hoping I wasn't about to drop a dead mouse onto my kitchen table, I gave the vase a firm vigorous shake.

"Eeew," I cried, closing my eyes as a furry brown figure tumbled out the opening.

Isabella popped up onto her haunches and leaned over the table, sniffing loudly as she issued a string of chattering observations. I placed a restraining hand on her slim shoulders and anxiously peered over the top of her head to the brown heap lying motionless at the center of the table.

"Not a mouse," I breathed out with relief as Isabella huffed a disappointed sigh.

It was, instead, a small stuffed animal. The toy looked as if it had been well loved by a child and perhaps washed several times; its synthetic brown fur was mottled and worn down in places. A thick black thread stitched a crooked smile across its mouth; two dull black buttons formed the eyes.

With a gloved hand, I gingerly turned the toy to its upright position. The animal appeared to be standing or sitting on its back haunches—the misshapen bulging of the creature's body made it difficult to tell which.

The scraping sound inside the vase had been created by a toothpick attached to the outstretched paw of an upper limb. Glued to the free end of the toothpick was a stamp-sized piece of paper. Isabella and I leaned over the table to examine it.

"It's the California state flag," I mused as I studied the printed image of a brown grizzly bear walking beneath a red five-pointed star. "The Bear Flag," I added, with an informative nod to Isabella, who murmured in concurrence.

"I guess that makes you a bear," I said dubiously to the tattered stuffed animal.

Isabella appeared unconvinced of this last conclusion. Her pointed ears swiveled sideways as she considered the strange-looking beast.

"What were you up to, Oscar?" I wondered aloud. My initial disappointment in the discovery of the green vase was now being replaced by the growing realization that I might have stumbled onto something far more valuable than a wad of fried-chicken-infused dollar bills.

This toy bear might well be a clue to one of Oscar's hidden treasures, I thought excitedly. I flipped the paper flag over and read the message printed on the opposite side.

Shiny gold lettering typed out the words: NEVADA CITY, CALIFORNIA.

Rupert didn't share his sister's interest in the inspection of the toy bear; he had ignored the human and feline commentary postulating on its potential significance. From his position on the floor beneath the kitchen table, his eyes remained fixed on the gaping hole in the wallpaper. Of the three of us, he was the only one aware of the kitchen's fourth occupant that morning.

Hidden in the shaded recess of the wall's interior framing, two shiny pinpoints glowed in the darkness, the luminous pupils of a tiny hairless mouse.

Chapter 5

A SPANDEX-CLAD VISITOR

I WAS STILL studying the toy bear's paper flag when I heard three cracking knocks against the front glass of the storefront below.

Whack. Whack. Whack.

"We're not open," I whispered down to Isabella as I dropped the bear back onto the table.

Bona fide customers were a rare occurrence in the Green Vase showroom. It had been over a week since the last stranger had stepped in off the street, and she certainly hadn't made any purchases.

"Mrs. Dempsey," I sighed as I remembered our last such visitor. "The tooth lady."

Rupert's head jerked up at me, his gaze temporarily leaving the hole in the wallpaper. The mere mention of Megan Dempsey's name still filled him with dread. The bustling matriarch of a family of five had made quite an impression.

I'd been sitting on the stool behind the cashier counter when a big-bosomed woman with bright lipstick and unnaturally white teeth opened the front door and asked for directions to North Beach. Midway through my hand-waving attempts to point her toward the corner up the street, she spied the antique leather dentist recliner in the back of the store.

"Oh, what do you have here?" she asked, stepping into the shop. Three rowdy children and a bedraggled husband followed her inside.

It turned out Mrs. Dempsey had worked her entire adult life as a dental hygienist. After years of propping open people's mouths and peering inside, she had developed a deep fascination with all things tooth-related.

Before I knew what was happening, the entire clan had proceeded to the back of the showroom. The three children were already bouncing on the dentist recliner by the time I caught up to them. Oblivious to her offspring's antics, Mrs. Dempsey bent over a display of rudimentary tooth removal devices from the Gold Rush–era.

"It's horrifying to think what people went through in those days," she said with a shudder as she pulled out her camera and began taking pictures to show her coworkers back home.

With a tired sigh, Mr. Dempsey bumped the

children off the recliner and collapsed onto its worn leather seat cushions. His wife set down her camera and picked up a pair of rusted metal pliers.

"Can you imagine what would happen if I tried to use *this* on one of my patients?" she asked her husband with an evil leer. She mashed the handles back and forth over his head as she aimed the pinchers at his mouth. Mr. Dempsey flattened himself against the back of the recliner, his expression one of genuine terror.

I didn't have time to worry about the torture Mrs. Dempsey was contemplating for her husband. The youngest of their children had begun to chase a terrified Rupert around the showroom. Isabella watched from the top of a bookcase while Rupert scrambled for cover. The little girl's wheezing, high-pitched voice filled the room as she squealed with delight, "Kit-*tee* . . . Kit-*tee*."

It took almost thirty minutes to get Mrs. Dempsey and her brood out the door. Rupert didn't emerge from hiding until dinnertime, nearly four hours later.

Customers, I had decided, were overrated— particularly the non-purchasing kind. Rupert and Isabella heartily agreed. I was beginning to appreciate the rationale of Uncle Oscar's customer-deterrent strategies.

With a grimace, I glanced down at my orange

nylon jumpsuit and thick rubber gloves. One look at this outfit should be enough to scare off even the most tooth-enamored dental hygienist.

A second series of raps echoed up from the showroom, and I glanced skeptically at the clock mounted onto the still-intact wall on the opposite side of the kitchen.

In my short year of experience, antique buyers, elusive creatures that they were, rarely visited Jackson Square before early afternoon. Even in my more optimistic days of running the Green Vase, I'd given up manning the cashier counter downstairs until after lunch. A sign posted on the front door clearly advised passersby that the showroom didn't open until 1:30 p.m. Whoever was trying to gain entrance to the Green Vase this sunny Friday morning was unlikely to be a shopper.

Given the sounds echoing up from the floor below, the persistent person on the street outside had apparently decided to switch tactics. I began to struggle out of my rubber gloves as the decorative brass handle on the showroom's front door rattled in its fittings. A moment later, I heard the metal grating of a key sliding into the door's lock. With a slight *clink,* the key turned in the keyhole's fittings.

"Hello?" I called out tentatively as the unmistakable creak of iron hinges signaled the opening of the front door. Both cats immediately turned to look toward the top of the stairwell that led from the kitchen to the showroom below.

"Hmmm," I mused uneasily. I picked up the scraper and slapped its flat metal side against the palm of my hand. I thought I had confiscated all the rogue keys to the Green Vase that inexplicably circulated among Uncle Oscar's friends and colleagues. Clearly, I had missed one.

Heavy footsteps clunked across the showroom toward the bottom of the staircase. There was an awkward stilted motion to the stride, as if the walker were carefully measuring his motions to retain his balance.

"Hello?" I called out again, my voice more demanding in tone. Still, the entrant below did not respond.

The voiceless, unnamed feet began hiking up the stairs, loudly clapping against each step as if they were encased in concrete. The repeating sound rattled through the second floor, jostling the dishes in the cupboard over the sink.

I glanced down at the cats. Isabella wore a dour, knowing look on her face as Rupert bounded happily across the room to the entrance of the staircase, his pudgy body wiggling in anticipation of the visitor's arrival. I put my hands on my hips and turned toward the top of the stairs, waiting for the intruder to enter the kitchen.

A dark rounded shadow emerged at the top of the stairwell. As the figure mounted the last few steps to the kitchen, the image of a black plastic helmet came into view. A pair of shiny reflective sunglasses obscured the man's eyes, but I had seen enough of the long narrow face smashed inside the helmet to confirm his identity.

The man raised himself another step in height. The momentum of the motion caused the helmet's black nylon strap to sway beneath his pointed chin. He cleared his throat importantly as his shoulders leaned forward to reveal a green nylon shirt crisscrossed with a purple and white argyle pattern.

The man smiled as Rupert hopped up and down in greeting. A black-gloved hand reached out to scratch him behind the ears. "Hey there, buddy," the man said playfully. Then, with a dramatic flourish, he cleared the last step and entered the kitchen.

Isabella and I stared skeptically at the bottom half of his biking gear: shiny green skintight leggings, partially covered by a pair of floppy black shorts. An odd-shaped bulge poked out from his posterior, the result, I suspected, of extra padding sewn into the seat.

The man lifted the helmet from his head and posed with his narrow chest proudly distended as if he'd just reached the summit of a mountain. The brown curls that typically sprang from his scalp had been mashed into a towering cone-shaped pile. His thin lips spread into a sly smile as he waited for applause.

We stood, curly-coned to goggle-strapped head, for a long moment before the man ripped his mirrored sunglasses from his face and squinted critically at me.

It was a testament to Montgomery Carmichael's self-assured cheekiness that after surveying my orange nylon coveralls, dust-covered face, and forehead-topping mask and goggles, he asked incredulously, "What's with the outfit?"

Chapter 6

FRIEND OF THE MAYOR

MY NOSY NEIGHBOR was a regular, if uninvited, guest to the Green Vase showroom and the apartment above. A closed or even locked door was no barrier to his intrusion. I had, unfortunately, grown accustomed to his spontaneous appearances in my kitchen, but I thought I'd confiscated all of his spare keys to my front door.

Monty ran an art studio across the street from the Green Vase, although the number of paintings on display there had dwindled substantially over the past year. He'd been spending the majority of his time at City Hall, where his prestige and influence—inexplicably—continued to grow.

Last summer, the Mayor had appointed Monty the city's commissioner for the historical preservation of Jackson Square. The post was meant to be ceremonial, as evidenced by its basement-level office and nominal remuneration. It was created to placate the city's many historical societies after the dissolution of the Jackson Square Board that spring.

The position's limited mandate had done nothing to dampen Monty's enthusiasm. He'd simply set out, through sheer bluff and bravado, to expand the boundaries of his authority.

The metal brackets poking out of the bottom of Monty's bike shoes clacked against the floor tiles as he hobbled across the kitchen to inspect the hole in the tulip-printed wallpaper.

I held out my hand, palm upward.

"Key," I ordered with a stern frown. He tossed it casually through the air to me.

"Is this the last one?" I demanded as Monty's eyes swept from my renovation gear to the protective sheeting I'd stretched across the kitchen counters.

"What's all this?" he asked, predictably turning a deaf ear to my question. His thin figure wobbled wildly as he pivoted on his metal-bottomed shoes to point a knobby finger at the hole in the wall. "Looks like a bit of off-permit work to me."

I sighed and rolled my eyes at the ceiling. While Commissioner, Monty had imposed a new set of guidelines regarding maintenance and repair of the city's historically designated buildings. These rules had changed frequently, morphing spontaneously to accommodate the capricious whims of the Commissioner. Despite numerous requests, I'd been unable to obtain a copy of these oft-quoted regulations. I had serious doubts as to whether a formal paper version even existed.

Nevertheless, Monty had proceeded to barge his way into all the homes and businesses in Jackson Square under the pretext of inspecting them for compliance. Anyone who resisted his entry was confronted with a blustery charade in which he waved a blank tablet in the air and threatened to begin issuing citations.

"You'll have to talk to Rupert," I replied flatly to Monty's raised eyebrows. "He tore into the wall last night." I crossed my arms over my chest, waiting for the act to play itself out.

Rupert adopted his best "Who, me?" impersonation, and Monty's admonishing expression broke into a broad smile. He directed his pointed finger at Rupert. "Lucky for you, I've given up the commissioner's position."

The whole of Jackson Square had breathed a collective sigh of relief a few weeks back when the Mayor promoted Monty to his cabinet, prompting his resignation from the commissioner's seat. Due to current budget restraints, his replacement had yet to be named. After Monty's tenure, we were all hoping the position would be eliminated—permanently.

Many puzzled, however, over Monty's new role in the Mayor's cabinet. As far back as anyone could remember, no mayor in the history of San Francisco had employed a personal life coach on his staff of advisors. Certainly, none had included an assistant life coach, the job title Monty had assumed.

While Monty touted his own credentials at every opportunity, an aura of mystique surrounded his boss, the Mayor's Life Coach. Despite numerous attempts by both the media and the Board of Supervisors, the anonymous figure had never been seen, heard, or even photographed. Every aspect of the man's identity remained cloistered in secrecy.

On the streets of San Francisco, perplexed citizens scratched their heads in confusion. What exactly was a life coach, they wondered, and why did the Mayor need one? Moreover, particularly in these tough economic times, how could the Mayor possibly justify a life coach's *assistant?*

Given Monty's frequent visits to the Green Vase, I'd had plenty of opportunities to quiz him on the topic of life coaching, but thus far, I had declined to do so. Quite frankly, I was afraid to ask.

Presumably, the life coaching staff at City Hall was tasked with pulling the Mayor out of the midlife crisis that had dogged him for the past several months. It had been a tough year for San

Francisco's beleaguered Mayor. He had never quite regained his gravitas following last summer's infamous frog invasion of City Hall.

There had been widespread press coverage mocking the Mayor's desperate panic-stricken retreat from the masses of frogs milling about the rotunda beneath City Hall's decorative dome. The Mayor had refused to return to his office until several SWAT team sweeps confirmed that every last amphibian had been evacuated.

The Mayor's attempt to explain the situation to a local television reporter had resulted in an awkward and embarrassing interview that he had eventually terminated by walking out. After that experience, he had declared a moratorium on further interaction with the press.

Prominent newspaper columnists had responded by openly questioning the Mayor's prospects in the upcoming gubernatorial race as well as his mental stability. Mayoral recall proposals began routinely appearing in the "Letters to the Editor" section of the *Chronicle*.

To make matters worse, a local prankster in a chicken costume who occasionally showed up at the Mayor's public appearances had modified his act to reflect recent events. His expanded routine now included an innovative frog-hopping bird dance, a video of which had become an instant download sensation on the Internet.

The Mayor's main political opponents had also

cashed in. The website for the President of the Board of Supervisors featured a frame-by-frame color photo analysis of the Mayor's indecorous departure from the frog-infested City Hall. The gubernatorial candidate for the opposing political party had adjusted his stump speech to include several oblique frog references, each instance generating raucous cheers from his supporters.

With the Mayor under constant assault from all quarters, his poll numbers had taken a swan dive.

After several tortured months of refusing to comment on or otherwise discuss the frog debacle, the Mayor had announced his withdrawal from the governor's race. He'd issued a brief statement and left town for an extended Hawaiian vacation.

When the Mayor finally returned to City Hall, he was accompanied by a new fiancée, a suitcase full of coconuts, and the elusive, seemingly invisible Life Coach. The lengthy vacation, engagement, and motivational guidance, however, had done little to buoy the Mayor's spirits. When spotted by a roving camera crew the previous week, he'd looked as if he wanted to crawl under a rock and hide.

Throughout all this turmoil, Monty had remained one of the Mayor's most ardent supporters. It was this unwavering adoration, I suspected, that had earned Monty the invitation to the Mayor's secret Hawaiian getaway. After a brief visit to the islands, Monty had arrived back in San Francisco with a light freckling on his normally pale face and the new head-scratching title of assistant—or apprentice, as he preferred to be called—life coach.

In recent weeks, the city's political rumor mill had been running hot with speculations that the Mayor would throw his hat into the race for lieutenant governor. Despite the political baggage of the frog-fleeing incident, pundits predicted he would be an easy front-runner in that contest, which was far less competitive than that for the office at the top of the ticket. If elected, there was a good chance the Mayor would take Monty with him to Sacramento.

Four Monty-free years, I thought with a longing sigh as I watched my green spandex-clad neighbor prance around the kitchen. It was almost too much to hope for.

At least Monty's obsession with San Francisco politics had temporarily distracted him from his previous favorite pastime. It had been several months since Monty had approached me with another bizarre theory regarding my Uncle Oscar's death—or lack thereof.

In the weeks following Oscar's passing, Monty had dreamed up numerous scenarios speculating on ways my uncle might have faked his death and assumed a disguise, perhaps in order to elude the likes of Frank Napis. According to Monty, it was entirely possible that a costume-camouflaged

Oscar was walking around Jackson Square, right under our noses.

I had at first let my imagination—and Monty's endless stream of ridiculous theories—persuade me that maybe, perhaps, there was a chance that Oscar was still alive. Truth be known, I preferred to think of him that way, off on a wild adventure instead of cold, dead, and buried in the ground. But I had long since dismissed those fantasies and, thankfully, so had Monty.

I watched as Monty's eyes darted from Rupert to the dusty green vase.

"Aha!" he said, spinning around the table to swoop it up. "You found a replacement." He brought the container close to his face and slowly rotated it under his nose, carefully inspecting the curves of the glass as he tapped the surface with his fingers.

"It's hard to say for sure . . ." he droned slowly as he turned the vase to squint down the opening into its interior. "But I'd have to say this is a match to the one you broke last summer."

I glanced grimly at the chunky cat sitting on the floor near my feet. "Actually," I said, clearing my throat with a light cough, "I'm pretty sure it was Rupert who did that one in."

Rupert looked up at me with another innocence-proclaiming expression.

"And what do we have here?" Monty asked, picking up the furry stuffed animal holding the paper flag. He sniffed the bear with the pointed tip of his nose, as if he were a wine connoisseur testing an elite vintage.

"It was in the vase," I replied. "I thought it was a dead mouse . . ."

"So you heard?" Monty asked excitedly as his eyes scanned the writing on the back side of the paper flag.

"Heard what?" I replied, confused.

"About Nevada City." Monty dropped the stuffed animal onto the kitchen table and gestured down at his shiny green leggings. "That's what I came over to tell you about. I'm heading up there this weekend."

Chapter 7

THE TOUR OF CALIFORNIA

I STEPPED WARILY back from the table, instantly concerned. During my brief tenure at the Green Vase, coincidences had a nasty tendency to result in disaster: a moment of hunger instantly sated by a cupcake whose frosting was spiked with a spider venom toxin, a transportation need suddenly fulfilled by a MUNI bus with faulty brakes. I had learned to be skeptical of any fortuitous convergence of circumstances, particularly when it landed so neatly in my lap.

"Why are you going to Nevada City?" I asked

suspiciously, the nerves along my spine contracting with apprehension.

Monty wasn't the least bit fazed by the conspicuous overlap in geographical references. "I'm representing the Mayor at the opening ceremony for the Tour of California," he said proudly. "I'll be making appearances for him at a couple of the host cities for the Northern California stages. Let's see, Nevada City, Sacramento, Davis, San Francisco . . ." He ticked off the names on his fingers as he spoke. "Of course the Mayor might decide to take that last one."

He thumped his narrow nylon-covered chest. "I've become rather important, in case you hadn't noticed. It's all set. I head out tomorrow."

I rubbed my temples, pondering. If the Mayor had started asking Monty to represent him at public events, he must be getting desperate.

"And—the outfit?" I asked, wincing. "Is that an assistant life coach uniform?"

"You know I prefer Life Coach *Apprentice*," Monty corrected me crisply. "This is my cycling gear." He strutted a circle around the kitchen table with a catwalk swagger. "What do you think?"

The baggy shorts hung loosely from his narrow hips, swishing against the spandex leggings as he walked. Rupert trotted behind him, curiously watching the wiggle of the padded cushion sewn into the seat of the shorts.

"I think it's quite slimming, don't you?" Monty turned his head from me to Isabella seeking approval.

"Wran," Isabella opined, her pinched face emphasizing her negative assessment.

Monty plopped down on the nearest chair, swiveling his hips to adjust the rear padding. "There's going to be a photo op at the start of the race, so I stopped by a bike shop this morning and got myself fitted."

His fingers plucked at the loose fabric of the shorts. "They tell me the cushioning makes the plastic bike seat more comfortable to sit on." He bounced up and down on the wooden chair, his narrow face scrunching up as he judged the effect. "I have to say, there's quite an improvement even with regular furniture. You know, they should put this type of padding in everyday clothing. I might have to start a new fashion trend with this."

I pointed to the black plastic helmet resting on the table next to the dusty green vase. "And the helmet? Do you have cufflinks to match the helmet?"

Monty smoothed the sleeves of his shirt. "Safety first," he admonished. "The race organizers wanted the Mayor to appear on a bike to help promote the event." He wrapped his hands around the helmet's bowl-shaped top and crammed it down onto his head. "California law requires government employees to wear protective headgear when riding a bicycle during the performance of their duties."

Monty drummed his fingers across the round curve of plastic covering his noggin. "They've loaned me a nifty set of wheels for the trip. It's got all the latest bells and whistles."

Ah, I thought with a wry grin. That perhaps provided the real reason Monty had been asked to step in for these cycling-related appearances. There was no way the Mayor's famous swept-back hairstyle could be maintained inside the cramped confines of a bike helmet—an issue about which Monty no longer had any concern.

It had taken several months' convincing, but Monty had finally given up trying to emulate the Mayor's hairdo. He'd developed an allergy to the hair gel needed to straighten, pin back, and cement his naturally curly hair into position. After an unpleasant episode with a head full of red rash and welts, he'd had no choice but to abandon the gel. You could still see a pinkish tinge on Monty's scalp when he stood in the direct sunlight.

Monty stroked the cutout divots and holes in the top of the helmet. "It's ventilated," he said, swinging his head rapidly back and forth like a wet dog. "Yep, I can feel the breeze."

"Okay, okay." I relented, holding my hands up to stop the demonstration before Monty fell off the chair. "It looks like you've got the equipment angle covered."

Monty leaned back in his seat. "Other staffers were interested in this gig, but I was easily the best choice—for the first leg of the race anyway," he said with an air of superiority. "What with my background in historical preservation and all."

I stared at him, puzzled, as he fumbled with the chinstrap to his helmet. Try as I might, I couldn't see the historical angle to a cycling event that was only a few years old.

"The tour begins this year in Nevada City," Monty replied to my confused look. "It was a mining boomtown in the 1850s. Most of the downtown buildings are designated historical landmarks. They've tried to preserve as much as possible from the Gold Rush–era."

He pointed at the floor, down to the showroom below. "I believe you have some familiarity with that time period," he added with a smirk.

I glanced back at the little stuffed animal sitting on the table. It had rolled over onto its side, but its outstretched paw still clutched the tiny paper flag. The beady buttons of the creature's eyes looked up at me bewitchingly.

For some reason, Oscar had hidden this Nevada City bear behind a raft of tulip-printed wallpaper. It wasn't the cash I'd been looking for, but I was growing more and more convinced I had found a clue to one of Oscar's valuable hidden treasures.

The possibility was too tempting. I had to investigate.

I couldn't believe I was actually considering accompanying Monty on this expedition, but if I were going to follow the trail Oscar had left behind, it seemed like the logical next step.

I sucked in my breath and hoped I wasn't making a huge mistake as I asked, "When did you say you were leaving?"

Chapter 8

THE DUFFEL BAG

THAT AFTERNOON, RUPERT huddled on top of the bed, glaring down at the black canvas duffel bag lying open on the floor. A frayed airline tag from the bag's last trip dangled from the handles, and its canvas fabric still bore a suspicious foreign scent. It had been several months since the bag's last outing, but Rupert remembered it vividly. This bag, Rupert knew from painful experience, could not be trusted.

An hour earlier, he had watched with intense loathing as his person lifted the bag off the closet's top shelf and loaded a small pile of clothes into its zippered compartment. A collection of toiletries had started to accumulate on the bathroom shelf by the sink. He knew exactly what was coming next.

A venomous hatred filled Rupert's fluff-covered chest as he glowered at the duffel. That *bag* was about to run off with *his* person.

Rupert sniffled sulkily. After all these years together, he thought they had an understanding, he and his person. It was quite simple, really. *He* allowed her to call him Rupert if *she* agreed to stay home and take care of him.

He was a cat, after all, and he had needs.

First off, there was the matter of his water dish. He preferred to drink his fluids out of a glass from the kitchen cabinet. No plastic pet bowls. No aluminum bins. Those were unacceptable; they left a strange aftertaste. He shook his head, as if remembering the unpleasant flavor.

Now, once the appropriate glass had been selected, it should be filled with water from the special filtered container in the refrigerator. After being poured, the water must be allowed to warm to room temperature before it was suitable for drinking. Then, as soon as the first cat food floaties began to accumulate in the glass, the whole thing must be dumped out, thoroughly cleaned, and refilled.

In Rupert's opinion, these were all perfectly reasonable requests, but not ones, in his experience, that were honored by your typical breeze-in, breeze-out cat sitter.

He stomped his feet stubbornly. Who was going to maintain the proper conditions of his water supply if the bag took off with his person? *Who?*

Then, he thought worriedly, there was the issue of tummy rubs. After a big meal, Rupert looked to his person to provide a warm lap for him to curl up in while she gently massaged the round pouch of his stomach. This procedure, he was convinced, was absolutely critical to proper feline digestion. He shuddered to think what might happen if he were deprived of this essential service. Who was going to rub his tummy while that duffel bag and his person were off gallivanting around Nevada City? he demanded in perturbed silence. *Who?*

Rupert ticked off a growing list of concerns regarding his pending abandonment. What if he got a kink in his back that needed massaging? What if his blankets got stale and needed fluffing in the dryer? What if the fog rolled in and he wanted the heater turned on? There was no end to the numerous calamities he might face.

That was the whole point, Rupert thought as his mind raced in growing panic. He might *need* something. What could be more important than staying here and taking care of Rupert?

Suddenly, Rupert sat bolt upright, his heart nearly stopping from a last alarming realization. The worst possible scenario had flashed before his eyes.

What if he got *lonely?*

The fluffy orange tip of his tail whapped against the surface of the bed in frustration. He puffed out another self-pitying sniffle. Honestly—that woman! What was she thinking?

Rupert stiffened his shoulders with resolve. He knew what he had to do. If his person thought she could leave him here all alone in the Green Vase with his bossy sister and that weird-looking mouse—well, she had another thing coming. Wherever that black duffel bag was going, he was going, too.

He crept to the edge of the bed. Carefully, he studied the zippered opening and sized up the distance. His claws dug into the comforter as he wiggled his back end and prepared for his leap. With a last defiant *"mreow,"* he sprang into the air.

A moment later, he disappeared inside the bag.

ISABELLA CURLED UP on a rug at the far side of the bedroom, skeptically observing her brother's mental machinations. She sighed dismissively as he leapt off the bed into the mouth of the duffel bag. No offense to her brother, but he was an amateur when it came to communicating with their person.

Isabella's brow furrowed as she thought of the toy bear they'd found earlier that day. She sensed that this was a significant revelation, a clue to one of Oscar's deeply guarded secrets.

Her white face pinched as she considered her person's pending departure. In most instances,

71

she preferred the comforts of home to a car trip. She hated being locked up in her carrier, unable to control the direction of the vehicle. But this was more than the typical excursion her person was about to embark on, and she would no doubt need Isabella's expert feline guidance.

Isabella twitched her whiskers as she came to the inevitable conclusion. She would have to convince her person to take the cats along with her to Nevada City.

As Isabella stared at the rustling duffel bag, pondering how best to instruct her person on this topic, she heard the familiar knocking engine of a pickup rumbling into Jackson Square.

Isabella trotted across the bedroom to the window overlooking the street. She propped her front feet on the edge of the sill and poked her head through the slats in the blinds. Down below, the pickup's rusted frame puttered to a stop in front of Monty's art studio. The driver's side door swung open with a loud creak, and a wrinkled old man in frayed overalls limped out of the cab.

Harold Wombler glanced up at Isabella's window as he rubbed a sore spot in the crook of his neck. Seeing her tiny white face in the blinds, he nodded an acknowledgment, his version of a friendly gesture.

Isabella watched as Harold hobbled around to the truck's back bed. His gnarled hands clamped down on the handle to the dented tailgate and dropped it into a horizontal position. With effort, he lifted a large object out of the bed and set it on the sidewalk.

Isabella's face registered bewilderment as she tried to figure out what Harold was doing with this strange wheeled contraption.

With a rueful grimace at Isabella's confused expression, Harold rolled the object to the street side of the truck to give her a better view. He pointed emphatically at a compartment positioned over the wheels. Then he turned to look up at her window to see if she'd understood his meaning.

Isabella's ears flattened against the side of her head. She leaned away from the glass, her blue eyes glaring a sharp rebuff to his suggestion.

Harold shrugged his shoulders at her, crimping his lips into a frustrated expression. This was the best he had been able to come up with under the circumstances.

With a resigned sigh, Isabella stretched her right paw through the slats of the blinds and tapped it against the window ledge, indicating her reluctant agreement to his proposal.

She dropped back down to the floor of the bedroom. Her slender pipe of a tail swished back and forth as the orange tips of Rupert's ears began to emerge from the opening in the duffel bag.

Her brother, she thought as she strolled across the room, was about to get a much-needed pounce.

Chapter 9
THE CAT-MOBILE

I WOKE THE next morning to a jarring bang against the front door.

Rubbing my eyes, I glanced sleepily at the nightstand beside the bed and then down to the alarm clock lying on the floor in front of it. Someone—or, more likely, some cat—had knocked the clock off the stand in the middle of the night, disengaging its settings.

My eyes jumped to the two furry bodies sprawled across the covers and narrowed suspiciously. Rupert and Isabella had begun registering objections to today's trip from the moment I pulled my duffel off the closet's top shelf. It had been several months since I'd left them alone overnight, but neither cat had forgotten the significance of a packed bag.

A further barrage of pounding prevented me from interrogating the alarm clock saboteurs. Muttering under my breath, I hopped out of bed and struggled into my T-shirt, jeans, and sneakers.

"Coming!" I hollered as I pulled a quick comb through my hair and scooped up the duffel bag. A pattering of feline feet trailed behind me as I hurried down the staircase to the second floor. All the while, the thumping against the downstairs door continued to increase in intensity.

"I should've had Harold install a doorbell," I said as I skidded across the kitchen and thudded down the stairs to the showroom. Turning the corner at the bottom of the steps, I stopped and stared at my tall, skinny neighbor as he swung open the front door.

"Or better yet, a Monty monitor," I added testily.

Before I had a chance to complain about yet another contraband key, Monty pushed a large bulky contraption through the entrance. His fingers were wrapped around the handle of what appeared to be a child's stroller.

The device had three rubber wheels arranged in a tricycle-style formation that supported a carriage constructed out of metal tubing and green nylon fabric. The passenger seating area was deep and wide enough to easily accommodate two toddler-sized children. The front and top portions of the carriage had been modified with a zippered net cover that kept the occupants secured inside while providing a window for them to see out.

"What do you think?" Monty asked smugly.

The wheels squealed against the wooden floor as he rolled the stroller back and forth in front of the cashier counter. He flicked a lever with his thumb, causing the wheels to screech to a sudden stop. "Nifty hand brake," he said, his voice as slick as a used car salesman's.

"What's it—for?" I asked tentatively, although I suspected I already knew the answer.

"For the trip, of course," Monty replied as he spun the stroller around in a tight circle to show me the opposite side.

A small plastic sign cut into the shape of a yellow triangle had been pinned to the carriage's nylon fabric. The sign depicted a silhouette image of the heads and shoulders of two cats below a bold black-lettered message: CATS ON BOARD.

Monty's face glowed with excitement as he pointed to the sign. "I call it the *Cat-mobile*." He leaned over the top of the stroller and unzipped the net cover.

"Top-of-the-line model," Monty boasted with a dramatic hand flourish. "Only the best for my feline friends."

Rupert bounded up to the buggy and lifted himself onto his back haunches, sniffing loudly as he looked inside. After a few preparatory tail swishes, he jumped into the stroller. His back feet caught the edge of the netting, impeding his progress, but he eventually squirmed his way into the passenger compartment. A moment later, his head poked out the opening. With a furry grin on his face, he looked approvingly up at Monty.

I shook my head at the cat-modified carriage. "This will never work," I protested, pointing to Isabella. Her tail bristled in offense as she glared at the stroller. "There's no way we'll get her in that thing."

Isabella sent me a sharp rebuking look, even more deprecating than the one she had just issued the Cat-mobile. Monty stepped back as Isabella stiffly approached the buggy. Slowly, she circled the exterior, closely inspecting the wheels and the passenger compartment's fabric covering. After a last icy glare at me, she issued a sharp *chirp* of warning to Rupert and leapt gracefully inside.

Reluctantly, I dropped the duffel on the floor and approached the stroller.

"They can't spend the whole trip in there," I said, putting my hands on my hips as I peered down at my cats. "They won't be allowed inside the hotel."

Monty pushed the cart forward, carving an arc around me. "I've got it all worked out. If we can't sneak them into the rooms, they can sleep in the parking lot. There's plenty of space in the van."

THE VAN—RUPERT'S orange-tipped ears perked up at the reference. He poked his head out of the carriage and licked his lips hungrily. For several months now, Rupert had been convinced that the primary function of Monty's cargo van was to transport not artwork—but fried chicken.

Rupert looked directly at his person and sent the clearest message he could muster.

"Take me to the chicken delivery van!"

An emphatic *"Wra-ooo!"* was all she heard.

HAROLD WOMBLER HOBBLED down Jackson Street toward the white cargo van parked against the curb alongside the red brick front of the Green Vase antiques shop. The threadbare fabric of the contractor's overalls hung limply from his bent arthritic frame. With each stilted step, the day's sunny breeze rifled through the gaping holes that flapped at the garment's knees.

Harold allowed himself the rare pleasure of a short smile. It takes a certain expertise to sculpt a pair of overalls into such a perfectly comfortable fit, he thought with pride.

An extra gust of wind whistled down the sidewalk, causing Harold's loose pant legs to balloon out behind his bony frame.

"Proper ventilation," Harold mused with satisfaction. "That's the key. Makes you feel as if you're not wearing anything at all."

He grunted out loud. While the occasional nudist wouldn't draw a raised eyebrow in some parts of the Bay Area, the well-heeled patrons of Jackson Square would certainly object if they caught sight of one here. Harold chuckled to himself, imagining the scene.

With a sly smirk, he turned to glance into the nearest highbrow antique store. The stiff-suited proprietor and his Prada-clad client stared back reproachfully. Harold continued down the street, adding an extra jiggle to his lurching gait for the watchers' benefit.

Midway down the next block, he reached the van. He crept stealthily along the outside of the vehicle until he could peek over the hood to the front windows of the Green Vase.

A stringy long-legged man in green spandex leggings pranced back and forth in front of the cashier counter. It was difficult to see past the man's flailing appendages, but he appeared to be pushing a large baby stroller around the showroom.

Feeling the ever-present drizzle of congestion seeping from his nose, Harold retreated behind the van and reached into a pocket for a handkerchief. He let loose a loud honking blow that filled the center of the cloth; then he stuffed it back into his overalls.

As Harold returned to his peeping position, he spied a woman with brown hair and thick-framed glasses standing near the front of the store. The woman faced the street, but her attention was focused on the stroller in front of the cashier counter. Her hands were planted defiantly on her hips. Harold could read the skepticism on the downward tilt of her face.

"Come on, Carmichael," he grumbled bitterly. "It's time to work your magic."

Harold's upper lip curled with disgust as he

watched Monty turn the stroller in a giddy circle around the woman. The springing curlicue locks on the top of his head bounced in time to his over-energetic demonstration of the stroller's cat-friendly features. Harold shook his head, grateful that he was on the opposite side of the glass, shielded from what was surely an ostentatious oration.

As Monty stepped back from the stroller, Harold knitted his eyebrows with concern. "Don't back off now, nitwit," he snarled. "Close the deal."

Just then, Harold spied two pairs of orange-tipped ears poking out the top of the carriage.

"Well then," he groused crankily as the expression on his wrinkled face began to soften. "About time."

While Harold continued to monitor the scene, the pudgier male cat hungrily licked his lips, straightened his posture, and let loose a long howl. The female sitting in the stroller beside him pawed the air imploringly, her open mouth presumably sending convincing cat sounds to her owner.

Finally, the brown-haired woman threw her hands up in the air, as if submitting to what she knew to be a ridiculous proposal. Harold waited until he was certain the woman had agreed to bring her cats with her on the trip to Nevada City before turning to hobble back up the sidewalk.

A long, painful block later, Harold's limping

figure reached the spot where he'd parked his truck. With an impish wave to the antique dealer glaring furiously from inside the adjacent storefront, he pried open the driver's side door and hefted himself into his rusted rig. After a last sarcastic grimace at the shopkeeper, Harold plugged the key into the ignition and chugged off down the street.

A block later, the pickup paused at a stop sign, and Harold lifted his baseball cap to smooth the greasy black hair crammed beneath. A recently acquired item, the cap was crisper and newer than anything else on or about his entire person. The cap's bright green fabric was as-yet unmarred by the grease and dirt stains that decorated the rest of Harold's clothing.

On the front of the cap above the brim, gold-colored thread traced out the image of a large bear riding a bicycle.

Chapter 10

ON THE ROAD

IT TOOK THE better part of an hour to pack up all the cat-related essentials needed for the trip, but Monty's van eventually pulled out of Jackson Square fully loaded with cat food, cat water bottles, two cat-filled carriers, and the cat-modified stroller.

The most important cat-related item rode in the back cargo area. Rupert had closely supervised the anchoring of the red igloo litter box to the brackets on the van's floor. Once the igloo was secured, Monty hung an old bed sheet from a rod in the ceiling to mitigate the inadvertent spray of litter into the rest of the cargo space. After a test run, which included a lengthy energetic digging session, Rupert gave the setup his official stamp of approval.

I leaned back against the front passenger seat with a sigh of exhaustion, still trying to figure out how I'd been talked into bringing the cats along on this trip.

"What a morning," I thought wearily as I stared up at the gray synthetic cloth that covered the ceiling.

The roof of the van was one of the only interior spaces that remained unmodified by Monty's creative hand. Most of the personalizing changes reflected his current fascination with the politics of state and local government. The van's front bucket seats had been fitted with leather seat covers decorated with the state seal of California. A necklace of campaign buttons dangled from the rearview mirror, whose flat reflective surface had been turned to a position more optimized for viewing the image of the driver's hair than that of the traffic behind us. Finally, affixed to the center of the plastic dashboard, a shiny-haired bobble-head figure of the Mayor bounced and wiggled with each bump, rut, and pothole on the street below.

Monty's fingertips tapped merrily against the steering wheel as he drove through the financial district. His green eyes focused on the road ahead, but the broad grin on his face indicated that his thoughts were elsewhere—no doubt envisioning his role in the upcoming ribbon-cutting ceremony and the coinciding photo shoot where he would be modeling his glamorous green bike gear.

The van chugged up the on-ramp onto the lower deck of the Bay Bridge and merged easily into the nearest eastbound lane. Despite our delayed departure, the bridge was only lightly populated with Saturday morning traffic. The bobble-head on the dashboard fell into darkness as the van slid under the shadow of the upper deck's grimy undercarriage.

Unlike the scenic view that greeted westbound commuters entering San Francisco on the bridge's top level, departing vehicles on the lower span were treated to a deeply rutted roadway topped by a bleak expanse of chipped concrete columns and cracked metal fittings. The crumbling construction didn't inspire much confidence, particularly when one considered the two hundred feet of empty airspace that filled the void between the bottom of the bridge and the choppy water of the bay.

Instinctively, I gripped the plastic armrest formed into the paneling of the passenger side door, mindful of the seismic demons that lurked beneath the bridge's shaky footings. It wasn't until the van popped out into the Oakland sunlight on the opposite side of the bay that I unclenched and breathed out a sigh of relief.

A glance back to the cargo area confirmed that the cats had both settled into the ride.

After making several loud snorkeling sniffs as the van left Jackson Square, Rupert had now assumed his regular slumbering position inside his plastic carrier. He lay flat on his back, his front and back legs curled up limply in the air. His breathing had transitioned into a heavy wheezing snore. He would likely be out for the duration of the trip.

The occupant of the second carrier, in contrast, remained alert and ready for action. Isabella sat stiffly erect, her head slightly hunched down so she could see out the carrier's front metal screen. Her right paw occasionally scratched the towel she was sitting on as her blue eyes honed in on the steering wheel. She looked up at me sternly.

"Mrao," she commanded. It was only twenty minutes into the trip, and Isabella was already asking to move up to the driver's seat.

With a placating smile at my frustrated cat, I turned back to face the roadway just as the van joined the interstate that would take us to

Sacramento and, beyond, Nevada City. Since we had at least two more hours to go, I decided to adopt Rupert's approach to traveling and snuggled down into my seat for a nap.

THE OCCUPANTS OF the van were unaware of the small convoy of vehicles accompanying them on the road to Nevada City that morning.

Eighty miles ahead, a perky pink convertible with a roll-down top and whitewall tires approached the outskirts of Sacramento. An elderly woman in a fluttering multicolored scarf and rose-tinted motor goggles manned the wheel. She wore a pleasant smile on her face as she gazed out at the bright red blooms of the oleander bushes growing in the interstate median.

It was a perfect day for a drive to the mountains, Dilla Eckles thought as her foot pressed down on the gas pedal and she weaved into the left-hand passing lane.

"Ah, the Bear Flag," she called out enthusiastically, speaking loudly so that she could be heard over the roar of the motor. "Oscar worked on that project for quite some time."

She glanced over at her husband's frail figure. He sat in the passenger seat, mummified beneath several layers of scarves and blankets. "The mountain air will do you good, dear," she said, her voice layered with concern.

Through a pair of mirrored aviator sunglasses,

Mr. Wang surveyed the low, sandy bottomlands that flanked the road. He took in a deep breath, summoning all the strength he could muster; the ache in his bones had grown more and more burdensome in recent weeks. With effort, he reached his left hand across the car's interior and rested it reassuringly on Dilla's knee. It was best, he'd decided, that his wife didn't know about the seedy brown sedan following them a couple of car lengths behind.

THE SEDAN WAS an older model vehicle, recently purchased for cash at a low-end used car lot. A thick color-dulling coat of dust and grime masked a rippling of dents in the side paneling. The front windshield's only visibility was through the portion of glass cleared by the arc of the wipers. Despite its decrepit outward appearance, the old sedan had more than enough power to keep the pink convertible in sight.

The driver leaned back in the worn bucket seat and thoughtfully stroked his chin. With a yawn, he wiped a crumb from his cheek, a remnant of the hasty breakfast he'd picked up on the way out of town.

Behind the dusty screen of the windshield, the driver's flat featureless face and thin, almost indistinguishable lips were as nondescript as the car. As the rusted rims of the sedan spun along the flatlands of the Sacramento Delta, Frank

Napis glanced up at a tiny stuffed bear hanging by a string from his rearview mirror. He tapped the bear with a stubby finger, causing it to swing back and forth.

Sitting in the passenger seat beside Napis, a second man stared out the half-moon section of clear glass on the windshield's right side. A narrow scar ran along the man's jawline, far more noticeable now that his head was shaved bald. His golden-brown locks had been shorn off nearly a year ago, when he'd been sent back to prison for the attempted poisoning of a woman who ran a Jackson Square antiques shop.

It had been a difficult internment at San Quentin for Ivan Batrachos. The pallor of his once-rich olive skin evidenced the strain of his confinement; his eyes bore a gray listless gloss.

This was Ivan's first full day of freedom, but he evidenced no trace of joy, relief, or celebration. He sat in the sedan, rigidly immobile except for a faint twitch that transmitted along the bulge of his right arm through to where his muscular hand formed a tightly clenched fist.

BACK IN SAN Francisco, Harold Wombler's rusted-out pickup pulled onto an eastbound lane of the Bay Bridge. He drove along the lower deck with a casual, relaxed air, not the least bit worried about the possibility of earthquakes or the span's structural integrity. If it was his fate to die in a watery grave of twisted metal, so be it. He wasn't going to waste a second of his life fretting about the possibility.

With a maximum highway speed of forty-five miles per hour, the truck would have been quickly outpaced by the other vehicles, even if it had left the city at the same time. But as the truck's ancient engine squeaked and squalled across the bridge, Harold had no concerns about catching up with the convertible, the sedan, or even the large white van. He knew where they were all headed, and he would get there eventually.

As the pickup began a slow, rumbling trek along the inland interstate route to Sacramento, Harold glanced over at his passengers, one of whom he'd picked up at the Green Vase on his way out of town.

On the frayed cushion of the truck's bench seat, avidly watching the colorful stretch of oleander flashing by on the median, sat a pair of small green frogs wearing feathery orange mustaches.

Next to the frogs rode a tiny hairless mouse, recently outfitted in a furry green jacket.

Chapter 11
NEVADA CITY

A COUPLE OF hours up the road, the tiny mountain town of Nevada City bustled with activity as it prepared to welcome the Tour of California. Banners greeting the cyclists were plastered across the windows of homes and businesses. Red, white, and blue streamers decorated fence posts and mailboxes; lampposts were adorned with pairings of California state and U.S. flags.

Cycling fans had begun to filter into town, filling the restaurants and bistros, dramatically increasing the percentage of spandex leggings walking the streets. Sidewalk conversations all trended in one way or another toward the upcoming race.

Spread across the lower hills of the Sierra Nevada, Nevada City's historic settlement straddled the top end of Highway 49, Gold Country's main transportation corridor. The town captured the woodsy, peaceful, easygoing essence of the surrounding pine-tree forest. The damp moisture of an elevated ocean breeze fed a fuzzy green layer of moss that covered the north-facing surface of almost every trunk.

Known primarily as a weekend getaway for mountain bikers, nature lovers, and the occasional mining enthusiast, Nevada City was located about an hour northeast of Sacramento, safely outside the hubbub of the capital city's sprawling suburbs. A steady influx of graying retirees swelled the ranks of the town's full-time residents, mixing with an eclectic group of artists, hippies, and life-enjoyment specialists.

The laid-back mountain community also saw its share of Bay Area yuppie-naires, cash-laden bankers, lawyers, and high-tech entrepreneurs seeking out the perfect wilderness setting for their enormous vacation homes. Over the last couple of years, these McMansion-style estates had popped up like mushrooms, seemingly overnight, in nearby meadows and forest clearings. As it turned out, the owners of these properties were just as transient in their departure as in their arrival—the state's recent economic downturn had led to a plumage of colorful FOR SALE and FORECLOSURE signs on many of these expansive front lawns.

The silent hills of the Sierra Nevada were unmoved by such fluctuations in fortune. They had seen boom and bust cycles before; they accepted both with equal passivity.

Time moved slowly through this region. The relics of an earlier era's flirtation with the fickle whims of the mining industry were strewn across the landscape. Discarded water cannons that once pummeled gold dust from eroding hillsides sat rusting in dried up riverbeds. Wooden flumes that had been used to funnel river runoff to these canons crisscrossed the forest.

During the height of the Gold Rush, the mining camps surrounding Nevada City had attracted some of the Sierras' highest concentrations of gold-seeking immigrants. The area's population exploded, leading to a proliferation of miner-friendly taverns and saloons along the town's main thoroughfare of Broad Street.

Several of Nevada City's modern-day establishments claim heritage back to that wild and woolly Gold Rush–era, although nowadays, they cater to a somewhat less grimy clientele. Certainly the two distinguished gentlemen bellied up to the wood-paneled bar on the first floor of the National Hotel bore little resemblance to the grisly miners who once straddled their seats.

As the leading television broadcasters for the sport of professional cycling, Will Spigot and Harry Carlin were celebrities in the biking world, their faces instantly recognizable to the sport's myriad fans. Spigot and Carlin had been covering the professional cycling circuit together for as long as either one of them could remember. They were a well-oiled team, accustomed to each other's commentating style and personal eccentricities. Cycling fans loved to listen to their banter.

Will Spigot was a white-haired fox of a man

with a slight build, sharp angular features, and a cheeky British wit. He relished the thrill of a close race, easily losing himself in the action until he was nearly as breathless as the panting riders whose progress he described.

Once the day's racing was done, Spigot turned his attention to life's finer comforts. He considered himself an expert on all aspects of high-end food, wine, and lodging, and he could provide extensive discourse and advice on these topics for every city, town, and hamlet that had hosted an international cycling stage within the past twenty-five years. He was a gentle, kindhearted man to all those around him—except when it came to the whims of his palate and the pleasures of a restful night's sleep. Waiters and hotel staff crossed him at their peril.

Spigot's broadcasting partner and long-suffering traveling companion was Harry Carlin, a fellow Brit and retired professional cyclist who had competed at the highest echelons of the sport during his day—long before cycling reached its current level of commercial success. As such, Carlin had a much greater tolerance for the hassles and inconveniences of travel. Truth be known, he rather enjoyed the humorous and unpredictable exploits that life on the road provided.

A rugged square-faced character, Harry was an intellectual, keenly interested in the world around him. He spent the cycling off-season on his farm in Africa, diligently researching the cultural and historical background of the coming stops along the racing calendar as well as any notable landmarks falling near the route. No tidbit of trivia escaped his study. Carlin worked hard to interject these obscure facts into his racing commentary—often over his partner's objections.

Will Spigot glanced around the bar at its dainty mirrors, vintage wall mountings, and glass-fronted liquor cabinet before turning his gaze to his broadcasting companion. Carlin, he suspected, was the one responsible for choosing the location for their pre-race telecast.

Spigot waited for the last of the monitors and mikes to be connected; then he cleared his throat and began his introduction.

"Welcome to Nevada City, California. We're coming to you live from the *historic* bar of the National Hotel."

The camera panned from Spigot's wry grin to Harry Carlin's earnest countenance.

"This is the start of a new era for the Tour of California," Spigot said affably. "For the first time since its inception, the starting date has been moved from February to May. This was due in part to the absolutely abysmal weather that plagued the Tour last year, when I believe it rained each and every day we were here—took me a month to dry out afterwards." He shuddered with remembrance. "We've been assured that won't happen *this* time."

Carlin nodded his agreement as Spigot continued.

"Apart from the weather, the change in the starting date is meant to bring California's tour into the meat and potatoes of the cycling calendar. It's only been around for a few short years, but the Tour of California has rightfully become one of the world's most preeminent professional cycling races. Many of the sport's topflight cyclists will be competing here this week. The event is now being seen as an important warm-up for the granddaddy of them all, the Tour de France."

He turned to look at his colleague. "Harry, we should have an excellent week of racing ahead of us."

Harry Carlin leaned toward the camera as it swung his direction. "Will, I couldn't agree with you more. It will all start here tomorrow morning in Nevada City, on Broad Street, right outside of where we're sitting. The riders will make a parade circuit through this quaint little town and then kick out onto Highway 49 for the ride down to Sacramento."

Carlin arched an eyebrow at Spigot. "You know, it's a rather interesting place, this Nevada City. Most of the buildings up and down Broad Street, including this one, go all the way back to the Gold Rush days."

Spigot's mouth twisted cynically. "Yes, well, a bit of history is all fine and good," he replied with a sour expression. "But you can take an idea a step too far. Not everything is meant to be retained and, ahem, *preserved*."

Carlin winced visibly. "Oh dear, this is about your room, isn't it?"

Spigot tilted his head skeptically. "I haven't had time to fully inspect the accommodations, but I must say, I have concerns."

"I'm sure we'll get the full report tomorrow."

"You bet you will."

"All right then, William," Carlin said with a chuckle. "Now, about the race . . ."

Chapter 12

IN THE VAN

MONTGOMERY CARMICHAEL STRUMMED his fingers against the dashboard's plastic rim, thinking about how much he loved his big white van.

It was an amazing machine, a tank and a mobile man-cave. Whenever he was behind its wheel, he felt invincible. There was no task he couldn't accomplish, no cargo he couldn't haul.

Several years ago, he'd unbolted the second and third rows of seats from the floor, creating a cavernous storage area in the back half of the van to accommodate the numerous pieces of artwork that flowed in and out of his studio. Today, he thought with pride, that same open space was loaded with his flashy new road bike, several pieces of luggage, two cat-filled carriers, and enough cat-related paraphernalia to support at least twenty cats for a week, if not longer.

Monty beamed out the front windshield as the van passed through the eastern outskirts of Sacramento. His right hand skimmed down the dashboard and flipped on the radio. Then, his long bony fingers twirled the dial, searching for a local sports' station.

"Aha, that's it!" he exclaimed as the static of two British voices began to emit from the van's speakers.

The broadcasters were discussing the next day's race route. After the riders left Nevada City, they would navigate a winding path through the forest until they reached the interstate. Once they crossed beneath, they would swing out into the delta for a wide loop before turning toward the finish line in downtown Sacramento. A spark lit Monty's eyes as the inspiration for an idea registered across his face.

He glanced over at the dozing woman in the passenger seat. *Perfect,* he thought with a mischievous grin. There'll be no opposition to this little detour.

Monty hit the blinker as he approached the next

exit ramp. A moment later, the van left the interstate for a narrow two-lane road that disappeared almost immediately into a dense thicket of pine trees.

From one of the plastic carriers in the back cargo area, a concerned voice called out, *"Mrao."*

RUPERT GAZED SLEEPILY up at his carrier's plastic roof as his furry body soaked in the soothing hum of the van's rumbling motor. His joints were perfectly relaxed and loosened from the vibration of the wheels rolling along the road below. He stretched his mouth into a wide yawn. He could ride like this for hours and hours . . . that is, until it was time to eat.

Rupert's mouth snapped shut as he considered the arrival of a future hunger. He lifted his head to look out over the soft cushion of his belly. He had expected Monty's van to be stocked with his favorite food, fried chicken. Certainly, there was enough room here in the cargo area for cooking equipment and a small stove, but he hadn't seen anything resembling fried chicken in the packages that had been loaded up that morning.

Rupert's blue eyes narrowed into slits as he stared at the corner of Monty's elbow, all he could make out from the crate's position on the floor. He would take this matter up with Monty at the next stop. That—and the strange clothes he'd started wearing. All that shiny green spandex was not a flattering look for a creature who had so little body fur to begin with.

Just like that mouse, Rupert mused drowsily as the image of the tiny bald rodent skittered across his brain. He cringed at the recollection of the animal's wrinkly pink skin.

Fur, in Rupert's fluffy-haired opinion, was the only way to go.

I WOKE TO a swerving sensation and the voices of two men with foreign accents coming from the radio. The men were engaged in a vigorous discussion apparently related to the upcoming bike race, but I had no idea what to make of their references to field sprints, breakaways, and a person who called himself King of the Mountains.

Of one thing I was certain: The van was no longer on the interstate.

"Monty?" I mumbled sleepily as the van slowed to navigate a sharp turn. Tree trunks bordered both sides of the road, inches from the edge of the asphalt. Every hundred yards or so, a dented mailbox appeared in the greenery. This route was much deeper into the forest than the one I had envisioned from the map.

"Are you sure this is Highway 49?" I asked skeptically.

"We're taking an alternative route," he replied confidently. He nodded at the radio. "I'm using Will and Harry's directions to get to Nevada City.

We're following the first part of tomorrow's racecourse—in reverse. Just sit back and relax. Embrace the unexpected. Take it all in. Imagine yourself on a bike, feet pumping at the pedals, the wind in your face, competitors at your wheel . . . Isn't it exhilarating?"

Monty's life coach mumbo jumbo wasn't doing anything to temper my concern. I sighed nervously as he leaned forward to steer around another sharp corner.

Twisting in my seat, I turned to check on Isabella. Her sharp eyes, I suspected, had not left the road the entire time I'd been asleep.

"Errau," she opined dubiously.

"Yep," I agreed as Monty swung the van into another fishhook-shaped curve. "We're lost."

Even if I'd had a sense of north or south when I first opened my eyes, I would have quickly lost it. There were no markers upon which to fix a mental compass. The trees were so tall they blocked almost all angles of direct sunlight. A thick carpet of pine needles covered the ground, obliterating any unique features that might have provided a distinctive marking. There was a disorienting sameness to the surroundings.

At least we'd left San Francisco with a full tank of gas, I thought with a sigh.

In search of a distraction from Monty's sure-to-be-lengthy detour, I reached into my pocket and pulled out the toy bear.

Bears, I considered as I stared at the figurine, were used symbolically on almost all of California's state logos. The image of a grizzly bear featured prominently on the state flag, the state seal, and most state-designated historical markers.

The bear references were an homage to the short-lived California Republic, formed in 1846 when a small band of Americans took over the tiny town of Sonoma and declared its independence from Mexico. The rough and rowdy group called themselves "Osos" or "Bear-Flaggers," after the bear-emblazoned flag they raised in the town square to celebrate their success.

Oscar had laid a trail for something bear or possibly Bear Flag related, I puzzled, sucking in on my lower lip. But what? I stared at the paper flag attached to the toothpick in the toy bear's paw. Perhaps I'd find the answer in Nevada City—that is, if we ever managed to get there.

I looked out the van's front windshield as we passed a green-roofed building with several tan trucks parked out front. I couldn't be certain, but I thought we'd passed this forest service station once before.

"Are you *sure* you know where you're going?" I asked with increasing anxiety.

Monty waved me off, never once doubting his estimation of our whereabouts.

"Trust me. We're right on track. Any minute

now, we'll pop out of these woods right into Nevada City."

Isabella grumbled from the back cargo area.

"Now, if I've got this right," Monty stretched the words out in anticipation, "it should be just around this next bend . . ."

The trees parted to reveal a green and white metal sign. Twenty feet beyond the sign, the road widened into an interstate on-ramp. The van slowed as we approached the intersection, and Monty cleared his throat.

The sign read: SACRAMENTO 5 MILES.

Chapter 13

CALAVERAS COUNTY

WHILE MONTY'S WHITE van sat idling in front of the westbound interstate on-ramp, Harold Wombler's pickup rumbled past on one of the opposite eastbound lanes.

Another mile up the road, Harold bypassed the prominent signage for the exit north to Nevada City and, instead, turned south onto Highway 49. The pickup set off along a meandering route that tracked across the rural farmland of the lower Sierra hills and valleys. On the bench seat next to Harold, his trio of tiny passengers leaned into the curves, happily watching the rolling green landscape.

After a pleasant hour's drive, the pickup entered the parking lot for the Calaveras County Fairgrounds. A green and white banner beside the road announced the day's seminal event—the county's annual Mark Twain Frog Jumping Competition.

"Here we are, then," Harold said to his charges as he pulled to a stop in a grassy field, alongside several trucks of similar vintage and condition to his own.

Harold gimped around to the truck's bed and opened a metal storage locker mounted behind the cab's exterior. He reached inside and pulled out an ice chest packed with an assortment of leaves and a container of chilled crickets.

Harold then opened the lid to a glass-sided terrarium and splashed in a generous amount of cool water. He selected a couple of leafy fronds from the cooler and scattered them across the bottom of the glass cage, topping them off with a few crickets. As soon as he pushed the terrarium into the truck's cab, the two frogs hopped eagerly inside.

After helping the mouse climb into the front chest pocket of his overalls, Harold secured the terrarium's ventilated lid, wrapped his fingers around the handle, and began the long walk up to the fairground entrance. It was a sunny afternoon, and he was breathing heavily by the time he approached the ticket booth.

The booth was located inside a white one-story building whose walls were decorated with the painted pictures of several leaping frogs. A row of California Bear Flags mounted onto the building's roof flapped in the breeze as Harold set the terrarium on the counter.

The two frogs peered politely through the glass at the ticket agent. Harold lifted the brim of his baseball hat to smooth down his stringy black hair and announced curtly, "We're here to jump."

The woman seated inside the booth stared back, a surprised openmouthed expression on her face as she studied the frogs' tiny orange mustaches. She'd seen a wide range of jumping contestants that day: enormous bullfrogs, long-legged marsh dwellers, and even a few toads. Not one of the other amphibian entrants had sported facial hair.

"That'll be six dollars," she said, her voice perplexed as she peered into the terrarium.

A moment later, Harold carried his frogs through the gated entrance and surveyed the scene.

At the front of the fairgrounds, a local singer warbled a lost-love country music song into a microphone. Behind her, children ran through a grassy field waving sticks wrapped with neon-colored cotton candy. Beyond, an asphalt-covered path led up a hill to a clutch of vendor stalls hawking hot dogs, bratwurst, and fresh-squeezed lemonade.

In the valley below the concession stands lay a collection of livestock barns, the largest of which was fronted by a stage and several rows of outdoor stadium seating. Harold followed the asphalt path to the livestock area, pausing every so often to read the Mark Twain quotations printed on the placards that lined the route. At the show barn, he joined a line of children waiting with their frogs for a turn on the jumping stage.

"No serious contenders here that I can see," Harold whispered hoarsely into the terrarium as the line slowly cleared in front of him.

At long last, Harold stepped to the front of the queue. A man in a broad-brimmed cowboy hat walked up and shook his hand.

"Let's see what you've got here," the announcer said, curiously studying the frogs and their mustaches. "Two contestants?"

Harold nodded gruffly. "One amateur. One pro."

"All *right-y* then," the man said with a raised eyebrow. "Let's have your, uh, amateur, first."

The announcer flicked the switch on a wireless microphone as he motioned for Harold to step onto the stage. Frog wranglers holding long poles attached to black nets formed a perimeter around the edge of the area, ready to capture any renegade jumpers contemplating an escape. As the announcer began to speak into the mike, his voice took on a pronounced twang.

"Ladies and gentlemen, we've got a real treat coming up next. Mister, uh . . ." He looked questioningly at Harold.

"Wombler," Harold supplied grumpily.

"Mr. Wombler has a rather *unique* pair of frogs for today's jumping contest. I don't reckon we've ever seen the likes of his amphibians in these here parts. Lean in close and get a good look, folks. These frogs are wearing little costumes!"

The announcer glanced up from the mustached frogs and whispered to Harold, "Don't you think that's a disadvantage? Weighing them down like that?"

Harold shrugged noncommittally. The announcer paused, temporarily flustered, before ushering Harold to a one-foot circle painted on the center of the stage.

"They'll be stylish if nothing else," he said cheerfully. "Please, Mister, uh, Wombler. Place your first entrant on the circle here."

Harold reached inside the terrarium, scooped up the smaller frog, and gently set him on the middle of the stage.

The little frog looked excitedly up at Harold. The red sliver of his tongue zipped out of his mouth and slapped the tip of his nose above his mustache.

"Now, sir, what's the frog's name?" the announcer asked, his voice booming through the speakers.

Harold rubbed the stubble on his chin, as if considering.

"Smiley," Harold replied curtly. "Jim Smiley."

"Smiley the frog," the announcer proclaimed as the crowd politely applauded. "I understand this is his first professional jump. Let's see what he can do."

The crowd grew quiet as Harold bent over and whispered to the frog. When Harold stepped back from the center, Smiley's back legs began to twitch. A moment later, he exploded into the air. The crowd erupted into cheers as the tiny frog's feet landed halfway across the stage. Harold pushed aside the nearest frog wrangler to retrieve Smiley while the announcer measured the distance between the circle and the jump mark.

"Fourteen feet, two inches!" the announcer gushed. "Best jump of the day!"

Harold nodded silently, a pleased smile creasing his wrinkled face. He reached back into the terrarium for the larger frog.

The announcer rushed over with his microphone. "Now, Mr. Wombler, please introduce us to your second entry—the, ah, veteran jumper."

"Daniel," Harold supplied bluntly. "This frog's name is Daniel."

"Well, Daniel," the announcer said, bending down toward the circle where the frog waited patiently. "Your little friend has set the mark to beat."

Daniel wore a serious, pondering expression on his pudgy face as he looked down his nose at the corners of his mustache. The audience edged forward in their seats, watching attentively as Harold nodded a go-ahead sign to the second frog.

Daniel rocked back and forth, concentrating on a spot several feet ahead. After a moment of intense focus, he launched himself into the air. Despite his heavy bulk, Daniel's jump was far more measured and graceful than the smaller frog's, his movements reminiscent of a bird taking flight. He stretched out his legs as he soared above the stage, and a slight breeze whiffled through the feathery hair of his mustache. Then, with a thudding *plunk,* he landed on the far edge of the platform, a foot or so farther than the previous jump.

The crowd broke into a raucous applause as Daniel waddled proudly over to Harold, who lowered the terrarium so that he could hop inside. The announcer hurriedly measured the distance to Daniel's jump mark.

"Sixteen feet, seven inches!" he exclaimed. "That's a Calaveras County Fair record!"

Chapter 14

BROAD STREET

A COUPLE OF hours later, the white van finally arrived in Nevada City.

"Here we are!" Monty proclaimed enthusiastically. "Like I said, right around the corner. I knew we'd get here."

Isabella grumbled a sarcastic congratulations from her carrier.

Rupert still lay on his back in the crate beside her. He yawned sleepily and stretched his front legs up and over his head. He was the only one who had enjoyed the long winding ride through the forest. All the sweeping turns had rocked him like a baby in a cradle. By the time we'd located the far-straighter thoroughfare of Highway 49's northern route, Rupert had fallen into a deep snoring trance.

The van entered Nevada City's downtown area and proceeded slowly up Broad Street. The sidewalks were packed with pedestrians, many decked from head to toe in colorful skintight cycling gear. Mobile vendors worked the street corners hawking all manner of race-related clothing and memorabilia. A variety of T-shirts and bumper stickers were on offer, along with a wide range of noisemaking devices designed to provide encouragement to passing riders during the race.

A painted cowbell rang just outside my window. Even through the glass pane, the metallic clanking jarred my eardrums. I don't know how the sound affected professional cyclists, but it certainly would have spurred me to pedal faster—if only to get away from the nuisance of its noise.

The cowbells had a much more positive effect on Monty. His green eyes sparkled as he soaked up the energy of the crowd. He couldn't wait to join them.

"Look at all these people," he enthused. His voice squeaked higher as he pointed to a couple walking their rides through the throng. "Some of them have their bikes!"

The commotion on the street finally woke Rupert from his slumber. He sat up in his carrier and tried to see out the front windshield as Monty slowly circled the van behind Broad Street to our hotel's parking lot.

There were only a few open spaces; much of the lot was occupied by television vans bearing brightly painted logos from state and local media. Gigantic satellite dishes were mounted on the vehicles' roofs; metal antennae spikes poked out from every angle.

In between the media vans sat several gleaming state-of-the-art tour buses. The riders spilled out of their homes-on-wheels into the busy parking lot where they mingled with media, sponsors, and support staff. With lean muscular bodies, minimal body fat, shaved legs, and short-clipped hairstyles, the professional athletes were easy to pick out.

We found a shaded space for the van several hundred yards away from the rear of the hotel, and I sent Monty out on his bike to explore. I figured the delicate process of trying to check into our rooms with the cats could wait until later—preferably after dark. In the meantime, I let the cats loose in the van to stretch their legs.

Rupert shook his head with a short chin-flapping vibration; then he proceeded behind the curtain to the red igloo-shaped litter box. By the time I'd set out the cats' food and water dishes, he was merrily digging away. I returned to the front passenger seat and rolled down the window, hoping to dissipate some of the smells associated with Rupert's ruckus in the cargo hold.

After a lengthy visit to the food and water station, Isabella sauntered to the front of the van and hopped into the driver's seat. Her tail wrapped tightly around her body as she sat primly looking up at the steering wheel. Her claws flexed, gripping the seat cover's leather fabric. Slowly, she turned her head toward me, an expression of entitlement on her pert face.

"I don't care how long you sit there," I said with a stern sigh. "You're not driving the van."

Isabella glared back, her blue eyes resolute. *"Mreow,"* she replied curtly.

Thoroughly satisfied with his litter box session, Rupert bounced into the front seating area to join us. He climbed happily onto my lap, the feathery poof of his tail sticking straight up in the air. I tried to dodge the inevitable tail whap to my face as Rupert turned around in a circle, kneading my stomach, his typical precursor activity to curling up in my lap.

"Okay, you two," I said, scooping up Rupert before he could collapse into his second nap of the day. "Let's see what kind of bears we can find in Nevada City."

WITHIN THE NETWORK of team buses and television trucks, a bevy of mechanics had set up shop on the asphalt, spreading out their bike stands and toolboxes so they could fine-tune the high-end cycles that would be used for the coming race. Wrenches whipped through the air, wheels spun, and tubes of lubricant squirted in every direction.

In the midst of all this frenetic activity, one man kept his head down, avoiding eye contact with the other mechanics. From the hunch of his shoulders, it was difficult to make out the narrow etching of the scar that ran down the left side of his face. Ivan Batrachos knew how to avoid drawing attention to himself.

No one noticed as he left his pile of tools and followed a woman pushing a large stroller across the parking lot.

IT TOOK AT least fifteen minutes for me to figure out how to unfold the Cat-mobile, but I finally managed to assemble it into its open configuration. After that struggle, loading the cats into the carriage compartment was a relatively straightforward, if not altogether scratch-free, procedure. Then, I locked up the van and directed the stroller toward the Broad Street end of the congested parking lot.

Isabella sat upright in the carriage, keenly looking out through the screened netting that covered the passenger compartment. For his part, Rupert began tunneling down into the pile of old towels I'd tucked in with him. He was not one to be dissuaded once he'd decided it was time for a nap. As Isabella's eyes stretched wide, taking in all the colorful sights, Rupert put his paws over his ears and wound himself into a determined white ball.

The area where we'd parked the van was mostly level, but the portion of the parking lot that led toward Broad Street was laid out across a steep side slope. Isabella issued a slew of cautionary comments as I maneuvered the stroller down the slick grade. All the while my hands tightly gripped the bar that formed the back handle, fearful of the wild ride the stroller might take if I lost control of it.

When we reached the sidewalk at the bottom of the parking lot, I stopped to look up and down the street, trying to get my bearings amid the sea of pedestrians.

On my right, the road dropped down to form an overpass over Highway 49. Broad Street's historic district spread out across a sloping hill above us to the left.

"Mrao," Isabella called out from the carriage.

"Up it is," I replied, flexing my leg muscles. I grunted as I began pushing the carriage up the sidewalk's incline. "It might be time for one of these cats to go on a diet."

Rupert wheezed out a loud I'm-ignoring-you snore.

I continued up the street, pausing every so often to weave around people mingling outside restaurants or perusing racing memorabilia from one of the many mobile vendors. Surprisingly few bystanders noticed the cats in the stroller. Most assumed the carriage compartment contained human passengers and politely jumped out of our way.

I was immersed in and yet separate from the crowds, a woman pushing a stroller loaded with cats through hoards of cycling-obsessed fans. I tried not to think of how ridiculous I looked as I searched the street for any reference to Oscar's toy bear or the California state flag it held in its paw. So far, the Bear Flags attached to the lampposts along Broad Street were the only potential clue I'd found, but that seemed reason enough to continue my slow climb up the hill.

As a small group moved to clear my path, I noticed a line of sandwich boards dotting the sidewalk ahead of us. Due to the heavy pedestrian traffic, I couldn't read the first advertisement until I was right in front of the placard. Bright green lettering on a white background read:

ON STAGE TODAY AT
THE HISTORIC NEVADA THEATRE:

A DELIGHTFUL LINEUP
OF THRILLING ENTERTAINMENT . . .

The area was too crowded to see very far up the street, but the theater, I suspected, was just up the hill.

I glanced down at the stroller. "Hmm," I said to Isabella. "Let's give this a look-see."

About ten yards farther on, we reached a second placard that pronounced:

TWO ENORMOUS ELEPHANTS
WILL NOT BELLY DANCE
FOR YOUR ENTERTAINMENT!

The *not* was in a dramatically smaller print, so that one had to squint to read it.

Isabella stared at the sandwich board for several seconds; then she issued her instructions.

"Mrao," she said sharply.

"It's a teaser, Issy," I replied with a laugh. "They're just trying to suck you in."

"Mrao," she insisted.

"Okay, okay," I said, shaking my head. I waited for an opening in the surrounding foot traffic; then I maneuvered the stroller around the placard.

Another block up the street, we stopped in front of a third green and white sign propped up against the side of a lamppost. It offered a similarly misleading enticement:

A TALENTED TROUP OF
IMAGINARY HIPPOPOTAMI
WILL PERFORM THE RUMBA!

"Hippopotami," I muttered with a grin, but Isabella was now even more determined.

"Wraaaow," she called out persistently.

"What would happen if I ever stopped taking orders?" I asked with an exasperated sigh, but I moved the stroller forward anyway.

We found the red brick two-story building that housed the Nevada Theatre at the top of Broad Street's long hill. Tall arched windows with black-painted shutters faced the sidewalk. A notice board set into the wall denoted it as "California's oldest original-use theater." Further details boasted of famous thespians and presenters who had appeared on its stage, including onetime San Francisco newspaper reporter Mark Twain.

The last piece of information immediately piqued my interest. Mark Twain had been one of my uncle's favorite writers. The previous summer, I'd found an old photo of Oscar dressed up as Twain—his costume had included the writer's signature rumpled linen suit and bristly white mustache.

My pulse began pounding as I pushed the stroller up to the fourth and final billboard, displayed outside the theater's front entrance. The crudely drawn image of a bear took up the left-hand side of the poster space. Isabella began frantically pawing at the stroller's top netting as I read the writing next to the animal:

A WILD CALIFORNIA
GRIZZLY BEAR
WILL NOT BE SERVING
COCKTAILS INSIDE!

Chapter 15

CLEM

THE FRONT DOORS of the theater were propped open, an indication, I assumed, that the show was about to begin. I pushed the stroller over the threshold and paused in the entrance, letting my eyes adjust to the dusky interior.

The walls of the lobby were covered with a rough concrete plaster, giving the room the feel of a cold damp cave. It was an eerie contrast to the warming bustle on the street outside.

The place had a recently vacated aura. A table pushed up against the back wall contained the remnants of what appeared to have been a sizeable spread of hors d'oeuvres and snack food. A handful of leftover sandwiches, each one cut into a triangle with the crusts removed, lay on a tray alongside a few scattered cookies and a lone deviled egg.

Rupert suddenly woke from his slumber and stretched his head upward, sniffing hungrily against the stroller's top netting.

"You just ate," I hissed down at him.

He gave me a confused look as he smacked his lips together. His last meal in the back of the van was already long forgotten.

I tapped Rupert's head through the netting and

turned my attention to the door leading into the theater's auditorium. Red velvet curtains had been pulled back to facilitate entrance into a semicircular stadium of seating. An easel-mounted placard beside the curtains identified the evening's performer as traveling Mark Twain impersonator Clement Samuels.

I grinned at the sign and whispered down into the stroller. "Doubt that's his real name, Issy."

She murmured her agreement as I peeked through the curtains to the auditorium. The overhead lighting had been dimmed, and the members of the audience had taken their seats. The room was filled with the respectful silence of a preperformance hush.

I didn't see anyone selling or collecting tickets, so I nosed the stroller inside and rolled it down a wide aisle near one of the back rows. With a light thud, I flipped the red vinyl cushion of the nearest chair into its horizontal position and sank into the anonymity of the darkness.

Craning my neck, I could just make out the front rim of a balcony positioned above my row of seats. Given the numerous pieces of lighting and sound equipment poking out over the ledge, the second floor looked as if it was closed off to the audience.

I dropped my gaze to the darkened area around me. The auditorium's walls and floor were constructed of the same concrete substance as those in the lobby. If the theater was as old as it claimed, I mused, extensive renovations must have been done to the original structure.

At the bottom cusp of the seating area, a focused flood of light poured down onto the stage, where an open checkerboard surface awaited the afternoon's performer.

Looking out across the audience, I noticed the front spotlights reflected the tops of mostly white-haired heads. The majority of today's patrons, I suspected, were local theatergoers. The occasional cycling tourist mixed into the crowd was easy to pick out.

After a crackling of static, a man's deep, resonant voice, warmed by the soft edge of a Southern drawl, echoed from behind the stage. "Friends, Romans, countrymen—and a few bewildered bystanders drawn in from the street. Welcome to the Nevada Theatre!"

A whiskery, rosy-cheeked man in a tattered black bow tie and a rumpled linen suit strolled gallantly onto the stage. He stroked the corners of a white mustache as he approached the microphone stand. Then, standing center stage, he turned toward the audience and pumped his wild flyaway eyebrows.

I stared at the actor, momentarily transfixed. The unkempt eyebrows, the bended curve of his shoulders, the twinkle in his eyes as he assessed the crowd—all these features were strikingly similar to the man in the black-and-white photo

I'd found almost a year earlier in the basement beneath the Green Vase—the photo of my Uncle Oscar posing as Mark Twain.

I tried for a moment to recall the details of the photograph so that I could perform a mental comparison between my costumed uncle and the actor on the stage. But quickly, I abandoned the idea. Of course there'd be a strong resemblance between the two men, I told myself with a firm reasoning gulp. They were both impersonating the same historical figure.

"Ladies, gentlemen, and"—the man paused for effect—"*assorted beasts.*" I gripped the handle of the stroller as he winked toward the rear of the auditorium. "Again, welcome to this afternoon's program. Now, I presume introductions are unnecessary?"

He stopped expectantly, as if waiting for confirmation from the audience. As the silence stretched out, he turned his whole body sideways, cupped his hand around his right ear, and leaned out over the front row of seats.

"What's that I hear?" he called out belligerently, stamping his lace-up ankle boots in exaggerated irritation as he spun to face the audience. "Surely, my reputation precedes me?"

Beneath the overgrown mustache, the man's lips puckered petulantly. He unbuttoned the loose-fitting linen jacket and stroked the paunch of his collared white shirt.

"Don't tell me that you are unaware of my extensive collection of work?" He put his hands on his hips defiantly. "Come now, I have not been dead that long. Someone in the audience must have read my writings . . ."

He scanned the crowd in frustration. His face grew pained as his voice pinched with disbelief.

"See here, I have it on good authority that my subversive propaganda has thoroughly infiltrated the educational system of this country . . ."

He began to pace back and forth indignantly. "A voluminous collection of texts explicitly crafted to inspire outrageous pranksterism and impish deviltry?"

The man's face reddened with mock outrage. "Manifestos which have corrupted generations of malleable young minds with their recountings of tomfoolery . . . and *Huck-Finnery*?"

The slightest whisper of a wink twitched the man's left eyebrow, triggering a few nervous giggles in the audience.

He leaned over the stage to examine a nine-year-old boy sitting in the front row next to a protective elderly woman in a silk scarf. The boy's eyes bulged as he plastered himself against his seat-back.

The actor's face broke into a gentle, reassuring grin. "Ma'am, is this your grandson?"

She nodded with a reserved smile.

The man beamed down at the boy. His voice

silked a rich comforting tone. "Ah, so innocent appears the bloom of youth."

He shifted his gaze back to the woman and thumped the lumpy bridge of his nose.

"Do not be deceived by this crafty little devil," he barked harshly. "The youth is a scheming and conniving beast—one of the most dangerous creatures known to mankind!" He leaned back on his heels with an appeasing grin. "I should know. I used to be one."

A ripple of laughter ran through the theater, and the man spread his arms wide. "We're all friends here. There's no need for the formality of our full Christian names," he said genially. "You can just call me . . ."

He picked up a four-foot-long wooden dowel stick and tapped it against a placard set up on an easel near the edge of the stage. It was identical to the one I'd passed in the foyer introducing the Mark Twain impersonator.

He cleared his throat with a loud "ahem." Then, with an extra jab of the pointer, he stated, "You can call me Clem."

Chapter 16

THE VIEW FROM THE BALCONY

HAROLD WOMBLER'S GREEN baseball cap bobbed through a sidewalk full of cycling fans as he lumbered up Broad Street toward the Nevada Theatre. A red cotton fabric flashed in the holes at his knees as he walked. After testing the late afternoon's crisp mountain air, he'd slipped on a precautionary pair of thermal underwear beneath his frayed overalls.

A prudent wardrobe choice, he thought to himself as he tugged the stretchy fabric to adjust the fit, but not nearly as comfortable.

From the front chest pocket of Harold's overalls, a pink nose popped up to check out the scene. Comfy in his tiny green jacket, the mouse twitched his whiskers as he soaked up the sights and smells of Nevada City.

In his right hand, Harold gripped the handle to the terrarium, taking care not to swing it as he walked. Before leaving the pickup, he'd refreshed the plant cuttings and tossed in a couple more chilled crickets. The two frogs rested comfortably on the wet leaves, their stomachs working to digest their afternoon snack. Every so often, the larger frog turned his head to stare proudly at the blue first-place ribbon tied to the terrarium's handle.

When he reached the top of the hill, Harold glanced briefly up and down the street to make sure he wasn't being followed. Not seeing anyone of concern, he ducked into the lobby of the Nevada Theatre.

Other than the food table positioned next to the auditorium's curtained entrance, the room was empty. Harold listened to Clem's voice echoing from the stage as he snatched up a triangular-shaped sandwich with his free hand and stuffed it into his mouth. Still chewing on the oversized bite, he shuffled over to a red velvet rope that had been looped across a flight of stairs leading to the balcony. With a last glance at the empty lobby, he goose-stepped over the rope and climbed the steps to the second floor.

A few seconds later, Harold stepped onto a landing packed with lighting and sound equipment. Booms, bulbs, and speaker boxes competed with one another for space. With difficulty, Harold made his way to the front row of seats and placed the frog terrarium on the ledge overlooking the auditorium. The frogs waddled to the side of their glass cage so they could peer down onto the patrons below. Harold carefully squeezed in behind the frogs and craned his neck over the top of the terrarium.

After a quick search of the audience, Harold spied a familiar pair of heads sitting in the middle of the theater: a woman with curly gray hair and, beside her, an elderly Asian man who was nearly bald. Dilla and Wang, he grunted silently. The Vigilance Committee was present and accounted for—Montgomery Carmichael had been left off the roster for the Bear Flag operation, which was plenty fine with Harold. That man had become even more unbearable since his recent promotion at the Mayor's office.

Harold rotated his head to study the space directly beneath the balcony. A woman with long brown hair sat next to a stroller containing two white cats. Through the carriage's net cover, a furry face with pointed orange ears looked up at him inquiringly.

Harold's bleary bloodshot eyes locked in on Isabella's clear blue ones. He jerked his head several times to the left; then he tapped the tip of his nose.

Isabella tilted her head up against the netting, cautiously pressing the flat pad of her nose against the underside of the zipper's metal slider. Following Harold's guidance, she began to move her head in quick jerking motions to the left, slowly inching the slider across the teeth of the zipper. The brown-haired woman sitting beside the stroller failed to notice as a cat-sized opening formed in the net cover.

Harold shifted his focus to the stage. The actor's cadence gradually began to increase as he built to a moment that would capture the audience's full attention.

When Harold saw the actor lean toward the front row, he motioned a go-ahead sign to Isabella. The actor growled viciously at the audience, causing the brown-haired woman to jump in her seat. Her attention remained fixed on the actor's bear impersonation as a flash of white fur leapt gracefully from the stroller.

Harold pushed back from the railing, a satisfied expression on his face. He reached into a pocket on the left side of his overalls. His thin lips twisted into a smirk as he unwrapped the package to reveal a toy bear holding a tiny paper flag in its outstretched paw.

Noiselessly, Harold eased his way to the rear of the balcony. Then, carrying the frogs in their cage, the mouse in his pocket, and the toy bear in his free hand, he quietly returned to the lobby.

IN A DARK corner of the balcony, where he'd sat watching Harold's entire charade with Isabella, Ivan Batrachos silently stroked the thin line of the scar that creased the left side of his face.

Chapter 17

THE WORDS OF MARK TWAIN

CLEM TAPPED THE microphone as the applause to his opener died down. "Now that we're all introduced," he continued jovially. "I'd like to move on to the main topic of today's lecture. This afternoon, I'll be discussing one of the more curious events from our state's early history."

He tilted his head conversationally. "The incident I'm about to relate to you happened a few years before I arrived on the scene, but I spoke to many firsthand witnesses, and I'm convinced my information is reliable and accurate."

Clem coughed lightly into his fist before amending. "Well—let's say *generally* reliable and *mostly* accurate." He shrugged his shoulders with a sheepish grin. "You have to allow me a few modest embellishments here and there."

His eyes flicked toward the back of the theater as he licked his lips dramatically. "Today, I'm going to tell you the story of the Bear Flag Revolt."

I edged forward in my seat as Clem leaned out over the front of the stage. Clearly, I had come to the right place, I thought as he suddenly assumed a threatening grizzly-bear stance and growled at the young boy in the front row. I felt myself jump, in tandem with the boy, who once more flattened himself against the back of his chair.

Clem chuckled reassuringly, "No, no, I promise, there aren't any *real* bears here tonight."

My hand instinctively reached into my pocket for the stuffed bear from Oscar's kitchen as my eyes stayed riveted to the action at the front of the auditorium.

"For a very brief time in the summer of 1846 . . ." Clem wacked the dowel stick against the rim of the stage as he pumped his eyebrows at the boy in the front row. "A very brief time, don't blink or you'll miss it."

Winking, he swung the stick up and over his shoulder. "California declared itself an independent republic. The Bear Flag Revolt was the beginning—and the end—of that independence movement."

Clem leaned the dowel stick against the microphone stand, tucked his hands into the small of his back, and began pacing back and forth across the stage.

"As I said, the Bear Flag Revolt took place in 1846. June fourteenth to be specific. Back then the West was a vast unknown territory, claimed by many, owned by none. It was a land of men. Men who were unfettered by the restraining yoke of a society's rules and regulations"—Clem reached up to the bent crook of his nose; dramatically pinching his fingers around the tip end, he squeaked out—"and its regiments of sanitation."

The crowd murmured in amusement.

"I'm not talking about those gold-grubbing Forty-Niners you here in Nevada City are so familiar with." Clem cleared his throat with a note of self-deprecation. "I count *myself* in that classification."

Straightening his shoulders, he self-consciously stroked the thin gray strands that covered the crown of his head. "No, I'm recollecting a time before those starry-eyed masses surged across land and sea to California's gold fields. This was a different group of explorers. Intrepid souls who came West hankering after something far more elusive than the gold nuggets that tumble through these frigid mountain streams."

Clem grumbled a shivering aside under his breath. "Blast those tormenting nuggets . . ." He shook his head as if to clear the memory.

"No, this was before the state took on its golden luster. In her early days, California attracted a different type of reckless visionary . . . ruthless, cunning men who were intent on fame, glory, and a permanent place in history—and they were willing to do anything to get it."

Clem dragged a wooden stool to center stage and eased himself onto the seat. "The old-man version of me needs a few props," he explained apologetically before resuming his dialogue.

"Our story begins with one such character, a

young gentleman who would become the leader of the Bear Flag Revolt: Captain John C. Frémont. He was in the U.S. Army Corps of Engineers—the part of the military responsible for drawing up maps of this country."

Clem politely cleared his throat. "Early on in his career, this here Frémont earned himself a nickname. It was a clever moniker, one that young John Charles wore with pride. He thought it was a compliment. You see, they called him 'the Pathfinder.'"

Clem issued a sly smile to the boy in the first row. "Beware of nicknames, lad," he said, slapping the top of his knee. "I don't know if Frémont ever caught on to the punch line about his nickname. He was a rather sensitive, touchy kind of fellow, and it's quite possible no one ever bothered to explain the joke to him for fear of the volcanic temper tantrum that might erupt."

Raising a finger toward the ceiling, Clem explained. "You see, the Pathfinder was known for blazing trails through the wilderness . . . his particular specialty was *finding paths* that had already been mapped out by others."

A roll of laughter passed through the crowd.

"Now," Clem admonished, wagging his finger at the audience. "This is not to say that our Pathfinder lacked ingenuity or that he in any way shied away from danger. Oh no. Long before his landmark visit to California, he'd demonstrated he was full to the brim with conniving initiative as well as the blindest form of bravery."

Clem cocked his right eyebrow. "John Frémont took a shine to the beloved daughter of the country's most powerful senator. Jessie Benton hadn't passed her sixteenth birthday when she fell under his romantic influences; she was more than ten years his junior—and stratospherically above his social status.

"Senator Benton right near took our sapling Pathfinder to the woodshed when he found out they'd eloped. If it weren't for the new Missus Frémont's intervention, her husband might well have been reduced to splinters. Cut down in his prime, so to speak."

Clem grinned impishly. "Seeing as Jessie had hidden all the meat cleavers and commandeered the keys to the gun cabinet, Senator Benton had to come up with some other means of dealing with his unsolicited son-in-law.

"Benton wasn't one of the country's leading politicians for nothing," Clem said, tapping his temple wisely. "He quickly came up with a plan. He arranged for a new mapmaking mission for the Pathfinder, one that his overly ambitious, glory-hungry heart could not possibly turn away from, one that would send him on horseback all the way across the continent to the wilds of the Oregon Territory."

A chuckle rumbled up from Clem's chest.

"*Oregon* immediately became Senator Benton's favorite word. He repeated it over and over again in his mind. He bought himself a dog and named it Oregon, just to have an excuse to call it out."

Stroking the rumpled collar of his suit jacket, Clem stood up from the stool and beamed at the audience. "Benton knew the trip to Oregon would take the pesky Pathfinder a year, if not more, to complete. It would send him on a perilous journey through scorching desert heat and jaw-locking blizzard freezes . . . through lands chock-full of scalp-severing Indians, ravenous mountain lions, and ornery outlaw bandits."

Clem stretched his face into a serene smile. "Yes, Senator Benton had the perfect expedition for this daughter-stealing Frémont," he said, rolling blissfully back on his heels. "He could hardly wipe the grin from his face as he watched that infernal Pathfinder set his compass, mount up, and begin his long ride west. Benton felt certain he'd seen the last of him."

Ruefully, Clem shook his head and leaned forward again, lowering his voice conspiratorially. "He had no idea what chain of events he'd set in motion."

"THE BEAR FLAG Revolt," I mused to myself. "Maybe that's what Oscar left the clue about. What do you think, Issy?"

I glanced down at the stroller. Rupert was

stretched out luxuriously across the inside of the passenger compartment. His sleepy blue eyes blinked happily up at me.

It was at that moment I noticed the six-inch opening in the net cover.

"What happened to Isabella?" I whispered urgently.

Rupert replied with an uninformative yawn that ended in a cat-food-smelling belch.

Chapter 18

SEARCH AMONG THE SEATS

I SPUN MY head back and forth, searching the surrounding area for any sign of my missing cat.

"Issy," I hissed as Clem continued his oration from the stage. A few heads turned to scowl at my interruption.

A searing panic gripped my chest as I re-zipped the netting to make sure Rupert didn't join his sister in the escape. Still flopped lazily on his back, he appeared unconcerned about her disappearance.

I hunched down as low as possible and slid off my seat, catching the rebounding cushion with my hand to keep it from banging against the seat-back. Rupert watched curiously as I scooted around the stroller and crawled down our row on my hands and knees.

"Issy," I whispered again, ducking my head to check the concrete floor beneath the seats in front of me.

I reached the end of the row and poked my head around the armrest of the last seat. The carpeted path leading down the theater's center aisle was disturbingly vacant.

Several more heads turned to glare at the strange woman creating the commotion at the rear of the auditorium. My face flushed with embarrassment, but I was far too worried about Isabella to let their stares impede my search.

"Isabe—" I swallowed the rest in a gulp of relief as I spied a furry white glow peeking around the lobby's red velvet curtains.

"Don't move," I mouthed silently.

Isabella sat on the floor and demurely looked in my direction.

Trying to make as little noise as possible, I returned to the stroller and eased it out of the back row. I drew a few last irritated looks before Rupert and I exited the auditorium.

We found Isabella waiting patiently for us in the lobby. Her sharp blue eyes stared up at me expectantly.

"What are you doing?" I whispered reproachfully. Despite my harsh tone, I was immensely relieved to have found her.

"Mreo," she replied pleasantly as I stepped around the stroller and bent over to pick her up.

From that crouched angle, my line of sight matched up with the bottom rim of a display case mounted on the wall next to the auditorium's curtained entrance. Distracted by the food trays on the table in front of the wall, I hadn't noticed the case when I'd passed it earlier. Clem's amplified voice faded into the periphery as my eyes honed in on a furry figurine sitting in the far corner of the display.

It was a little stuffed bear holding a tiny paper flag colored to match that of the state of California.

HAROLD WOMBLER CROUCHED behind the stairs to the balcony, silently munching on a second triangular-shaped sandwich. He watched the woman with the long brown hair as she peered into the glass display case at the toy bear.

Harold gummed his dentures, satisfied with the result of his efforts; then, still carrying the terrarium, he slipped quietly through a side door leading out to the parking lot.

Seconds later, Ivan Batrachos tiptoed out behind him.

Chapter 19

THE NEVADA CITY BEAR

ISABELLA HUNG IN my arms as I stared at the toy bear. It was in better condition than the one I'd found behind Oscar's kitchen wallpaper, but otherwise, it appeared to be almost identical.

"Mrao," she said, tapping the display case with one of her front paws.

"How did you . . . ?" I wondered, leaning in closer to inspect the bear.

Isabella muttered a response under her breath, offended that I would question her clue-hunting expertise.

I set Isabella on the floor between my knees and placed my hands on the surface of the case. The glass front moved easily beneath the pressure of my fingertips, making a grating sound as I slid the top panel to one side. Threading my hand through the opening to the back corner, I stretched my fingers to catch the outer tip of the bear's paw and pluck it out.

As I removed the bear from the display case, I thought I heard a slight shuffling near the stairs to the balcony—but Clem's voice was still booming from the theater, so it was impossible to be sure. A quick glance around the lobby convinced me that it was still empty. I put the bear on the ground next to Isabella and, as quietly as possible, pulled the glass front back into place.

The bear didn't appear to have any relevance to the other subject matter in the case, I noticed as I scanned the rest of the contents in the display. The main exhibit contained a black-and-white photograph of the Nevada Theatre from the late 1800s. A short article posted alongside the photo described the theater's long history as well as some of the famous figures who had graced its stage, most notably Mark Twain.

I already knew much of the history of Twain's California experience. He had arrived in San Francisco in the mid-1860s, fresh off a disappointing mining stint in the Sierras. After a few months working a local reporting beat, a job he had vehemently detested, Twain had transitioned into writing short stories and essays for Bay Area literary magazines.

Twain's first nationwide success came with *The Celebrated Jumping Frog of Calaveras County*, but even this triumph failed to bring in enough income to pay the rent. Increasingly desperate for funds, he decided to try his hand as a public speaker. He transformed his humorous writings into a comedic stand-up routine.

Despite Twain's lack of stage experience, his show was an instant hit. After a successful start in San Francisco, he took the act on the road. His first performance circuit trekked across Northern

California, eventually passing through Nevada City.

In order to gin up interest in the tour, Twain papered each town along his route with over-the-top adverts and fliers bearing messages similar to the billboards the cats and I had followed up Broad Street.

I looked around the empty foyer, trying to imagine a young Mark Twain, still rough around the edges, nervously summoning his best bravado before marching inside the theater to begin the night's show.

"So what does this second bear have to tell us?" I asked, returning to the task at hand. I retrieved the toy bear from Isabella, who had by now thoroughly sniffed it over. Tilting my head, I squinted in the lobby's dim lighting to read the gold-lettered writing on the opposite side of the bear's flag.

"Sutter's Fort, Sacramento," I murmured out loud as another roar erupted from inside the theater. Between the noise of the crowd and my intent studying of the flag, I failed to notice the footsteps creeping across the lobby toward us. I looked up with a start at Isabella's disgruntled *"Mrao."*

"What a love-a-lee ki-ki-kitty," a man said in a stilted, stuttering, high-pitched voice. I dropped the bear into my jacket pocket as I twisted on my knees to face him.

"Umm . . . yes. Thank you," I mumbled in return. Something about his voice provoked a squirrely sensation in my gut.

The man wore a theater attendant's cheap cotton vest over a faded T-shirt that bulged around the belt-line of his dark-colored jeans. On his feet, I spied a pair of black leather tennis shoes.

"Do you have a t–t–tick-et?" the man asked as he adjusted a green visor pushed up against his brow.

The visor seemed a strange addition to his theater attendant's uniform. It shaded the top half of his eyes, leaving me to focus on his unusually plump lips, which resembled those of a fish.

Before I could answer, the man hunched down toward Isabella. "Sh-sh-she's pretty," he wheezed.

My hand wrapped protectively around Isabella's shoulders as he reached out to pet her head.

"Hisssss," Isabella spat at him.

"I'm s-s-sorry," he stuttered, quickly retracting his hand. He pointed to the yellow and black CATS ON BOARD decal pinned to the side of the stroller. "B-b-but we don't allow p-p-pets inside the theater."

"Right," I replied. "Of course." Isabella continued to glare up at him as I grabbed her around the middle and stuffed her into the stroller's passenger compartment. She and Rupert huddled together, suspiciously eying the theater attendant.

"Oh, you've g-g-got two c-cats," he observed haltingly.

I gripped the stroller's handle and spun it toward the exit. The odd tenor of the man's voice was making me extremely uneasy. "We were just leaving," I said briskly.

The attendant waved at us, his plump fishy lips spreading into a strange smile as I hurriedly shoved the stroller out the theater's front doors.

The sun had begun to set on Nevada City, and Broad Street's crowds were starting to peter out. Past the corner of the theater's red brick building, a few feet down the sidewalk, I parked the stroller and knelt down to check on the cats.

"That guy gave me the heebies," I said with a shudder.

"Mrao," Rupert piped up at me. Isabella looked at her brother as if she agreed with his assessment.

As I puzzled at my cats, the image of the theater attendant flashed before my eyes. For a moment, he stood in my mental picture, awkwardly leering. Then, his appearance began to change.

The visor vanished from his head, and the thick plump of his lips deflated. The face beneath the disguise, so flat and featureless, had easily hidden behind the distracting visor and the stuttering lisp.

I turned back toward the entrance of the theater, my cheeks flushed with recognition. My pulse began pounding with the realization that I had just been face-to-face with Frank Napis.

140

Chapter 20
POST-DINNER REPORT

A TELEVISION CAMERA panned the darkening slope of Broad Street's twinkling hill, taking a moment to focus on the painted wooden sign of the Mine Shaft Saloon before sweeping across the street to the green and white balcony on the second floor of the National Hotel.

Will Spigot and Harry Carlin sat at a round metal table on the balcony, their faces spotlighted by production equipment. Microphone wires snaked up the backs of their lightweight sport jackets and wound discreetly around their ears.

The silver-haired Spigot leaned in toward the largest camera as a harried producer counted down the seconds to the start of their next broadcast segment.

"Welcome to our continuing prerace coverage for this year's Tour of California. Eight stages over eight consecutive days covering a race route that will take us the length of the Golden State."

The camera widened its frame as Spigot turned to his partner. "And it all gets going tomorrow morning."

Harry smiled warmly into the lens. "I can hardly wait. Let's take a moment to review the route."

The camera zoomed in on Harry's ruddy face as

the television monitor in front of him split its screen to show a stylized map of California. The cities and roads had been removed to allow for a thick red line that highlighted the race route.

"You can see on the map here that we kick off tomorrow morning in the Sierra Gold Country. Stage One will begin on the street below us. After the riders leave Nevada City, they'll wind their way through several acres of stunning pine-tree forests until they reach the flatlands of the upper delta. That will take them into a sprint through downtown Sacramento."

The cameraman swung his lens back toward Spigot. He ran his tongue over the slim line of his upper lip and began the description of the race's second stage.

"Day Two will take us out across the lower Sacramento delta, west to the shoreline of Lake Berryessa. After circling a portion of the lake, the riders will cut through the vineyards of the Napa Valley, climb over the lower coastal mountains—there'll be some twisting roads through that stretch—and finish up in the town of Santa Rosa."

Spigot's lean face scrunched into a hungry expression. "Harry and I have been invited to dinner at a Sonoma winery that evening. That should be a spectacular meal . . ."

Carlin coughed lightly as the producer waved his hands in a circular motion, urging the broadcasters to hurry along and keep on topic.

"Tuesday will see us leaving out of San Francisco, heading south on Highway One down the coast," Carlin said smoothly. "The riders will cut inland for a couple of climbing segments up and over the Santa Cruz Mountains before arriving in the town of Santa Cruz. The Stage Three finish line will bring them right up to the famous Santa Cruz Beach Boardwalk."

Carlin turned toward his partner, raising his eyebrows, trying to cue him to launch into the summary of Stage Four. But Spigot was still fixated on the dinner reservation.

"Those folks in Sonoma—*they'll* know how to properly cook a piece of fish," Spigot opined indignantly.

Carlin cleared his throat again as the producer tapped his watch impatiently. "Ahem, returning to the route, then, Day Four of the course takes us from San Jose to Modesto . . ."

"Unlike the chap working behind the curtain at tonight's little bistro," Spigot muttered bitterly.

Carlin nervously eyed the now wildly gesticulating producer. "And then the, uh, yes, the next stage takes the riders inland through California's Central Valley, its breadbasket, so to speak."

"It was a perfectly honest piece of salmon, from what I could tell," Spigot cut in grumpily. "Before that cook got hold of it."

Carlin pressed on. "Stage Six takes us up into the San Bernardino Mountains . . ."

"Coated it with that wretched pepper and paprika concoction . . ."

Carlin wiped perspiration from his brow. "Stage Seven is an individual time trial through the streets of downtown Los Angeles . . ."

"Seared the taste buds right off my tongue." Spigot gripped his stomach, moaning in pain. "And now that toxic paste is working on my intestines . . ."

"Well, you did tell them to make it extra spicy," Carlin snapped as the producer threw his hands up in despair.

Spigot shrugged his shoulders as if surprised by Carlin's sudden outburst.

Carlin took in a deep breath. Then he concluded, "Finally, the last stage of the race wraps up just north of Malibu, in what will surely be a thrilling—"

"I say," Spigot interjected, leaning over the edge of the balcony, "what's that going on down below?"

The cameraman followed the motion of Spigot's head and aimed the focal point of his equipment at the sidewalk beneath the balcony, where a gangly-legged man in green spandex leggings weaved wildly through the crowds on a bicycle. Pedestrians scrambled to jump out of the way as he careened from side to side. Angry shouts were hurled at the wobbly rider, drowning out his frantic apologies. The front wheel of the bike hit the curb of an intersecting side street and plunged into its gutter, causing the man to somersault over the front handlebars and land, padded rump first, on the pavement.

"Poor fellow," Spigot said sadly as he turned toward the camera and cocked his right eyebrow knowingly. "I reckon he had the fish."

Chapter 21

THE STOAT

I STOOD IN the gathering darkness, staring at the doors to the Nevada Theatre, still reeling from the realization of my encounter with Frank Napis. If nothing else, I tried to reason optimistically, the presence of Napis was a clear indication that I was on the track of one of Oscar's hidden treasures. I just wished I had some idea of what I was searching for.

The metal brackets on the soles of Monty's bike shoes clapped against the concrete as he marched up the hill, pushing his bike beside him. A five-foot-long flexible stick of plastic was taped to the frame's back end. Flapping at the top of the stick was a green triangular-shaped flag that proclaimed the rider of the bike to be the "Official Representative of the Mayor of San Francisco."

I turned to study his advancing figure, frowning in concern as he approached. The right sleeve of his nylon shirt was torn open, and the skin on his exposed elbow was raw with road rash. The reason he was walking rather than riding his bike also became obvious: The front tire was completely flat.

"What happened to you?" I asked as he staggered to a stop beside me.

"Lucky . . . to . . . be . . . alive!" Monty gushed emotionally between deep air-sucking breaths. "A bike like this . . ." He coughed hoarsely. "It's really quite complicated to ride."

My mind drifted back to the treasure hunt as Monty began a long-winded explanation of his biking accident. *Bears,* I thought intensely. Oscar's clue related in some way to the little stuffed bears.

"To begin with, there's the pedals," Monty said, pointing at the bike, then at the soles of his feet. "You have to fasten the brackets on the bottom of your shoes into little nubbed clips on the pedals—all while balancing on top of the bike. It's darn near impossible to keep the thing upright while you're trying to get your shoes hooked into the pedals. That was the *first* time I fell off . . ."

I tucked my hand into my jacket pocket and fingered the pointed tip of the latest toy bear's flag. Bears with flags, I pondered to myself. The state flag of California . . . commonly referred to as the Bear Flag . . .

"Then I had some problems with the gears. As it turns out, it's not so easy to shift between twenty-five settings. You flip a lever the wrong way, and everything gets gummed up."

I continued with my internal bear musings. The first bear's flag had directed me here to Nevada City, where I'd found a Mark Twain impersonator discussing the Bear Flag Revolt. Uncle Oscar had been absolutely enamored with Mark Twain, but it had to be a coincidence that I'd run into the impersonator at this specific time and place—or was it . . . ?

"Once I finally got moving, the disc brakes nearly did me in. All it takes is one light squeeze of the handle, and the wheels freeze up immediately. I went flying over the handlebars down the hill there in front of the National Hotel. Ripped the sleeve of my jersey . . ."

I turned my attention to the second toy bear. The stuffed animal was similar in size and shape to the one I'd found behind the wall in the kitchen. The writing on this flag was directing me to Sutter's Fort in downtown Sacramento.

Monty continued to babble about his injuries as I pulled Clem's flier from one of the stroller's side pockets to check the location of his next venue. I sucked in my breath as my finger skimmed the performance listings. The following afternoon,

Clem was scheduled to appear at Sutter's Fort.

Staring at the night sky above Monty's head, I summed up my observations. There was something disturbingly contemporary about this trail of clues that Oscar had presumably laid out before his death over a year ago—and, not to mention, strikingly convenient. Sutter's Fort, in downtown Sacramento, was also near the finish line for tomorrow's stage of the race.

". . . somersaulted through the air and landed with a *splat* on the pavement. Knocked the wind right out of me. It was a near death experience, I tell you."

Sutter's Fort, Sutter's Fort. I repeated the phrase, searching for a connection in my memory banks. Somewhere in Oscar's book collection, I'd read about the fort's involvement in the Bear Flag Revolt. If I remembered correctly, Captain Frémont, the Pathfinder Clem had described in today's stage performance, had spent time at Sutter's Fort.

Monty was beginning to wind down his tale of woe and endangerment. "It's a good thing I brought along some spare shirts," he said in a more practical tone. "Wouldn't do to show up for the opening ceremony looking like this."

"Let's get you back to the hotel," I said suddenly. "I packed a first aid kit in the van." Monty's inability to operate the mechanics of a high-end bicycle was not entirely unexpected.

"Bandage me up, Florence Nightingale," Monty said, swooning dramatically.

"All right, all right," I replied absentmindedly as I wrapped my hands around the stroller's handlebar and steered Monty and his wounded bike back down the hill.

My next course of action would be to brush up on the details of the Bear Flag Revolt. I just hoped I'd brought along the right book.

WE RETURNED TO the parking lot about ten minutes later. While still packed with vehicles, the earlier bustle was beginning to die down. Most of the riders were off to dinner and an early bedtime so they would be fresh for the one-hundred-plus miles they would spend on the road the next day.

From the back cargo area of the van, I dug out the first aid kit and handed it to Monty.

Then, I reached for a bag of books I'd tossed in when we loaded the cat supplies, and began searching for a certain dog-eared paperback that might have the information I was looking for. After a moment's digging, I found it on the bottom of the sack.

Rupert sat on the van floor next to Monty, closely watching as he began dabbing his wounds with an alcohol-soaked towelette. I crawled into the front passenger seat and found Isabella perched on the driver's side cushion, staring longingly up at the steering wheel.

"Wran," she insisted.

"It's not physically possible," I replied, shaking my head at her. "Look at how far down the pedals are. Trust me. No cat could drive this van."

"Ruh," she muttered grumpily, clearly unconvinced.

With a sigh, I flicked on the van's interior light and laid open the book on the center console between our two seats.

Bernard DeVoto's *The Year of Decision 1846* was over five hundred pages of small, dense font. Even in paperback form, it was a hefty weight to lug around. The volume had been written in the early 1940s by a historian whose wry crankiness rivaled that of my Uncle Oscar's. The book was packed with obscure details mined from every possible source its author could dig up. Suffice it to say, DeVoto had been Oscar's kind of history buff, and it was no surprise that the book was well-worn from constant reference. My uncle's nearly illegible pencil marks were scrawled across many of the margins.

Isabella scanned the upside-down text as I flipped through the pages, looking up index citations to the Bear Flag Revolt.

I stopped at an entry with extensive doodling across its top header. The page described the creation of the original Bear Flag, which was raised on June 14, 1846, by a group of American rebels who took control of the tiny town of Sonoma.

The flag was constructed by William Todd, nephew of Mary Todd, the wife of then-senator, and later, U.S. president, Abraham Lincoln.

For the rectangular base of the flag, Todd cut a stretch of white fabric from an old shirt. Next, he sewed a strip of red flannel across its bottom length. In the upper left-hand corner, he used red paint to create a five-pointed star—an imitation of the emblem then associated with the independent state of Texas. Facing the star, Todd sketched the upright figure of a bear. Across the lower-middle of the flag, Todd printed the phrase *California Republic*.

According to DeVoto, the original flag was destroyed during the devastation of San Francisco's 1906 earthquake when the building where it was being stored burned to the ground.

I tried to block out the overwrought expressions of pain coming from the cargo area as Monty painted his elbow rash with iodine. Having seen enough of the bandaging process, Rupert hopped over the center console and crawled into my lap. Stroking his head absentmindedly, I pulled the latest bear from my pocket and studied its miniaturized version of the California state flag. The Bear Flag, as it was commonly referred to, was meant to simulate the one raised by the rebels at Sonoma.

"Wait a minute," I murmured slowly, returning my attention to the section of the book describing

William Todd's flag. The bear on the state flag was depicted on all four feet, but the description in DeVoto clearly stated that the original bear had been "standing on its hind legs."

A dense block of my uncle's scrawled handwriting was crammed into the margin next to the text. I grabbed a flashlight from the glove compartment and shone it down onto the page, trying to decipher Oscar's annotation. After a minute's squinting, I finally translated the writing. The words read as if they had been copied from another reference:

Local Indians, passing through Sonoma after the revolt, ridiculed the animal on the flag, calling it a pig or a stoat.

"Stoat?" I asked, puzzling at the last underlined word. "What's a stoat?"

I looked questioningly at Rupert, who was now flopped across my lap. The tip of his tail lightly tapped my leg, the extent of his response.

"Wrao," Isabella offered as I pulled out a pad of paper and tried to recreate the original flag using DeVoto's description. Monty was a much better artist, I thought, but, judging from the whimpers still emanating from the back of the van, his skills were temporarily unavailable.

My lips rolled inward in concentration as I sketched a large rectangle with a colored stripe across its bottom length. The star on the left-hand side was relatively easy to place, but the bear was a far more difficult challenge. After several attempts, I finally traced the crude outlines of an upright grizzly bear. I scrunched up the side of my face, trying to see the pig resemblance.

"I can't say I've ever seen a pig standing upright," I said, still perplexed by the Bear Flag anomaly. With a shrug, I shaded in the area around the bear's stomach, filling out a more piglike belly.

"Stoat, stoat, stoat . . ." I repeated the word over and over, but no image came to mind. "I have no idea what a stoat looks like."

I looked up through the front window of the van to the back side of the hotel. It was the same historic vintage as the other venues up and down Broad Street and, I suspected, would have some sort of lobby or sitting area that might offer a bookshelf to its guests.

Isabella followed my gaze. *"Mreo,"* she said encouragingly.

"Yep," I agreed with her. "I bet they've got a dictionary."

Chapter 22

THE NATIONAL HOTEL

I CALLED OUT to Monty, who had almost finished dressing his wounds in the back of the van. "Can you stay with the cats while I check on something inside the hotel?"

There was a loud clunking as he clambered up toward the front seats.

"I've still got to check in," he said, his head appearing over the center console. He'd put on another clean cycling shirt that was identical to the one he'd torn earlier. "How about we all go in with you?"

I twisted my head around to look at him. "*All* of us?" I asked skeptically, trying to avoid Isabella's affronted gaze. I lowered my voice to a tense whisper. "Wouldn't it be better to sneak them in after we get the room keys? I'm sure they don't allow cats inside."

Rupert looked up from my lap with a questioning grunt.

Monty waved off my concern. "Pop 'em in the Cat-mobile. No one will know the difference."

He backed out through the cargo area and unfolded the stroller on the pavement beside my door. I removed the CATS ON BOARD sign from its side. We'd have better luck sneaking the cats

154

into prohibited places, I reasoned, with a more incognito approach.

Rupert was still making disgruntled noises about the hotel's feline exclusionary policies when I loaded him and his sister into the carriage. After I double-checked that the mesh cover's zipper was securely fastened, we headed off across the parking lot to the hotel's back entrance.

A swinging gate in a white fence opened to a concrete-paved courtyard behind the hotel's main building. The combination of brick and wooden siding had been painted in sections of white and dark forest green, the same motif as the front balcony that overlooked Broad Street. We walked past a couple of smaller cottages that flanked the courtyard's rear side and approached a screen door leading into the hotel's main wing.

Bold block letters greeted us on a hand-painted sign affixed to the middle of the door: NO PETS.

Monty waved it off dismissively. He leaned over the stroller and whispered reassuringly to its furry occupants, "I'm sure they don't mean *you*."

Nervously, I unzipped the net cover and reached inside to fluff the towels up around Rupert and Isabella.

"Stay very quiet," I cautioned the cats as Monty propped open the door and helped me lift the stroller over the threshold.

We stepped into a narrow hallway lined with plaques, most of them black-and-white photos featuring Gold Rush scenes of Nevada City. At the end of the hall, we arrived at a longer corridor that ran the length of the building. After conducting a quick recon, Monty directed me to the left.

Following the *clumpity-clunk* of Monty's cycling shoes, I pushed the stroller past the top of a staircase that dropped down to the hotel's lower-front street level. The stairs were accompanied by a pair of heavy wooden banisters that matched the overall theme of red carpeting and fleur-de-lis-covered wallpaper we'd encountered thus far.

The hotel's somewhat primitive administrative offices were positioned just opposite the stairs. A gated window provided guest access to the registration desk, whose office equipment, while not dating back to the Gold Rush, definitely qualified as antiquated.

Farther down the hall loomed a large salon. If the abundance of wallpaper I could glimpse from this angle was any indication, that room seemed the most likely location for a bookcase and, I thought hopefully, a dictionary.

As quickly and as nonchalantly as possible, I pushed the stroller past the registration desk and scooted down the hallway to the salon. The woman seated in the area behind the gated window took no notice. She was facing the opposite direction, poring over an appointment book as she spoke into a phone's large plastic receiver. Monty leaned against the counter, waiting for her to finish so he could check into the suite of rooms that had been reserved for the Mayor.

"We're all booked up for the weekend," the woman told the caller plaintively. "I'd say that goes for everything within a thirty-mile radius. There's a bike race here tomorrow, you know."

I parked the stroller in the center of the salon and turned a slow circle, taking in the surrounding furnishings and décor. Outside of Oscar's kitchen, I'd never seen such a heavily wallpapered room. I counted three, no four, different patterns plastered across just one wall. Only the glass windows that framed the balcony had escaped the wallpaper's plastering reach. Perhaps this, I thought wryly, was where Oscar had acquired his fascination with the stuff.

Back at the front desk, the woman hung up the phone's receiver and turned to face Monty. Snippets of their conversation floated out into the salon as I continued my search for a dictionary.

"You say you're checking in for the Mayor of San Francisco?" the clerk asked skeptically.

The middle of the room had been left open to facilitate guest traffic, but a clutter of antiques and memorabilia were stacked up around its edges. Several humongous pieces of wooden furniture were cloistered against the walls, including a heavy wood-paneled piano that looked to weigh at least half a ton. Brass trinkets and lace doilies decorated every flat surface.

I found a vintage typewriter tucked into a recess behind the stairwell, which continued from the salon to the hotel's upper floors. The machine's lettered keys pronged out from the keyboard like fangs—the device looked as if it were more suited for eating a piece of paper than printing on it.

As I bent over the typewriter, the desk clerk's words echoed into the salon, the volume of her voice rising in tandem with her suspicions. "You don't *look* like the Mayor of San Francisco. Your hair's too curly," she protested. "I've seen pictures of him. He's got that swept back gangster-style hairdo."

I moved on from the typewriter to a photo album spread open next to a stack of pamphlets advertising wedding services. Nuptials appeared to be the hotel's main focus—that is, when the town wasn't hosting a cycling event. I put my hands on my hips as I scanned the area. Where might they be hiding the dictionary?

"Assistant life coach?" The woman now sounded truly perplexed.

"Ahem." Monty corrected the clerk, the sound of his voice increasing to match hers. "I said I was the Life Coach *Apprentice*."

"What in *tarnation* is a life coach?"

I smothered a giggle as I spotted a small

credenza squeezed into an empty space behind the piano. On it lay a thick age-crusted dictionary. I quickly thumbed through the pages to the *S* section.

"Is this a joke?" the clerk demanded warily. "Are you with one of those reality TV shows? Am I on *Candid Camera*?"

I ran the tip of my finger down the column until I found the listing for *stoat*.

"Ermine," I reported in a loud whisper to Isabella, who was watching me closely through the stroller's mesh netting. Rupert had curled up for a nap when I'd tucked him into the towels and was now happily snoring away, oblivious to the commotion at the front desk.

My lips puckered in thought as I studied the picture of the creature next to the listing in the dictionary. "It looks like a mink or a ferret. It's kind of slender—with a long furry tail." I reflected back on the DeVoto description of the animal on the original Bear Flag. "It *is* standing up on its hind legs . . ."

Returning to the stroller, I pulled out the tablet with my earlier sketch of the Bear Flag. I rotated the drawing of the pig-modified bear to the left and right, trying to figure out how to modify the animal to make it resemble a stoat. After a couple minutes of attempting to mentally superimpose the stoat image over that of the bear, I used my pencil to add a long, thick tail.

"Wrao," Isabella said thoughtfully when I showed her my drawing.

"I know," I replied, puzzling at the picture. "That doesn't look like any bear I've ever seen."

Chapter 23

THE BRICK

A WAVE OF white-haired patrons poured out of the Nevada Theatre, happily chatting about the evening's performance as they strolled down Broad Street. While there were a few dissenters, most agreed Clem had made an admirable attempt at his Mark Twain impersonation.

The citizens of Nevada City were quite particular about their Twain impersonators—the town had hosted dozens of Twain-inspired actors over the years. This, however, was the first time anyone could remember a Twain character working the Bear Flag story into his routine.

Trailing behind the departing theatergoers, Dilla and Wang were the last of the audience to leave the theater. Dilla skipped looping circles across the sidewalk as Wang, with the support of his cane, hobbled a slow straight line.

"He was pretty good, don't you think?" Dilla trilled merrily.

Wang managed a weak smile in response.

"I can't wait to see what's on tap for tomorrow,"

she said, gazing up at a nearby streetlamp and the pairing of American and California state flags mounted just below its light fixture. "Sacramento should be beautiful this time of year."

Wang continued his turtlelike pace down Broad Street's steep hill, his wizened face pinched in thought. He nodded absentmindedly to his wife as he pondered what Frank Napis might be planning to do with the information he had gained inside the Nevada Theatre.

PAST THE LOBBY, through the empty theater, down a narrow flight of concrete steps to the area beneath the stage reserved for stagehands and performers, the afternoon's Mark Twain impersonator shuffled sideways through the slim width of a dressing room doorway.

Clem carried a large plastic shopping sack in one hand; the strap of a bulky duffel bag was slung across the opposite shoulder. After a short struggle, he managed to fit both his body and the packages through the opening. Dropping his bundles on the dressing room floor, he turned to lock the door.

The room was long and narrow, its eight-foot length ample space for an actor to change costumes, apply makeup, and practice lines before a performance. One of the longer walls was taken up by a rectangular-shaped mirror, which rested on top of a slender wooden dressing table.

Clem shrugged out of his rumpled linen suit coat and, with a casual flick of his wrist, tossed the jacket onto the angled hook of a burnished brass coat rack.

Rolling his shoulders, he stretched his neck to the left and right, squeezing out the inevitable tension that had built up over an hour's worth of theatrical work on the stage. He swooped his arms and upper torso into a few awkward yoga moves that probably did more harm than good. Then, he bent over the dressing table and stared intently at his reflection.

The basement-level dressing room had a vintage, aged look. It had escaped the modernizing renovations that had been performed on the theater's upper level, leaving the brick walls exposed to the interior. The only recent maintenance of note was a fresh coat of baby blue paint that lightened the otherwise dark windowless space.

Over the past hundred-plus years, an endless parade of notable human faces had primped and preened in this dressing room, and the painted bricks had taken careful note of each and every one. Decades of facial images were stored within their collective memory, an unwritten record documented in their compacted clay, sand, stone, and mortar. The role of historical observer was an important aspect of their existence, one the bricks considered almost as important as the task of holding up the building. It was with this responsibility in mind that they eagerly scrutinized the reflection of the man who had just entered the dressing room.

There was a vague familiarity about his wild flyaway eyebrows and bristly mustache. So, too, the thick protrusion of his nose, which was slightly bent along its bridge as if it had seen action in a bar brawl or two. The bricks mulled over these distinguishing features as they closed in on a match to one of the thousands of faces in their memory, conferring first among themselves to ensure that they were all in agreement.

A wall took its strength from the unity and collaboration of its members. If even one brick ventured to speculate outside of the collected consensus, it risked bringing down the entire structure. Rarely did the bricks have difficulty reconciling their thoughts and, on this issue, they easily came to a unanimous decision. Yes, they concluded, the imitator bore a striking resemblance to the original.

The bricks watched as Clem gently patted the left front pocket of his collared shirt.

"Hello there, little friend," he said as a tiny whiskered face poked out of the pocket.

A murmur of excitement passed through the wall. What's that? the bricks puzzled, curiously edging against one another to get a glimpse of the creature that crawled shyly from the pocket and into the palm of Clem's hand.

The bricks quickly came to a clear identification. *It's a mouse!* they exclaimed in proud giddy unison. But a moment later, an undercurrent of confusion rippled through their ranks.

Strange that the little mouse has no hair . . . Odd that it's wearing a furry green jacket . . .

Clem heard the slight floating whisper of the bricks, but he dismissed the sound as merely the natural creaks and moans of an old building. After setting the mouse on the dresser, he strode across the dressing room to the spot where he had dropped his packages. He picked up the shopping sack, carried it back across the room, and placed it on a shelf next to the dressing table.

Ooh, that tickles, the bricks thought, giggling to themselves as Clem dug around inside the bag, causing it to brush against the wall. His right hand finally emerged holding a small plastic makeup case, which he laid on top of the dressing table.

Clem returned to the area in front of the door and picked up the duffel bag. With effort, he wrapped the bag's strap over his right shoulder and lugged it across the room to the shelf. The bulging contents strained against the teeth of the zipper that ran down the duffel's length.

The wall winced as Clem turned, smacking the bag against it. A grumble of complaint issued from those bricks receiving the brunt of the impact. The building braced itself, preparing to accept the weight of the bag, as Clem swung it toward the wall and thunked it down onto the shelf.

After a moment of paralyzed apprehension, the wall oozed out a sigh of relief. The duffel, the bricks now realized, was more bulk than weight. How silly of them to have worried, they chuckled. This building had stood for a hundred and fifty years. There was nothing in this bag the wall couldn't handle.

Clem let out a slight groan as he paused to massage his right shoulder where the strap had rubbed against his skin.

Come now, huffed the bricks. That wasn't so heavy really. Try holding up a building. Awash in self-confidence, the bricks continued their silent watch.

Clem turned back to the dressing table and sat down on a short stool in front of the mirror. The mouse tilted its head to watch as Clem fixed his gaze on his reflection, licked his upper lip, and reached up to his left eyebrow. His stubby fingers wrapped around one end of the brow and, with a slight ripping sound, quickly peeled it off.

The bricks hummed inquisitively. *What do we have here?*

Clem tucked the first eyebrow into the makeup kit and began working to remove the second. A moment later, the mustache followed the eyebrows' rapid departure from his face.

The bricks watched uneasily, crowding against one another as they tried to size up Clem's changed appearance. Costuming was, after all, a routine practice among actors, the bricks tried to reassure themselves. This wasn't such an unusual scene.

Clem scrunched his face and wiggled the tip of his nose. Cupping his right hand over the nostrils, he tugged on the base of the nose with his left. With a sucking *pop,* a large portion fell off into his hands.

The bricks strained to get a better look at the fake putty-nose that Clem placed on the dressing table. Clem glanced at the ceiling as the building let out another long, groaning creak.

Very convincing, the bricks agreed. They'd never seen an artificial nose convey such a convincingly lifelike transformation.

Mesmerized, the bricks ogled the strange man in the mirror, marveling at his altered image. His flat face lacked any unique characteristics, making it instantly forgettable. His eyebrows had been plucked so thin that the arches faded into the background of his pale wrinkled forehead. The permanent nose that had hidden beneath the monstrous putty creation was small and utterly unremarkable. If a random sampling of noses were rounded up from the street, the bricks would have had difficulty picking this one out of the lineup.

The bricks tittered back and forth, checking and rechecking the new reflection as they searched through their collective memories for a match to one of their previous visitors, for any inkling of recognition. But the featureless face was impossible to grasp hold of; it kept slipping through the cracks between them.

With a brisk slap of his cheeks, Clem spun around on the stool, suddenly facing the wall. The bricks retracted involuntarily as he stood up and walked toward them. Surely, he hadn't detected their spying eyes, they tittered nervously. No human had ever suspected the wall's secret surveillance.

Clem stopped at the shelf holding the duffel bag, and the bricks let out another gushing sigh of relief. They watched anxiously as he struggled to pry open the bag's zipper. At long last, the teeth began to unhitch, and a gap formed across the duffel's top side.

Despite their growing apprehension, the bricks contorted within the confines of their mortar, trying to inspect the bag's contents. A perplexed silence swept over the wall as it examined the furry brown cloth that bulged out of the bag's opening.

Slowly, Clem eased the layers of material from the mouth of the duffel, taking care to ensure the fabric didn't catch on the zipper. Once he'd lifted the bundle free of the bag, he raised one edge of the cloth to his shoulders and let the rest unfold down to the floor.

Gripping the top hem of the fabric, Clem shook out the wrinkles of what appeared to be a furry suit. Then he turned the costume around to wiggle a long, thick tail attached to the opposite side.

The bricks shuddered with morbid fascination, trembling to imagine what might happen next, and yet utterly unable to look away. They had seen plenty of unusual human beings in their time: all manner of outlandish freaks, brazen scoundrels, and social deviants. But they had never witnessed an after-performance display quite like this. All this odd behavior was causing a fair amount of consternation among the bricks—and more than just a little bit of a dangerously individualized thinking within the wall.

Several of the bricks began to wring and knot in worry as Clem untied his lace-up boots and kicked them off his feet. Then, holding the furry cloth out in front of his body, he fed first one leg and then the other into the bottom half of the costume. After the loose-fitting fabric swallowed his shirt and pants, he pulled a long interior zipper all the way up to his neck.

Clem now turned to the shopping sack. The bricks watched as he reached inside it and retrieved a globe-shaped headpiece. He swiveled his head back and forth, cracking an interior neck joint, before sliding the massive structure down over his face.

The wall wondered in fearful amazement at the furry figure that stood before it, trying to determine what kind of creature this costume was meant to emulate.

They searched fruitlessly through their memory banks, comparing the costume to pictures, emblems, and icons they had seen before. If pressed, the bricks concluded, they would have to place their bet on a bear. Bear symbols were common in these parts—but no bear image they'd ever come across had possessed such a tail.

Clem scooped up his makeup kit from the dressing table and dropped it into the duffel bag. He plucked his linen jacket from the coatrack and tucked it neatly on top of the kit. Bending over, he slipped his shoes back on his feet, where they were almost completely covered by the costume's long legs. After a last check around the room for any forgotten items, he zipped the bag shut.

With a slight flourish, Clem leaned over the dressing table, and the tiny mouse scampered up his fur-covered arm until he found a pocket hidden in the front chest of the costume. Then, giving his tail one last wiggle, Clem slipped the strap of the duffel bag over his left shoulder and strode confidently out the door.

The bricks released an exhausted sigh. Well, that

was something, they murmured to one another. Not your everyday dressing room scene, that was for sure.

But what, exactly, had they just witnessed? What was the story with that costume? And where was the man going in that getup? Many of the bricks were skeptical of the bear identification, but none of them wanted to break the unity of the initial classification.

"I know, I know," a tiny squeaking voice broke through the silence.

The voice came from a small brick, turned sideways so that most of her surface area faced into the wall. She had been inserted the previous year as a replacement for an old beloved brick that had, unfortunately, fractured and split. There was still much mourning among the bricks for their lost friend, and they looked upon the replacement with mistrust and suspicion.

This was not the first time the newer brick had tried to speak her mind. Her ideas were odd and, many thought, ill-considered. She had a frightening tendency to break the rules that all the other bricks lived by, and she seemed oblivious to the danger of her un-vetted opinions. More than once, she had risked near annihilation of the entire structure with her peculiar off-stream commentary.

Such a minor player in the observations, particularly one with so little experience in the trade, was not expected to contribute to these discussions. A young, untested brick like herself should be focusing all of her attention on supporting the wall, not challenging the carefully structured, rigid uniformity that ensured the building's preservation and integrity.

But the sideways brick was persistent and certain in her information. The whole wall cringed with dread as her squeaky voice piped out, "I know what the costume is supposed to be."

The wall held its breath, waiting for the announcement that would surely bring about its immediate destruction.

She paused, hoping one of the other bricks would engage her in this discussion, but they remained stonily silent.

Finally, her voice peeping in excitement, she exclaimed loudly, "It's a kangaroo!"

Chapter 24

DOWNGRADED

I WAITED IN the salon of the National Hotel while Monty continued his efforts to check in to the Mayor's reserved suite of rooms. After a long discussion about his assistant life coach credentials, the hotel clerk finally reached beneath the counter and selected a room key. Reluctantly, she held it out to Monty.

"Take the hallway on your left to the courtyard. The Garden Room is on the far side next to the parking lot."

Monty coughed loudly as his fingers clamped around the key. "Garden Room?" he asked plaintively. "Is that the, uh, Mayoral Suite?"

The woman stared at him as if she thought he'd lost his mind. Her lips pursed resolutely, and the lines of her face hardened into a take-it-or-leave-it expression. Her fingers still firmly gripped the key—she looked as if she were about to change her mind altogether.

"I'm sure this will work just fine," Monty said meekly. With a tugging jerk he extracted the key from the woman's clenched fingers.

Monty scampered nervously down the hallway as I followed, pushing the cats in the stroller. His pace increased when he reached the door to the courtyard. I reached the exit in time for the swinging door to slam shut against the stroller's front bumper.

Isabella's uninterpretable comments grumbled up from the carriage as I propped open the door and struggled to shove the stroller through it.

"This isn't so bad," Monty called out from the opposite side of the courtyard. He stood in front of what looked like a small brick shed. A sign above the door helpfully identified it as the Garden Room.

I watched dubiously as he fed the key into the

lock. It seemed unlikely that a suite of rooms would be found inside.

Good thing I packed my sleeping bag, I thought ruefully.

With a loud creak, Monty pushed open the door and stepped into the room. I hung back in the courtyard, waiting for his report.

"Weeellll . . ." He strung the word out for what felt like an eternity. From the strangled tone of his voice, I gathered this was a somewhat smaller accommodation than what he had been promised by the Mayor's secretary. I prepared myself for the worst and followed him inside.

Arms crossed over my chest, I stood on the threshold surveying the room. It held a twin-sized bed and a dresser. There wasn't room for anything else. A narrow aisle between the bed and the wall led to a tiny bathroom. Despite the lack of space, the room did feature an abundant covering of wallpaper.

With a sigh, I returned to the stroller. I called back to Monty as I began rolling it toward the parking lot.

"We'll be in the van."

A MAN IN a green cotton vest and matching visor scurried beneath the stage of the Nevada Theatre. The black rubber soles of his sneakers squeaked against the concrete floor as Frank Napis hurriedly searched the basement area, peeking into every last dressing room and broom closet. His face grew more and more frustrated as it became clear that the person he sought had already left the building.

After a last agitated effort to hunt down the elusive Mark Twain impersonator, Napis stomped across the stage, snatched the green visor from his head, and slammed it into a trash can.

A few blocks from the Nevada Theatre, a figure in a furry kangaroo costume walked casually down one of Broad Street's sidewalks and disappeared around a corner into a darkened alley.

Chapter 25

AN EXCELLENT DRIVER

THE MOON AWOKE from its daytime slumber, feeling lighter and decidedly more invigorated in its slightly slimmer figure. With a brief yawn and an arching stretch, it leapt up the banks of the bay and headed out across the delta. Acres of fruit orchards passed beneath its glow as it leapfrogged over row after row of perfectly groomed trees.

A short time later, the moon approached the sprawling metropolis of Sacramento. After a quick cleansing dip in the water beneath the burnished-gold frame of the Tower Bridge, it strolled into the capital city's downtown area for a short waltz around the blooming grounds surrounding the statehouse.

Stretching out a slender luminous hand, the moon plucked a plump orange from a leafy tree and slurped up a mouthful of the fruit's sticky sweetness. Still licking juice from its fingertips, it proceeded down Sacramento's tree-lined sidewalks, past Sutter's white-walled fort, until it picked up the icy cold trail of the American River.

A rising sea breeze at its back, the moon hiked into the Sierra foothills, looping to the east until it reached the ruins of an old abandoned sawmill. It surveyed the rickety structure with a proud sigh of reminiscence. This was the site of one of its most impressive instigations of mischief. Dipping a toe into the surface of a nearby stream, it sent out a twinkle of mystical moonlight that caught, for a brief instant, the reflection of the golden nuggets that once tumbled within.

Still brimming with nostalgia, the moon turned north, skimming across the pointed tips of a pine tree forest as it traced the track of Highway 49. When at last it reached the sleeping mountain hamlet of Nevada City, it took a quick scan of Broad Street's nighttime scene. In the bar on the first floor of the National Hotel, a boisterous crowd of locals cheered the bartender who sang into a karaoke microphone while pouring an endless round of drinks, never once spilling a drop.

With interest, the moon watched as an elderly woman dressed in a feather-topped hat pushed a feeble Asian man in a wheelchair through the bar's front door. I might stop in later, the moon thought shrewdly. But first, I need to check on my charges.

The moon proceeded briskly to the parking lot behind the hotel. In contrast to the saloon, this area was silent and dark. After weaving around several parked tour buses, it crept stealthily up to the front windshield of a large cargo van and cautiously peered inside.

A slender white cat lay curled up on the driver's seat, deep in sleep. The moon slid over the dashboard and, with a long willowy finger, caressed the smooth crown of the cat's forehead.

Isabella rolled over onto her back so that the moon could stroke the silky fur of her chest. The claws on her front paws gripped the air as the moon reached inside her head and plucked out the spindly thread of her dream.

Isabella stood on the driver's side seat cushion, her front paws draped over the steering wheel while she piloted the van down a twisting mountain road. The window to her left was rolled down, letting in a crisp, refreshing breeze that ruffled through her hair. The engine hummed beneath her, a willing servant to her every command. She had never felt so free, so empowered.

The van careened down the winding road, following the asphalt path into a gully and over a narrow wooden bridge. A roaring stream flowed below, churning a white foam over the slick boulders that lined the water's bed. On the opposite side, the vehicle soared up the steep rise of the next hill, quickly climbing toward a perfect blue sky.

A pleased purr rumbled in Isabella's chest as she expertly maneuvered the steering wheel, guiding the van through the dense woods of soaring pine trees. In the fabled land of her imagination, her back foot magically mashed down on the accelerator, even as she keenly gazed out through the front windshield.

With a blissful purr, Isabella glanced over at her copilot. Rupert sat in the front passenger seat, a seatbelt safely strapped over his chest. A broad smile spread across his furry face as the wind caught the loose pockets of his puffy cheeks and plastered his whiskers against the side of his head. Every so often, he reached over to munch a bite from the box of fried chicken they'd picked up at the drive through of a fast food restaurant they'd passed on the way out of town.

All the while, Isabella heard but chose to ignore the muffled complaints of the two human figures locked in the wire-fronted cages in the back cargo area.

Try to tell *me* I can't drive a van, Isabella thought scornfully. I'm an excellent driver.

The moon giggled at the cat, her twitching legs, and the fantastic adventure she was having, if only in her mind.

LEAVING ISABELLA TO the pleasures of her dream, the moon crawled over the center console into the van's back cargo area. A large sheet covered the left-hand side of the cargo space, masking the location of a red igloo-shaped litter box. The moon took one curious sniff inside the igloo and instantly abandoned all interest in the domed contraption. It directed its attention, instead, to the sleeping bag stretched out on the opposite side of the sheet.

A woman with long brown hair lay fast asleep inside the thick flannel-lined fabric. Her bifocal glasses were carefully folded up inside their protective leather case, but the freckled bridge of her nose still bore a reddish indentation where the connecting curve of the plastic frames had pressed down during the day.

The woman's head rested on an extra-long pillow, which she shared with a furry orange and white cat. Light snoring sounds whiffled out of Rupert's mouth as his body snuggled beneath the blankets.

The moon carefully lifted a sun-lightened strand of hair from the woman's cheek as it peeked into her head for a quick sample of her dream. After a moment, the moon drew back, perplexed by the peculiar stream of images it had glimpsed inside.

A grizzly bear roared up on its back haunches, growling viciously at a five-pointed red star. As it howled, the bear's belly began to swell, pudging out into a wide bulging pouch. The image rotated to the now-rotund animal's rear, where its stubby tail lengthened into a thick thumping appendage.

Then the creature began to hop . . . very distinctly . . . like a kangaroo.

Chapter 26

THE STARTING LINE

I WOKE THE following morning feeling remarkably refreshed for having spent the night asleep on the van's metal floor. After filling up the cats' food and water dishes, I cracked the windows and checked that the van would remain in the shade for the next twenty minutes while I ducked into Monty's room to freshen up. Carrying my toothbrush and shower kit, I crossed the parking lot to the hotel's back entrance, fully expecting I'd have to pour a bucket of cold water on Monty to get him out of bed.

To my surprise, I found my typically late-rising neighbor already decked out in his cycling gear, sitting at a metal table in the middle of the courtyard, sipping a coffee and reading the local paper. Apparently, he had been up for some time—the citrus scent of his aftershave had already diminished to sub-sneeze strength.

"Is that a *third* green jersey?" I asked, noticing the fresh-out-of-the-box sheen of his shirt. It looked too crisp to be the one he had changed into after his cycling accident the previous evening.

Snapping the newspaper, Monty arched an eyebrow at my tousled hair and blotchy, sleep-ridden face.

"Saved some hot water for you," he replied, tossing me the room key. "Chop, chop," he said briskly as I headed inside for my shower. "We've got a busy day ahead."

A COUPLE OF blocks away, Dilla Eckles walked out onto the front porch of a small Nevada City bed-and-breakfast. It's a shame we're headed back to San Francisco so soon, she thought with an appreciative glance at the morning sun shining down on the manicured yard.

Her brow furrowed with concern as a light breeze fluttered the pink scarf around her neck. Her husband had been quite adamant that they return to the flower shop as quickly as possible. She had a sneaking suspicion she knew the reason why.

IN THE FENCED-in yard behind the bed-and-breakfast, John Wang sat in a wheelchair beneath the protective shade of an elm tree. Harold

Wombler huddled next to the chair, grumpily conferring with the invalid.

"You're sure Napis knows the next location?" Wang asked softly, his wizened face deep in thought.

Harold nodded with a sour grimace. "My source was unequivocal."

"I'll brief Dilla on the way back to the city." Wang said with a slight wheeze. "Your source, are you still sure we can trust him?"

Harold spat at the ground. "We have to."

Mr. Wang stroked the long, spooling thread of his beard, a nonvocal agreement with Harold's assessment. After a long minute, he finally spoke. "I suspect that is what Oscar intended."

IT TOOK A bit more convincing to get Isabella into the stroller on the second day of our trip, but I eventually convinced her that with thousands of pedestrians and several hundred bicycle tires cruising the streets, the inside of the stroller was the safest place for a cat to observe the start of the race. At long last, the three of us left the van and headed off toward Broad Street—Monty had departed earlier to meet with the race organizers.

The cats and I rounded the corner of the hotel parking lot to find that Nevada City had been transformed overnight. The downtown area had been taken over by a traveling circus of hospitality tents, vendor booths, and temporary metal barricades.

Oodles of people had gathered on Broad Street, which was now closed to vehicular traffic. It was a festive family affair, with mothers holding little hands, fathers carrying toddlers on their shoulders, and one intrepid antique dealer pushing a large stroller containing two orange and white cats.

From a temporary stage positioned beneath the National Hotel's green and white balcony, an announcer jabbered details and statistics about the coming race to a growing throng of spectators. One by one, the riders were introduced to the crowd as they checked in and received their race numbers.

Rupert and Isabella were the only cats I saw at the event, but the local canine population was out in force. Representatives of almost every breed and mix were on hand to enjoy the sunny starting line, from pony-sized wolfhounds to stubby-legged wiener dogs. Some sported colorful bandanas around their necks; others wore lightweight coats over their bodies. I think Isabella managed to hiss at each and every one of them.

A half hour and several disgruntled dog encounters later, the race was finally ready to begin.

The riders massed behind the yellow starting

banner, a melee of shiny painted metal, mirrored sunglasses, colorful nylon shirts, and turtle shell–shaped plastic helmets. Each cycling team was identified by a unique color scheme; the team members matched one another right down to the color of their socks.

A loose formation of riders congregated behind the starting ribbon that stretched across Broad Street, ready to set out on the parade lap through Nevada City. It would be slow going for the first couple of kilometers as the riders were primarily concerned with avoiding any dangerous pileups in the crowded city streets. The real racing would begin once they hit the open road outside of town.

The music that had been blaring off and on all morning faded out, replaced almost immediately by the raucous commotion of the noisemaking devices dispersed throughout the crowd. Rows of fans pressed in toward the street as the chief organizer of the race shepherded Monty's green goblinlike figure to the starting line.

Above the scene on the National Hotel balcony, the producer crouched in front of Will Spigot and Harry Carlin as he counted them down to the live broadcast.

Four, three, two, one . . .

WILL SPIGOT TOOK in a deep breath and began.

"It's a beautiful morning here in downtown Nevada City. The time has finally come. The start of the first stage of the Tour of California will get under way any moment now." He turned toward his partner. "Harry, the Tour has never seen crowds like this."

"Without a doubt, Will," Harry Carlin agreed as the cameraman widened his shot to capture the heads and shoulders of both broadcasters. "And, I have to say, we have one of the best seats in the house. We have a view up the entire length of Broad Street, and let me tell you, it is literally *packed* with people."

The camera returned its focus to Spigot. "The rest of this week we'll be set up at each day's finish line, but we wanted to be here this morning for the big send-off." He tilted his head toward Carlin for an aside. "It's just as well that I didn't have far to go this morning. That bed I slept in last night did a right number on my back."

"Oh dear," Carlin said, his face blushing uncomfortably as the producer's head jerked up in alarm. "You didn't enjoy your room then?"

Spigot bridled with indignation. "I'm all for historic, mind you, but there are some aspects of modern society that should not be shunned. Plumbing, hot water, and, above all else, *bedsprings*." He shook his head wearily. "Look here, I'd wager that bed has been around since the establishment first opened. Probably last slept in by some old coot miner. I should have shaken out the bedsheets to look for gold dust!"

Eying the producer's exasperated prompting, Carlin broke in to change the subject. "The, ah, riders are lined up and ready to go. All of the team cars are assembled behind them. Any second now, and we'll be under way."

But Spigot wasn't finished recounting his night's travails. "Do you know," he interrupted, waving his hand to attract the cameraman's attention, "I think I saw a mouse in my room. I woke up in the middle of the night, and the little creature was sitting on the edge of my bed. It was the strangest thing. It didn't have any fur, and I think it was wearing a . . ."

The camera swung abruptly back to Harry Carlin. He looked temporarily startled, and then sputtered, "All that's left now is the ribbon cutting. That must be the designated VIP stepping up to do the honors. There he is, walking out in front of the riders."

"What—the man in the shiny green tights?" Spigot interjected. "Say, isn't that the bloke we saw on the sidewalk last night?"

ISABELLA AND I watched as Monty stepped up to the ribbon with an excited, expectant air. The smile on his face reflected a magnificent grin. He was already imagining the glorious photo that would hit the papers the following morning.

Monty brushed a hand through his towering brown curls before tamping the plastic bike

185

helmet down onto his head. The organizer of the race handed him a gigantic pair of scissors, indicating that the moment had arrived. Photographers leaned in from either side of the street to get the perfect ribbon-cutting shot. Monty raised the scissors, gripped the handles, and extended the mouth of the blades.

Just as the organizer nodded for Monty to begin, a voice shouted out, "Hey, there's the Mayor! It's the Mayor of San Francisco!"

A group of men burst from the crowd near the starting line. They charged in front of Monty as one of the scissor blades caught the rim of the ribbon, shearing it in half. Flashbulbs blinded us all—which was just as well.

Each of the men who'd jumped into Monty's photo shoot wore rubber masks mimicking the Mayor's long face and sculpted, swept-back hairstyle. The rest of their bodies were completely bare.

Chapter 27

THE WILD, WILD WEST

"CRIMINAL CHARGES," MONTY muttered bitterly as he climbed into the van's front passenger seat. "They should round them up and press criminal charges."

The group of streakers had slipped away into

the melee of bicycles, security personnel, and photographers, easily eluding the flailing grasp of the crazed man in the shiny green spandex leggings. The start of the race had been delayed a full twenty minutes while the organizers sought to regain control of the starting line.

Monty's cheeks were flushed and streaked with grime. The purple argyle pattern on his cycling shirt was stained with the contents of a chocolate ice cream cone and a pink-colored energy drink, both of which he'd run into while chasing the streakers through the crowd.

I stared straight ahead through the van's front windshield, desperately trying to keep a straight face as Monty continued to stew over the scoundrels who had upstaged his photo op. He shook his head again. "I just can't believe it."

"Well," I replied, struggling to strike a conciliatory tone. "At least the picture is sure to make all the local papers."

Monty was not amused by this prospect. He threw a towel over his head and collapsed into the passenger seat's cushions. "Wake me up when we get to Sacramento," he moaned plaintively.

It is not unusual, here in the Wild, Wild West, to come across free-spirited individuals with an unorthodox approach to style, fashion, and, yes, even the necessity of clothing. On a warm spring day after a long rainy winter, certain young Californians find themselves overwhelmed with an exuberance that can be released, it seems, in only one way—particularly when the lowering of their inhibitions is encouraged with the promise of some extra weekend drinking money.

A FEW BLOCKS off Broad Street, several young college students gathered around Harold Wombler's rusted-out pickup. As the recently reclothed men handed back the rubber Mayor masks, Harold grumpily peeled off dollar bills, doling out twenty-five per streaker. One by one, the young men disappeared with their payments into a nearby bar, eager to convert the morning's earnings into glasses of cold beer.

Harold counted out a final wad of cash and handed it over to the last of the streakers. There was a faint fried chicken scent in the air as he folded up his wallet and tucked it into a pocket of his overalls. He added a few more crickets to the frog terrarium on his front seat; then he climbed into the cab and rumbled off toward Sacramento.

Chapter 28

DOWNTOWN SACRAMENTO

WILL SPIGOT'S VOICE described the scene as television cameras panned the Sunday afternoon crowd waiting for the riders to arrive.

"Welcome back, folks. It took some doing, but

we've made the journey here to downtown Sacramento. We're stationed across from the State Capitol, right above the finish line for Stage One of the Tour of California."

The camera briefly switched frames to a wide shot of the broadcast booth before focusing in on the commentators.

Harry Carlin smiled warmly to the viewers. "I must say, it's a beautiful spot we've got here. As we look up L Street where the riders will be coming in, we see a gorgeous row of palm trees, and beyond that, Capitol Park, which is absolutely blooming right now with all manner of brightly colored vegetation."

Spigot arched a wary eyebrow. "Do you know, Harry, there are orange trees sprinkled throughout that park? Shady characters, those. You've got to watch your back in there. The fruit is enormous, and the trees don't give you any warning when they decide to let go of one. If you hear a rustling above your head, it's time to duck and run for cover."

"Yes, well, hmm," Carlin replied. "I'll keep that in mind. Meanwhile, the weather conditions for the race couldn't be better. The sun is shining down on this lovely boulevard, but the temperature is still relatively mild. There's a light breeze in the air, but it won't do more than give the riders a nice cooling as they make their final laps through the downtown area."

Spigot stroked the point of his narrow chin. "What do you think of the run in to the finish line, Harry? Are we going to see a sprint today?"

"It's three circuits around the downtown loop, flat, with plenty of room for the teams to line up their sprinters. I'd say we've got perfect conditions for a real neck-and-neck all the way to the line."

Spigot leaned forward eagerly. "Yes, we'll tell the crew to get their cameras ready, because this might well be a photo finish." He glanced at a sign being held up by their producer and cleared his throat. "Now, let's catch you up on the action out on the road so far.

"After the, ahem, *delay* getting out of the starting gate, there was an early breakaway of about ten riders. The peloton—that's the term we use for the main group of riders—has kept them on a tight leash, though. There's never been more than about a twelve-minute time gap between them, and with the flat terrain of the last fifty kilometers, the peloton should have no trouble catching them before the finish."

Carlin glanced slyly at Spigot. "Is that your prediction, then?"

"That the peloton will catch the breakaway?" Spigot nodded his head emphatically. "Yes. Absolutely."

Carlin smiled warmly. "I think we're in agreement there. Can't see it playing out any other way today." His expression grew more serious. "Let's see. We also need to brief you on a bit of a mishap the riders ran into on the road outside of Auburn."

"Oh, this was a spectacular crash," Spigot said luridly as he hunched forward and tapped the arm of a production assistant. "I think we have the video to show you . . . Ah, there it is. See that rider in the bright pink shirt? He's right in the middle of the pack. The road takes a slight turn coming around the bend. There must have been some loose gravel on the surface and . . . oh! Down he goes!"

Carlin somberly cleared his throat as the television screen zoomed in on a thrashing pile of bodies and bikes. "Yes, well, as you can see, he took a good part of the peloton with him. Luckily, everyone was able to piece themselves back together again. A couple of bikes had to be switched out, but the team cars are always prepared for that. There were a few scrapes and bruises on the riders, no doubt."

Spigot was still plastered to the gory picture on the monitor. "Ooh, see there? That one's got a nice-looking rash on his upper thigh. That's going to hurt in the morning."

"You know, William," Carlin said professorially. "This crash happened very near a place of great historic importance to the state of California. Do you know what that is?"

Spigot turned toward his broadcasting partner, his narrow face flattening into a cynical expression. "No, but I'm sure you're going to tell me."

"They were but a few kilometers away from the sawmill where James Marshall discovered the first gold nuggets that set off the California Gold Rush," Carlin said enthusiastically.

Spigot smirked wryly. "Perhaps that's what that pink-shirted rider was thinking of when he miscalculated that turn. Shame, that. Well, as we said, everybody made it safely out of the pileup, and the riders are now approaching Sacramento. Soon, they'll enter a loop that will make three laps through the downtown area. The breakaway is still out in front of the peloton, but the gap has gone down dramatically over the last half hour. Harry, how much of a lead have they got now?"

Carlin bent over a small computer located on the side of the broadcast booth that collected data from the riders' progress out on the course and used it to calculate their predicted finish times.

"Let me check the computer . . . there it is. The peloton is trailing the breakaway group by just under two minutes."

Spigot shrugged confidently. "Ack, they'll be caught. Does the computer say they'll be caught?"

There was a pause while Carlin fiddled with the keyboard. "The computer thinks they'll be caught," he confirmed confidently.

Spigot nodded wisely into the camera. "Don't tell that to the boys up front. They think they've got a shot at staying away to the finish line. They're still dreaming of victory."

Carlin switched his attention to the color monitor transmitting the live feed from the course. "We can see from the picture on the video cameras that the lead riders are now turning the corner at L and 26th to begin their first downtown lap," he said, squinting at the screen. "That building in the background is Sutter's Fort, I believe. Say, that's another historic venue I meant to tell you about . . ."

WITH ISABELLA'S DIRECTIONAL assistance, I managed to navigate around several race-related roadblocks to find a shaded parking space for the van on the far side of the park that held Sutter's Fort.

Monty was still snoozing loudly when I cut the engine. I turned back to Isabella and put my finger to my lips. She reached out her paw to tap on her carrier's metal grate.

After rolling down the driver's side window a couple of inches, I carefully opened my door. I stepped quietly out and, holding my breath, gently pressed it shut. I hurried around to the rear of the van and gripped the back door handle.

With a hopeful grimace, I pulled the lever toward me. There was a slight clink of metal and a low squeal of hinges, but Monty appeared to still be fast asleep when I reached into the cargo area and lifted out the stroller. Once I'd reconfigured it to cat-carrying mode, I crawled back in to get Isabella.

"Wrao," she demanded impatiently as I unhooked the latch to her door.

Rupert was dozing peacefully, so I decided to leave him in the van with Monty. He let out a wheezing snore as I opened his carrier and set a bowl of water on the floor beside it. Then, I scooted a retreat out the back.

With a last check on the van's two sleeping occupants, I cracked open a second window and locked the doors. Several tall redwoods blocked the overhead sun, shading the van. I felt confident the interior would remain cool for the short time it would take Isabella and me to check out the fort.

A group of ten furiously pedaling cyclists zoomed by on the cordoned-off race route as I began pushing the stroller down a sandy path leading into the back side of the park. A sandwich placard set up on the grass next to a clump of redwoods caught my eye.

TODAY AT SUTTER FORT:

THE WORLD'S BEST CYCLISTS
ARE OTHERWISE PREOCCUPIED;

SEVERAL A-LIST CELEBRITIES
ARE IN TOWN BUT WILL NOT BE APPEARING.
INSTEAD, WE'RE SURE YOU'LL ENJOY
THE PRESENTATION OF

MARK TWAIN
IMPERSONATOR

CLEMENT SAMUELS.

Chapter 29

SUTTER'S FORT

WE FOLLOWED THE inevitable trail of teaser placards around the park to the front of Sutter's Fort. Isabella called out an alert at each one to ensure I didn't lose my way.

Surrounded by green grass and yucca plants, the historic state park was a frequent day-trip destination for local schoolchildren. A large group of short-statured munchkins milled around the fort entrance as I approached.

Constructed in the early 1840s, these whitewashed brick walls had formed the cornerstone of Swiss immigrant John Sutter's ambitious trading and agricultural enterprise. In its heyday, the stronghold of Sutter's Fort provided a full-service rest stop for travelers through the region—those depleted from the trek over the Sierras and those gearing up for the climb. Sutter was well on his way toward achieving his vision of a new Swiss empire when he lost it all in the sweeping social upheaval of the Gold Rush.

Soon after the discovery of gold near a watermill in the nearby Sierra foothills, Sutter's vast estate was overrun by hordes of fortune-hunting Forty-Niners. Sutter was besieged from all sides: he couldn't keep gold-seeking trespassers off his property, and he couldn't persuade his gold-infatuated employees to stay on it long enough to complete their work. Sutter's once-vast manual labor force abandoned their posts to search for gold, leaving fields unplowed and stock untended. The estate crumbled before his eyes. That which wasn't ransacked by vagrant miners quickly fell into ruin from lack of maintenance.

I paused to survey the thriving city surrounding the park square. What had once been the focal point of an agricultural empire encompassing some fifty thousand acres now sat, incongruously, in the middle of Sacramento's downtown business district. A sizeable medical center, a church, and several office and apartment buildings looked out on the remnants of the square sentry and cannon portals Sutter had positioned atop each of the fort's four corners.

In addition to his vast estate, I reflected as I dodged a spontaneous game of tag that had broken out near the fort's flagpole, Sutter had also been known for his eccentricities. In the years before his precipitous downfall, Sutter paraded around Northern California as a self-proclaimed general, an assertion that no doubt irked the territory's Mexican rulers. But since the closest Mexican troops were over a hundred miles to the south (under the command of the legitimately titled General Castro), there was no formal objection to Sutter's delusional proclamations.

As the Sacramento Valley began to attract increasing numbers of independent-minded Americans, however, the Mexican authorities became more and more wary of Sutter's growing spread. It was at Sutter's Fort, after all, where locals first heard rumors that the Mexican government was planning to tighten its loose apron strings on the region, send in troops to round up the American immigrants, and force them all to either declare their allegiance to the Mexican authorities or leave.

Many suspected U.S. Army Captain John Frémont was the one responsible for spreading these inflammatory rumors—the explorer made several stops at Sutter's Fort during his mapping expedition of the Oregon Territory. Frémont had high expectations about both the future of California and the role he would play in bringing it into the American fold. The Pathfinder's blustery entrance to the scene triggered a chain of events that would forever change control of the region—whether the American government was ready for it or not.

I PUSHED THE stroller up to the ticket counter as Clem's resonant stage voice echoed from inside the fort. While fishing through my shoulder bag for the admittance fee, I caught a glimpse of Clem's linen-clad figure standing on the flat top of a horse wagon in the fort's open center area. He was about to begin his act for an audience of enraptured schoolchildren and their adult caretakers.

I slid my five-dollar bill across the counter to the park attendant manning the ticket booth, thankful that she was too distracted by the next busload of children queuing up behind me to notice the feline passenger in my stroller. Isabella sat quietly but attentively in the carriage compartment as I pushed the stroller into the fort's rectangular courtyard.

The fort's open interior spread out over more than an acre. A ringed layer of rooms was built inward from the fifteen-foot-high, whitewashed brick wall that formed the perimeter. The main living quarters were located near the center of the fort, while the perimeter rooms were designated for livestock pens, leather tanning, and a small row of holding cells.

A group of volunteers decked out in period costume simulated tasks around the grounds to help visitors envision what the fort had been like in its pre–Gold Rush prime: a pair of men in heavy leather aprons demonstrated blacksmithing, a woman and two children in homespun pioneer garb prepared a gooey bowl of dough in one of the kitchens, and a soot-covered cook stirred the coals of a freestanding wood stove as he monitored a previously made lump that was now baking into bread.

Amid all this busy activity, Clem commanded the wagon's makeshift stage, which was set up in the middle of the courtyard. He wore the same costume he'd used for his Nevada City performance: a rumpled linen suit, tattered black bow tie, and lace-up ankle boots. His feet thunked heavily across the wagon's rough wooden boards as he started in on the beginning of his monologue.

"Now, I presume that introductions are unnecessary?" Clem asked as he leaned out over the edge of the wagon toward the front row of children and made a series of exaggerated facial contortions. I smiled as the youngsters tittered in amusement. A little girl's enthusiastic hand shot up, and she called out excitedly, "I know who you are! I know who you are!"

An exhibit on the history of the fort was housed in the rooms built into the perimeter wall to the right of the entrance. Since I had a few minutes to spare before Clem caught up to the part of the performance where I had left him at the Nevada Theatre, I wandered into the open door of the display area to look around.

As I pushed the stroller inside, Isabella and I were immediately greeted by a life-sized wax figure of John Sutter. He was a pale, balding, mustached man in a long coat, buttoned vest, and frumpy neck scarf. From his sharp disapproving gaze, I got the distinct impression that General Sutter would not have appreciated my intrusion onto his property.

That, or he hadn't been fond of cats, I thought as Isabella stared up at him, her brow furrowed in a bewildered manner.

"He's not real, Issy," I assured her as the stroller bumped over the rough concrete floor past the wax figure.

I followed the indicated path into the rest of the exhibit. A series of posters detailed Sutter's early life in Europe, his journey to California, and his relationship with General Mariano Vallejo, the local representative of the Mexican military who had resided in the unmanned garrison at nearby Sonoma. With no troops serving under him, Vallejo's "General" moniker had been almost as impotent as Sutter's.

Clem's voice continued in the courtyard as I rounded a corner into the second room of the exhibit. "Our story begins with John C. Frémont . . ."

Right on cue, I found myself face-to-face with a

portrait of the famous Pathfinder. He was depicted as a serious young man with an innocent-looking expression engulfed by a thick tangled beard. Positioned next to Frémont was a picture of the Bear Flag with which he was now so inextricably linked.

The Bear Flag in the frame was a photograph of a replica that had been created at the fifty-year anniversary of the Bear Flag Revolt. This flag had the same general layout and design as the current state flag. A five-pointed star was affixed on the upper left-hand corner, and a red banner ran across the bottom. Next to the star stood a bear, positioned with all four feet on the ground beneath it.

I studied the flag's bear, recalling the passage from Oscar's DeVoto book that had described the original animal as "standing on its hind legs." Who had changed the position of the bear on later flags? I wondered again. And why had Oscar written the notation about the bear into the margin next to that text?

Local Indians, passing through Sonoma after the revolt, ridiculed the animal on the flag, calling it a pig or a stoat.

"I could see someone confusing this bear with a pig," I mumbled to Isabella as I stared at the beast's heavy floor-scraping belly, ". . . but a stoat?"
"Wrao."

I glanced down at the stroller where Isabella was pawing at the netting.

"*Wrao,*" she repeated.

"No, no," I replied sternly. "No more escapes . . ."

And then I saw what had caught Isabella's attention. There on the dusty floor beneath the Bear Flag display case, propped up against a dimly lit corner, sat a little stuffed bear holding a California state flag.

My fingers trembled as I reached down to pick it up. I blew off a dusting of spiderwebs as I turned the tiny paper flag so that I could read the two lines of gold-lettered script on the back: BEAR FLAG MEMORIAL, SONOMA PLAZA.

Chapter 30

A DELICATE CONSTITUTION

MONTY SLOUCHED IN the van's front passenger seat, his bony frame limp with sleep. His face twitched with the slight crease of an eager-to-please smile.

"Why yes, Mayor, absolutely," he mumbled groggily. "I'd go with the dark blue tie. It brings out the color of your eyes."

His head flopped wildly from one shoulder to the other. "No, no, I'd use the sterling silver cufflinks," he said, his speech markedly slurred. "They make you look more gubernatorial."

Monty smacked his lips together. "Sacramento? Mayor, sir, you know my heart's in San Francisco . . ."

A trickle of drool began to run down Monty's chin as he continued to sputter out words from his dream. "Me? Why, I'd be honored. You'd be leaving the city in capable hands, I can assure you . . ."

His lower jaw dropped to his chest, leaving his mouth gaping open. A large fly zoomed through the two-inch opening at the top of the passenger side window and buzzed curiously toward the black hole.

Monty's lips suddenly clamped shut, thwarting the fly at the last moment. His mouth formed a slobbering pucker as he murmured, "Just need to get my photo album started . . ."

HAROLD WOMBLER'S PICKUP slowly circled Sutter's Fort State Historic Park, weaving around the barricades set up for the bike race as he looked for Monty's large white van. He found it parked in a slot beneath a clutch of redwoods, around the block from the fort's main entrance.

After scoping out the surrounding area to ensure he wouldn't draw immediate police attention, Harold pulled to a stop in the middle of the street, double-parking behind the rear of the van. With an aching groan, he engaged the parking brake, gathered the frogs into their terrarium, and clambered out the cab of the pickup.

Harold walked stiffly around the van and peered into the passenger side window. His bleary eyes narrowed as he surveyed its sleeping occupant. Snore-distorted words floated up from the human heap crumpled in the seat.

"Me?" Monty's lips flapped with a whoosh of expelled air. "You want to nominate *me* to take your place?"

Harold's lips curdled with disgust as a large fly approached the dribble oozing from Monty's open mouth. Grumbling under his breath, Harold pressed his face against the passenger side window and smacked the palm of his free hand against the door's metal panel.

Jolted awake by the sound, Monty's lips snapped shut, trapping the fly inside his mouth. His instinctive swallow was followed by a sour grimace as the fly's struggling body caught in the back of his throat.

"Sweet . . . mother of pearl, Harold!" Monty gasped with a choking cough. "What are you doing here?"

CLEM HAD JUST started the second part of his narrative when Isabella and I emerged from the exhibit area and returned to the courtyard, the third bear safely secured in one of the stroller's side pockets. I rolled Isabella to a position at the back of the crowd and settled in to watch the rest of his performance.

"Now then, after several months of travel through the country's midsection, our fearless Pathfinder finally arrived in the Western territories. Captain Frémont was dutifully fulfilling his mission to remap the forests of Oregon when he discovered an unfortunate feature of life in the Pacific Northwest."

Clem leaned forward, wisely cocking an eyebrow at the children standing in front of the wagon. "Those folks take their weather in the liquid form."

He leaned back on his heels. "There are some that don't mind the occasional light mist, the odd sprinkle, the regular afternoon shower, the daily downpour . . ." He wagged his finger briskly back and forth. "Our Pathfinder was not one of them."

Clem struck a pained expression. "Frémont had mold growing in his saddle blanket, fungus taking root between his toes"—he jerked his left leg out over the edge of the wagon's stage—"and an inexplicable itch creeping across his entire body. It was more than any man could tolerate!" His shoulders shuddered violently as he pulled his leg back in.

"You see, our Pathfinder had a delicate constitution," Clem said, his voice taking on a whining tone. "It became more and more delicate the farther into Oregon he traveled." He wrapped his arms around his body and shivered. "As the calendar turned to its winter months, and all that rain started coming down as snow, Frémont decided he'd had about enough of *Oregon*.

"Forget about tramping through those cold, wet forests," Clem declared with a disparaging guffaw. "He could make the map up on his own!"

Clem tapped his temple with a stubby forefinger. "Being a student of geography, our Pathfinder knew exactly where to find a warmer climate." He brought his finger out in front of his body to point at the crowd. "He headed south—to California!"

HAROLD GRIMACED AS Monty rolled down the window.

"What're you doing here, Harold?" Monty repeated sleepily.

"I'm a cycling fan," Harold spit out coarsely. He tapped the brim of his baseball cap and pointed at the bike-riding bear sewn onto its front.

"Right, of course," Monty replied. He glanced skeptically down at Harold's ragged overalls. "I wouldn't have pegged you for the type."

The loose skin on Harold's cheeks sucked sourly inward as Monty smoothed his hands over the front of his nylon cycling shirt. "What do you think of my biking gear?"

He didn't wait for Harold's response. "Hey, did you see the start of the race this morning?"

he asked indignantly. "I couldn't believe those guys . . ."

"Where's your traveling companion?" Harold demanded grittily.

Monty swung his head toward the empty driver's seat. "Hmm," he mused. He twisted his torso to check the van's back cargo area. "That's a good question," he murmured, slightly perturbed.

Harold rolled his eyes. He shoved the frog terrarium through the open window and thrust it into Monty's lap.

"Hold on to this, you worthless git. I'll be right back." With that, Harold stalked off toward the entrance of the fort.

The two frogs looked curiously up at Monty as he peered down into the terrarium, his narrow face registering wonder and amazement.

"Did you grow that hair or are those fake mustaches?"

CLEM STROKED HIS chin thoughtfully as he paced across the floor of the wagon in front of the enraptured schoolchildren.

"There was one more thing that attracted our Pathfinder to California—other than its hospitable climate. The Oregon Territory, you see, was already firmly within the clutches of the American government."

Clem waved a dismissive hand. "There was a niggling little dispute with England over where to draw the northern border, but that issue was well on its way to being sorted out by the diplomats." He kinked his pinky finger in the air and made a loud slurping sound. "Over a cup or two of tea."

The children giggled at Clem's antics. Stroking his mustache, he grinned an acknowledgment and continued.

"California offered Frémont the one thing he desired the most—even more than dry socks. That was fame and celebrity. He'd had his first taste, and he was hungry for more."

Clem raised the point of his finger to elaborate.

"Frémont's young wife, Jessie, had translated the mapmaking notes from his earlier expeditions into a series of widely read travelogues. These tales of wild adventure captured the nation's imagination and inspired many Americans to hop on their wagons and venture west. As seen through the adoring eyes of his spouse, Frémont and his mountaineer sidekick Kit Carson became literary heroes. Thanks to Jessie's creative pen, Frémont was a legend around the wagon-trail campfires.

"Fame is an addictive elixir," Clem said, shaking his head. "That first sip of stardom left Frémont with a powerful thirst—and he knew where and how he might quench it."

He nodded to the front row of children. "Right next door to Oregon, there was another Western territory that was clearly destined to fall to the

Stars and Stripes. California was ripe for the picking. All it needed was the right man to step in and help push it over the edge. A hero to lead the disorganized masses to their rightful destiny."

Clem lowered his voice to a conspiratorial whisper. "Frémont decided that *he* was the man for the job."

HAROLD GIMPED THROUGH the fort's entrance and plunked a stack of five-dollar bills on the ledge of the admissions booth. As the park attendant tucked the money into her cash register and handed over his ticket, she smiled and said, "Smells like someone's cooking fried chicken around here."

Grunting a response, Harold carefully edged his way toward the spectators surrounding Clem's wagon. His bleary eyes honed in on the woman with the long brown hair standing at the back of the crowd, next to the cat-occupied stroller. With a satisfied grimace, Harold took notice of the new toy bear sticking out of the stroller's side pocket.

As he began to back out of the courtyard, Harold scanned the state park employees, particularly those in period costume, for signs of any additional imposters. Satisfied that the Mark Twain impersonator was the only addition lurking among the fort's regular play actors, he turned and limped toward the exit. He gave a short finger wave to the tiny whiskers poking out of Clem's shirt pocket before retreating from the fort's walled interior.

Despite Harold's careful scrutiny of the grounds, he had missed one unscripted costumed character.

As Harold disappeared through the gate, a pasty-faced John Sutter emerged from the exhibit area near the courtyard's inner perimeter.

Chapter 31

MANIFEST DESTINY

THE FIGURE DRESSED as John Sutter ambled casually around the outer edge of courtyard, his dusty overcoat and frumpy collared shirt giving him the convincing appearance that he belonged with the other period actors inhabiting the fort. He approached a bench about twenty feet behind the crowd circling Clem's wagon and slid noiselessly into the seat.

Sutter watched as Clem strode back and forth across the wagon, his rosy cheeks glowing from the direct sun shining down on his peppery mustache and flyaway eyebrows.

"Of course, Frémont wasn't the only one with his eye on California," Clem advised his listeners. "The U.S. President was eager to incorporate the Mexican Territory into the American fold."

He let loose a low whistle and pumped his

eyebrows at the audience. "James Polk. Now, there was a rascally devil if I ever saw one—"

Clem's face froze as his gaze landed on the man seated on the bench at the rear of the crowd. After an awkward pause, he coughed nervously and resumed his dialogue, but his voice began to sound hurried, as if he were skipping ahead in his lecture.

"Polk came to the presidency with a single-minded obsession," Clem said, spreading his arms wide. "Expanding America to encompass the whole of the land stretching toward the western shore. He believed it was our destiny, our manifest destiny."

Clem dropped his hands to his sides, but barely paused to catch his breath before pressing on.

"That being said, in the spring of 1846, the Polk administration's military agenda was fully occupied by the situation in Texas. The U.S. had recently annexed the fledgling independent state, and a confrontation with Mexico appeared imminent. Polk was in the process of marshalling the nation's ragtag army down to the Rio Grande, the battlefield that would likely determine the fate of the President's expansionist ambitions."

Clem stroked his mustache, once more glancing anxiously toward the back of the audience.

"While the White House geared up for the coming confrontation in Texas, the California Territory was put on the back burner. Polk had spies on the ground—American Consul Thomas Larkin in Monterey and his Vice-Consul William Leidesdorff in Yerba Buena. He knew from their reports that the Mexican presence in California, particularly the northern region, was almost nonexistent. Moreover, they'd assured him that many of the Mexican generals stationed here were amenable to becoming U.S. citizens. All the while, hundreds of Americans continued to move into the area. Future U.S. annexation of California seemed inevitable to almost all observers. Polk reasoned that if he could wrangle the Mexicans to the negotiating table on Texas, he could lump California in with any resulting treaty."

Clem crossed his arms over his chest, strumming his fingers against the sleeves of his jacket.

"In the meantime, the Polk administration issued clear instructions to its California operatives to maintain peaceful relations out West. A couple of navy ships were positioned out in the Pacific, so that they could move in and secure the most important California harbors should the U.S. and Mexico formally declare war over Texas. Larkin and Leidesdorff were under strict orders to encourage an amicable transition for the California Territory—one that would avoid any unnecessary military involvement, because those resources were already stretched thin."

Clem drew in a deep breath and locked his gaze upon the John Sutter character before concluding. "That was the strategy of President Polk and his advisors. That was *their* plan. They didn't count on the Pathfinder."

Chapter 32

THE LURE OF THE YELLOW JERSEY

THE MAIN GROUP of riders sped around the corner of L and 26th near the edge of Sutter's Fort State Historic Park. The peloton, containing eighty or more cyclists, was about to begin its second downtown lap toward the finish line for Stage One of the Tour of California.

A motorcycle hummed along in front of the pack, the driver carefully navigating the race route as a cameraman hung off the back of the machine, angling for the best shot of the action. Another camera crew hovered in the sky above, videotaping wide-angle views from a helicopter. All these visual feeds were looped back to a mobile computer center near the finish line, where technicians spliced them together for the live television broadcast.

A wrinkled old man in ragged overalls stood on the curb, watching as the peloton swept toward him, a zinging buzz of high-tech gears grinding away at top speed. In one hand, he held

the handle of a glass-walled terrarium containing two distinguished-looking frogs wearing
feathery orange mustaches. The frogs' heads
swiveled on their short, stubby necks as they tried
to follow the blur of motion.

A stiff, man-made breeze ballooned against the
frayed fabric of the man's overalls, pressed back
the skin of his loose hanging cheeks, and nearly
knocked the green baseball cap from his greasy-
haired head. One of the riders tossed a plastic
water bottle into the air, causing the man to duck
and the frogs to tumble inside their jostled cage.
The discarded bottle rolled to a stop at Harold
Wombler's feet as the tail end of the group
zoomed past.

Beneath the sea of bobbing plastic helmets, the
riders' faces were chiseled into expressions of
intensely focused effort. The peloton had easily
caught the ten riders from the original breakaway, but as the racers pedaled the first downtown
lap, a lone rider had made his own individual
sprint away from the pack to take the lead. He had
managed to jump out nearly a minute in front of
the peloton, but they had no intention of letting
him stay there.

The collective speed of eighty riders aero-
dynamically grouped together was a force no
single cyclist could hold off—at least not for any
substantial amount of time. For over a hundred
miles of riding, the teams had been preparing

themselves for a sprinter's finish, and they weren't about to let this renegade rider spoil the plot.

Several blocks ahead, the lone cyclist rode down the stretch leading to the finish line, desperately wishing he were one lap farther down the course. Eager crowds three and four people deep lined the route, cheering as he pounded at his pedals. The finish-line banner stretched over the street in the distance, a heartbreaking illusion of glory. He tucked his head down and begged his screaming muscles to continue their effort.

If he could just hold on to this slim lead . . . if he could just stay out in front of the charging peloton . . . if he could just make it one more lap . . . he would start the next leg of the race wearing the coveted yellow jersey.

IN THE BROADCAST booth above the finish line, Will Spigot shook his head ruefully.

"It's a funny thing, what the yellow jersey can spur a man to do. Our little friend here has no chance, none, of making it to the finish line ahead of the pack, but he's let that elusive yellow lady blind him to reality. The lure of the yellow jersey—that's what I chalk this up to."

Spigot licked his lips and leaned over the counter of the broadcast booth. "For all of you neophytes watching at home, let me explain how the yellow jersey is awarded. As we progress through the eight stages of the race, the time each rider takes to go from the day's starting point to its finish line is added together for a total race time. At the end of each racing stage, the yellow jersey is awarded to the rider with the lowest overall time.

"In order to succeed in the competition for the yellow jersey, a rider has to perform well on flat, windy stretches, like we have on the run in to Sacramento this afternoon, as well as steep mountain passes, like the ones we'll see in the days to come. It takes a rare combination of skill and endurance for one rider to be able to succeed across multiple road conditions, but even that's not enough to win a stage race like the Tour of California. Each elite rider with a chance of competing for the overall win needs a hardworking team to help him through the inevitable difficulties that will crop up over the course of the week."

Leaning back, Spigot tapped a pencil on the top of the counter. "That's the primary storyline, if you will. The overall headliner. Each day of the race, however, one or more of the lesser riders will form a breakout group in front of the peloton, putting all of their efforts into winning just that day's stage. It's a tiring and exhausting endeavor, because the riders in the breakaway don't get the aerodynamic benefit of riding in the peloton. And, as we've seen today, the attempt

216

rarely pays off. Tomorrow, they'll be back in the pack, working to support their team's overall contender. But it's that slim hope that they might make it to the finish line ahead of the main group that keeps them trying for it. And for stage one, of course, the prize is extra special. At the end of today's racing, the overall time and the Stage One time will be the same—meaning that today's stage winner will also earn the yellow jersey."

Spigot cocked his left eyebrow at the camera. "That's what has sparked the imagination of our little friend out there—the hope that he might win today's stage and wear the yellow jersey at the starting line tomorrow. It's a rogue move, I'll give him that. But the peloton is surging full speed behind him, and I'd wager a fine steak dinner that he won't be able to hold them off."

The camera panned out to pick up Spigot's broadcasting partner in its frame.

"Now, Will," Harry Carlin prompted gently. "That's a nice summary, but don't forget to tell our listeners about the sprinters. We expect one of them to win the stage today."

Spigot raised a bony finger. "Ah yes, the sprinters. Because so few cyclists are capable of competing for the overall win, many riders have developed specialties in a specific type of racing. Their goal is not to win the overall race—instead their objective is to hone their skills to a specific type of racing in order to improve their chances at getting a win on stages that best suit their abilities.

"Today we're going to see the sprinters showcase their talents. These riders have trained their muscles to kick their bikes forward in a last spurt of extreme speed a hundred meters or so in front of the finish line. A stage like today, with a long flat finish, is tailor-made for the sprinters' teams, but in order for them to have a shot, the peloton will have to catch this last breakaway rider before he finishes the final lap."

Spigot glanced over at Carlin. "Does the computer think he'll be caught?"

"The computer says he'll definitely be caught," Carlin said, a chagrined smile on his ruddy face.

"Yes, well, the computer is usually right about these things," Spigot replied, nodding his head wisely. "And I don't think the sprinters fancy letting him steal their thunder on this one."

He leaned out over the edge of the booth, looking down at the finish line as the lone rider sped past. "Don't tell *this* bloke it won't work. He's a stubborn one, that. He's going to give it his all, right up until the end."

Chapter 33

GAVILAN PEAK

CLEM STRODE TO the far side of the wagon and reached for a water bottle from one of the park personnel. Thirstily, he unscrewed the plastic cap, brought the opening to his lips, and tilted his head back. His Adam's apple bobbed up and down as he guzzled half the bottle in a single gulp.

I stood next to the stroller, near the rear of the audience, puzzling over Clem's strange behavior. Midway through his routine, he'd begun acting as if something had shaken his confidence. What's more, every so often, he appeared to glance back to where I was standing. I pushed my glasses farther up my nose, perplexed. Surely he couldn't see Isabella inside the stroller from that angle and distance.

Clem wiped his mouth on the sleeve of his linen jacket and turned toward the spectators with a sideways smile. "When we last visited with our Pathfinder, he was fleeing the rain-soaked forests of Oregon for the warmer weather of California. After a brief stop in Yerba Buena, the settlement that would later become San Francisco, he headed down to Monterey to meet the American Consul, Thomas Larkin."

Pumping his eyebrows, Clem paused for a wry

smile. "Consul Larkin was an odd little fellow. He was a timid, bookish man who fretted constantly. He worried over breakfast; he worried over lunch. By the time he got to dinner, his stomach was so knotted-up from his day of worrying, he could hardly bring himself to look at a plate of food, much less eat it."

Clem leaned back and thunked his hands across the plump girth of his stomach. "Larkin took one look at Frémont and nearly collapsed into a fit of anxiety."

Tugging on his collar to loosen his bow tie, Clem bent down toward the children standing in front of his wagon. "Our Pathfinder had already assumed the character he hoped to play in Jessie's next book, and he was eager to show off. He'd outfitted himself with a pair of buckskin pants and a floppy, wide-brimmed hat. The hair on his head and beard had been growing wild for months. He looked like a cross between a gunslinging outlaw and a woolly-haired gypsy."

Clem's mustache twitched as his eyes flicked once more to the back of the crowd. I watched as a steadying expression passed over his face. It was as if he'd mentally determined to ignore whatever was throwing him off his routine. His voice strengthened as he continued.

"Captain Frémont's arrival in Monterey didn't go unnoticed by the Mexican authorities. General Castro, the head of the local presidio, wanted to know what an American army officer was doing in his neck of the woods."

Clem raised a stubby finger skyward. "Frémont responded that he was a famous mapmaker—a Pathfinder, so to speak—and he was just stopping by as part of his geographical explorations."

Clem scratched his chin thoughtfully. "Now, Castro may have been exiled to the outer edges of a forgotten parcel of the Mexican empire, but he wasn't the dullest tool in their shed of generals. Monterey and its surrounding environs were well mapped out, and none of its current inhabitants had any trouble finding their way around town. They certainly didn't need this flamboyantly dressed American to guide their way."

Clem blew out a guffaw. "No, Castro wasn't buying this story. And after he received reports that Frémont was stirring up the local Americans with all sorts of rebellion talk, Castro politely invited Frémont to take his mapmaking expertise elsewhere—outside the boundaries of the Mexican Territory of California."

Clem cowered on the edge of the wagon, wringing his hands in emulation of the nervous American Consul. "Larkin was beside himself with worry. He was convinced Frémont was about to provoke an international incident—the kind the President of the United States had tasked him with preventing. So Larkin pleaded with Frémont to return to his designated post—in *Oregon*."

Clem popped back up, slapping his hands together with a loud clap. "Our Pathfinder would not be so easily deterred from his self-appointed mission," he said, wagging his finger. "Frémont huffed out of town all right, but he didn't go far. He and his men hiked up the nearest mountain overlooking Monterey to a place called Gavilan Peak. This gathering of, ahem, mapmakers, built themselves a roaring campfire and invited the local Americans up for a powwow. It wasn't long before all sorts of crazy insurrection talk began to be thrown about the embers."

Clem stroked his mustache thoughtfully. "Now, of course, an expedition such as this needs a constant resupply of provisions, fresh transport, and the like. Since Frémont and his men were several days' ride away from Sutter's Fort, he decided to, ah, *borrow* what they needed from a local Mexican farmer.

"That was the last straw," Clem said, shaking his head. "Castro gathered his troops and prepared to march up the peak to arrest Frémont as a horse thief."

Clem struck a pose of mock innocence. "Naturally, Frémont was outraged that such a charge should be levied against him, a man of such stature and celebrity. Frémont called his rum-drunk men to action. It was time for them to stand up for their principles . . ."

Clem drew back from the stage and scratched

his whiskery chin. "Yes, well, hmm, principles." He looked out across the audience with a skeptical expression. Then, clearing his throat, he continued, "It wasn't exactly clear what principles the Pathfinder and his men were vowing to defend, but Captain Frémont nevertheless proclaimed Gavilan Peak—or at least the immediate area surrounding his campfire—to be the liberated and highly principled property of the United States government. Frémont vowed he would be bloody and lifeless before he surrendered the smallest inch to those greedy, obstinate, horse-hoarding Mexicans . . ."

Clem's voice trailed off as he issued the audience a sly wink. Then, abruptly, he pulled himself inward to a crouched, cringing position.

"Meanwhile, Larkin had worked himself into a foaming frenzy, certain that he would be blamed should this Don Quixote Pathfinder get himself fricasseed. Frémont was vastly outnumbered, and the closest American forces that might be summoned to rescue him from Castro's men were on a Navy ship several hundred miles out in the Pacific Ocean. Larkin mustered his last ounce of gumption and told Frémont to pack up his floppy hat and buckskin pants and hightail it back to Oregon—before Castro marched into his camp and shredded him to pieces.

"It was an ignominious end to a one-sided standoff," Clem said as a wry smirk settled onto his face. "The Pathfinder finally convinced himself that his patriotism would be better served if he temporarily ah, *repositioned* his camp to a more strategic location.

"And so, tail tucked between his legs, Frémont gathered his small group of explorers and hiked down from Gavilan Peak. Reluctantly, he set his compass north and began trodding in the cold, wet direction of . . ."

Clem sucked in a deep breath, and then breathed out a loud, exhausted, *"Oregon."*

Chapter 34

STAGE ONE FINISH LINE

RUPERT YAWNED AND rolled over onto his stomach, an action that had the immediate effect of awakening his hunger. After a quick glance at what he could see of the van's cargo area, he stepped out his carrier's open door with a long stiff-legged stretch.

He took a sip from his water dish, smacking his lips together as he sampled the liquid. His person had brought along a bottle of the filtered water from the Green Vase's refrigerator. It was slightly staler than he preferred, but, given their current mobile circumstances, he could cope.

The food she had left out for him, however, was another matter entirely. He sniffed disdainfully at the dry giblets his person had sprinkled into his bowl. Once his expectations had been raised to the level of fried chicken, those crunchy orange triangles simply fell below the mark.

Twitching his whiskers, Rupert ambled to the front of the van to discuss the matter with Monty. Rupert had slept through much of the morning's stroller outing in Nevada City and had missed the streaker action at the starting line. He wasn't sure why Monty had been muttering about hooligans and criminal charges, but he had his own ideas on where his tall friend might direct his efforts.

He slunk around the back of Monty's chair, crawled up into his lap and began kneading his stomach.

"Oh, hello there, Rupert," Monty welcomed him. "What do you think of my shirt? Pretty cool, huh? The fabric's so lightweight and breathable."

Rupert paused for a moment and gazed solemnly into Monty's green eyes. Not your best look, mate, he thought silently. But I'd be willing to look past this horrendous wardrobe decision if you'd get me some real food.

Rupert resumed his kneading, this time poking the pads of his feet a little harder into the paunch of Monty's stomach.

"Hey, hey, watch the threads there, Mister," Monty said sternly, gently lifting Rupert off his chest.

Rupert decided to switch tactics. Purring loudly,

he summoned his best hypnotic trance. I'm hungry, he thought with intense concentration as he stared into Monty's face. You're hungry. Let's go get ourselves some fried chicken.

Rupert felt his hunger surge as his mind fixated on an imaginary plate of his favorite food. His stomach rumbled; his mouth salivated. Then, suddenly, he stopped to consider the size of Monty's potential appetite. After a brief reflection, he amended his mental message.

You're only a *little* bit hungry.

A motion of color in the rearview mirror caught Monty's attention. "Was that a rider?" he asked suddenly. He glanced from the mirror down to Rupert. "I think we're right next to the race route. Shall we go take a look?"

Take me to the fried chicken, Rupert repeated over and over again, his eyes crossing as he focused on Monty's forehead.

Monty opened the driver's side door and scooped Rupert up into his arms. Feeling somewhat optimistic, Rupert draped himself over his pal's slick green shoulders as Monty walked down to the corner where Harold Wombler stood on a curb next to a discarded water bottle.

"Hi again, there, Wombler," Monty said cordially. "Are you waiting on the racers?"

Harold turned to look at Monty, a crass expression on his loose, wrinkled face.

"What's that sound?" Monty asked as a mass of riders came around the bend.

Still gripping Monty's shirt, Rupert turned his head in the direction of the commotion. His entire body froze in panic as he temporarily forgot about his fried chicken fixation. Never in his short fluffy life had he seen such a buzzing whirring tornado of motion.

Aaaaah! Rupert thought, flexing his claws through the thin fabric of Monty's shirt.

"Aaaaah!" Monty screamed as a searing pain lanced across his chest.

INSIDE SUTTER'S FORT, Clem paused mid-sentence as a man's high-pitched, bloodcurdling scream rang out from the parking area behind the fort.

I glanced down at the stroller.

"Wrao," Isabella said sharply, drawing some curious looks from the children standing nearest to us.

"Better head back to the van," I whispered in agreement.

"HARRY, DID YOU hear something?" Will Spigot's forehead creased as he tried to interpret the sound.

"I believe it was a siren," Harry Carlin replied calmly. "Perhaps a fire truck or an ambulance. They have quite a few of those here in this country."

The television monitor behind the broadcasters flashed an image of the top curve of the race route's downtown loop. The video briefly honed in on the strange spectacle of a tall skinny man in a shredded green nylon shirt jumping up and down as he held a fluffy white cat over his head.

ISABELLA AND I returned to the van to find the back door propped open. Monty sat on the edge of the cargo area, his green legs dangling over the bumper. Shirtless, he was applying bandages to a number of deep red scratch marks on his chest. It looked as if his upper torso had been run through a lawnmower.

Rupert sat on the floor of the van next to him, curiously watching the second first aide process in as many days. He looked up at me as I approached, a hungry expression on his furry face.

"Wao?" he asked hopefully.

WILL SPIGOT FLASHED a wry grin at the camera. "Our riders have just made the last turn of the downtown loop, a few blocks to the east of us, and they're now charging down L Street toward the finish line. They're just specks of dust from our view in the broadcast booth, but you can see them clearly here on the video screen."

"There's just the little matter of our friend out in front there," Harry Carlin said with a wince. "He's put up a gallant fight, but the peloton are almost upon him. They're going to sweep past him, I'm afraid, and leave him in their dust."

Spigot had no sympathy. "It was a foolish move, wasn't it? The computer told us all along that he had no chance." He nodded to the video monitor. "Yes, see, there he is being pushed off to the side. Look at his face. He doesn't know what's hit him. After all that, he'll cross the line at the bottom of the pack."

With a shrug, Spigot turned his attention to the charging peloton. "The sprinters' teams are angling for position," he said eagerly, his eyes sparkling with anticipation. "They're setting up their lines, looking to catapult their top riders out across the finish line. It'll be down to the wire, this . . ."

Chapter 35

MOON OVER SACRAMENTO

THE MOON ROSE over Northern California into a clear Sunday evening. It glanced down at its ever-slimming crescent body, admiring the sharp, seductive points that had begun to form on its narrowing top and bottom. Swiveling its hips flirtatiously, the moon sashayed inland to Sacramento's brightly lit skyline.

The city was still celebrating the thrilling Stage One finish of the Tour of California that had swept through its downtown streets earlier that afternoon. In the grassy area outside the State Capitol buildings, fans milled about sponsor tents, buying souvenirs, perusing displays touting the latest technological advances in cycling equipment, and, of course, discussing the day's racing.

An enormous video screen positioned at the edge of the hospitality area played a constant loop of hastily spliced together footage of the down-to-the-wire finish. Several sprint specialists had challenged the pack in the last hundred meters, but the winning rider was a cherry-faced Englishman with a solid, squatty build who was known throughout the cycling world by his self-proclaimed title, "The Fastest Man in the World."

The video clip finished with a scene from the podium presentation. Basking in his latest victory, the Fastest Man leapt merrily onto the top pedestal to receive a bouquet of flowers and cheek-to-cheek kisses from local beauties in short skirts and tight-fitting blouses. A moment later, a representative from one of the race sponsors stepped up behind him to fit the yellow jersey around his shoulders.

Beyond the crowd, the rider who had led the peloton for the last lap and a half of the downtown loop lay spread-eagled in the grass, spent and exhausted from his exertions.

The moon skirted around the video screen and

found its way to the cycling teams' tour buses. In a cordoned-off area set up for media interviews, one of the sport's most famous cyclists—a man referred to by many as the Elder Statesman—held court amid a swarm of blinding flashbulbs and prodding microphones. He had recently returned to racing after a few years' retirement, deciding to give it a go at one more round of glory and, perhaps, one last yellow jersey.

Despite his lean musculature and brawny physique, the gray flecks in his closely cropped hair accented the fact that he was close to twenty years senior to the youngest riders in the race. While his aging body might struggle to maintain the level of fitness required for this demanding sport, his years of experience had given him a definite advantage when it came to handling the press. The iron muscles of his face exuded an air of confidence, a cloak he wore so effortlessly few dared to question it.

The Elder Statesman's silver-blue eyes surveyed the surging chaos of the scene around him. Then, with a few strong, simple words, he expertly corralled the sea of interrogators, calmly but sternly coordinated the order of their questions, and, bit by bit, measured out his responses, providing them no more information than he had previously determined he would release.

When the Elder Statesman had endured enough, he pulled out his mobile phone to signal that the interview was over, turned, and walked away. There was a slight hitch to his stride, coupled with the hint of a swagger, as if his cycling shoes and plastic helmet were instead a pair of cowboy boots and a brimming ten-gallon hat.

Like many of the abandoned media members, the moon gushed in awe at the Elder Statesman's departing shadow. Then, straightening its shoulders, it settled into the night's agenda.

After a short search, the moon located the big white van on the top level of a parking garage across the street from one of the downtown area's fancy business hotels.

The moon sent out an exploratory beam of light that crept stealthily up the van's front grill. After carefully picking its way around several smashed insect carcasses, the beam snaked along the surface of the hood, sent a probing spotlight up over the windshield wipers, and looked inside.

A dusting of short white hairs covered the driver's seat, but the female cat who had claimed this position the previous evening was nowhere to be found. Perplexed, the beam pushed further in toward the back of the van, pulsing the interior with the widest spotlight its shrinking crescent could muster—to no avail. The furry white mischief-makers were sleeping elsewhere that evening.

Momentarily stumped, the moon vacated the

van and plopped itself down on the rim of the parking garage roof to regroup.

Hmm, the moon pondered. They couldn't have gone far.

It scanned its light over the surrounding buildings. Every direction presented a facing of glass walls and windows. Slowly, patiently, the moon filtered through the options, discarding room after room until it located its targets on the twenty-second floor of a nearby hotel: two white cats with orange-tipped ears and tails were curled up on a window seat looking out across Sacramento's sparkling cityscape.

It was a beautiful suite of rooms, complete with sleek silver-accented furnishings, a full-sized couch and a flat screen television. But how, the moon wondered, had the crew managed to sneak the igloo-shaped litter box into the hotel? And where, the moon puzzled, were the two humans? Clearly, a second sleuthing mission was in order.

Back down on the pavement, the moon darted along the city streets, searching through restaurants and pubs for the cat caretakers. It wasn't until it returned to the festive area surrounding the State Capitol that it spied the missing pair in the dwindling crowds near the hospitality tents. The tall, skinny man swerved wildly along the sidewalk on his recently retooled bicycle while the woman walked a safe buffering distance to his side.

Spinning skyward, the moon took in a wider view of the area.

"Aha, there," it said smugly as it spied a figure in a brown kangaroo costume handing out free noisemakers to passersby, about twenty feet behind the mismatched couple.

The moon kicked back, satisfied with the results of the night's investigations. It was just about to roll out of town when the reflected sheen of a man's shaved head caught its attention. Standing beneath the trees in the gardens beyond the hospitality area, the bulk of the man's brawny figure was obscured from the views of the skinny cyclist, his female companion, and the gentleman in the kangaroo costume.

The moon watched, mesmerized, as the menacing man plucked an orange from the tree and held it in the palm of his muscular hand. Slowly, he began to squeeze the large round fruit, his expression one of concentrated fury as the sweet, pulpy juice dripped from his fingers, ran down his arm, and pooled in the grass at his feet.

Chapter 36

THE FLOWER SHOP

THAT NIGHT IN San Francisco's financial district, an elderly Asian man sat in a wheelchair on Montgomery Street's deserted sidewalk.

The empty thoroughfare had the abandoned air of an after-hours amusement park. The artificial canyon created by the mountainous office buildings that lined the street blocked out much of the surrounding city's noise and light. Debris of discarded sandwich wrappers, used coffee cups, and yellowed newspapers lay in piles pushed up against the cold stone and concrete edifices.

Inside one darkened foyer, a droopy-eyed security guard struggled to remain alert. He tapped his thumbs against the surface of his desk, blankly staring down at the polished marble floor. It was another slow uneventful night in the financial district—or so he thought.

Mr. Wang's frail body rustled beneath the heavy wool blanket piled over his lap. His bony fingers reached up and thoughtfully twisted the wispy gray beard that spiraled down from the tip of his chin. Tilting his face up toward the narrow wedge of evening sky visible between the rows of office buildings, he listened intently to the whisper of the moon.

In contrast to the quiet on the sidewalk, the flower shop behind Wang's wheelchair was abuzz with activity. A strong floral scent floated out the shop's open windows, an odor far more pungent than that provided by the fresh flowers that filled the front racks.

A scattering of purple tulip petals formed a path leading into the shop's interior. There, in the room's widest open space, two women suited in goggles, gloves, and aprons worked over a table laden with glassware.

Rubber tubing connected a collection of beakers and vials that had been arranged into a temporary chemistry lab. A trio of Bunsen burners shot flames up against a set of test tubes whose rounded bottoms contained a bubbling dark-colored liquid.

Dilla Eckles bent over a pile of tattered papers as beads of perspiration dotted her forehead. The familiar handwriting scrawled across the top page detailed the last of the author's numerous experiments with various solvents and distillation techniques used to purify a valuable extract from the petals. When ingested orally, the resulting formulation acted as a powerful antidote to a certain spider venom that caused delusions of drowning followed by a state of near-deathlike paralysis.

"How much more do we need?" Lilly Wang asked as she gathered another handful of stems from a box of fresh tulips. She began expertly plucking petals from one of the blooms, her smooth ponytail of silky black hair swishing back and forth as she worked.

Dilla eyed the clear liquid extract she'd collected from the flasks thus far. "Let's do a few more batches," she replied with a grateful smile at her stepdaughter.

Brushing the back of her wrist across the damp surface of her forehead, Dilla stepped away from the counter and glanced toward the windows that looked out onto the sidewalk in front of the store. On their way back from Nevada City that morning, her husband had finally confessed that Frank Napis was on the Bear Flag trail being followed by Oscar's niece. However, Mr. Wang had been frustratingly oblique about the intended purpose of this large volume of antidote.

With a sigh, Dilla stepped back to the counter to attend to one of the boiling glass containers. As she clamped a pair of metal tongs around the neck of a bubbling test tube, her shoe brushed against one of the half-dozen empty cardboard boxes stored beneath the lab bench. Each box bore the label of a local life sciences supply company and a cautionary statement that read: WARNING: LIVE ANIMALS.

The unloaded creatures were happily exploring their temporary flower shop home. Exactly ninety-nine nude mice played on a collection of spinning treadmills and transparent round tunnels in a row of glass cages stacked against the back wall.

These mice were strikingly different from their house-mouse cousins. They had been genetically altered for optimal testing of the spider toxin and its tulip extract antidote. As an unintended side effect of the alteration, the mice failed to grow the white coats typical of their species.

Dilla and Lilly looked up from the table as the front door swung open. Wheels squeaking, Wang rolled through the entrance and rounded the front rack of flowers.

He pushed his chair up to the edge of the lab table and reached out for one of the finished vials. Carefully, he poured the liquid into a small silver flask. After tightly screwing on the lid, he slid the flask into his robe's chest pocket.

"I've got to step out for a while," he said in response to the women's concerned faces. He pumped his thin eyebrows humorously. "Don't worry," he assured them as he patted the bulge in his chest pocket. "This isn't for me."

Mr. Wang maneuvered his wheelchair to the broom closet near the storage area at the back of the flower shop. The women followed, watching anxiously as he lifted himself from the chair and knelt to the closet's floor. His gray hand wrapped around the handle of a trapdoor and lifted it up.

For a short moment, he stood over the gaping hole, wobbling wildly.

Dilla leapt forward to steady him, but Wang regained his balance before she could reach him. Lilly wrapped an arm around her stepmother's shoulders as he swung a slippered foot into the hatch and began climbing down the metal rungs of the ladder drilled into the side of the wall below.

Wang was breathing heavily when he reached the floor of the tunnel, but he didn't stop to catch his breath. Slowly but surely, he hobbled in the direction of the basement beneath the Green Vase.

Chapter 37

A SECOND ATTEMPT

BRIGHT AND EARLY Monday morning, Monty and I loaded the cats into the van and headed out of town for the Tour of California's Stage Two starting line. Our next stop was Davis, a leafy, laid-back college town on the western outskirts of Sacramento's spreading metropolis.

Despite its proximity to the state capital, Davis retained a college town's quaint familiarity, offering a friendly, welcoming atmosphere for the thirty thousand students attracted to its expansive land-grant university. Due to its affiliation with Northern California's wine country, the university boasted a world-renowned viticulture program.

The school offered some of the only college courses in America where students were required to drink (or at least taste) wine in order to receive passing marks.

As we neared the Davis turnoff, I leaned my neck to one side, stretching out a sore knot of muscles along the ridge of my shoulders. All in all, the hotel room couch had been a relatively comfortable place to sleep, but I had nearly packed up for the van floor several times during the night to escape Monty's incessant snoring.

With a yawn, I glanced in the rearview mirror at the cats, who both looked far more rested than I did. They had each devised their own measures to block out the annoying buzz from Monty's nasal cavity. Rupert had tunneled into the cat stroller's blankets, while Isabella had disappeared inside the bathroom and pushed the door shut behind her.

I was still amazed at how easily we'd been able to sneak the cats and their necessities into the hotel room. Given all the cycling teams coming and going with their odd-shaped bike-related luggage, the porters hadn't noticed when we loaded the litter box onto a luggage cart, covered it with a bedsheet, and rolled it through the lobby.

As for hiding the cats themselves, the stroller had proved to be an invaluable piece of equipment. If you kept the buggy moving at a quick enough pace, most observers assumed that it contained human, not feline, passengers. Even in its stationary position on the elevator up to our room, neither the race-obsessed cyclists nor the stiff-suited businessmen in the lift with us had been interested in disturbing the sleeping "children" I had tucked inside the stroller.

I flicked on the turn signal as the van approached the green interstate sign marking the Davis exit. Monty had left the morning's driving to me, which was just as well. He was far too distracted by the upcoming ribbon-cutting ceremony to safely operate a five-thousand-pound vehicle.

He'd spent the entirety of the brief trip from Sacramento to Davis on his cell phone with the Mayor's Life Coach, apparently seeking motivational support for his second attempt at the starting line photo. It had taken several hours of pleading and an intervention from the Mayor himself to convince the race organizers to bump the local official who was originally scheduled for this morning's ceremony and allow Monty a second shot at a streaker-free photo.

I took a quick peek over at the passenger seat. Monty sat with his eyes squeezed shut as he spoke into the cell phone.

"Visualization," he said nervously. "That's a good suggestion. Yes, yes, I can see myself standing in front of the ribbon. I'm holding up the ceremonial scissors. I can see the blades closing in on the tape . . ."

I couldn't figure out why Monty was so fixated on obtaining a photo of himself cutting the starting line ribbon, but I had decided not to pursue this line of questioning. Where Monty was concerned, some mysteries were best left uninvestigated.

With a sigh, I steered the van down the main avenue leading into campus, following a trail of pointed arrows posted on neon-colored race signs to the designated parking lot for race-related vehicles. I was still working on a plan to persuade Monty to stop off at the Bear Flag Memorial in Sonoma on our way back to San Francisco. I'd wait until after he'd successfully completed his ribbon cutting operation to broach the subject.

A light drizzle began to smatter against the windshield as I pulled the van into an open slot. Given the heavy rain forecasted for the next several hours, the risk of streakers appeared low, but Monty wasn't taking any chances. He snapped his cell phone shut and cleared his throat importantly.

"Now," he instructed as I struggled to disengage the key from the steering column. "I want you to keep your eyes on the crowd. If you see anything suspicious—anything at all—give me the sign, and I'll have security sweep the area around the starting line."

With an exasperated eye roll at the ceiling, I

yanked the key from the ignition and waited for Monty to finish brushing the wrinkles from his shirt. He had started the day in yet another green cycling jersey with the exact same purple argyle pattern across its front. By my count, this was shirt number four.

"Seriously, Monty, how many of those shirts did you bring with you?" I asked incredulously.

IN A PARKING lot behind one of Davis's many fraternity houses, Harold Wombler stood next to his pickup's dented fender issuing instructions to an eager group of freshmen initiates in black trench coats and tennis shoes. Afterward, each pledge departed for the racecourse starting line carrying a rubber mask fashioned into the caricaturized hair and face of the Mayor of San Francisco.

As he saw the last of his stooges off, Harold climbed into the truck's cab to await the start of the race. He cranked the rickety engine to start the heater and turned toward the amphibian passengers beside him on the front seat.

"Amazing what you can convince young people to do these days."

"WELCOME TO A rainy Stage Two of the Tour of California."

Harry Carlin attempted a cheerful greeting as Will Spigot stared forlornly out the front of the

243

broadcast booth next to the Stage Two finish line in downtown Santa Rosa. Cold streams of water ran down the outside of the booth's windowpanes. The colorful banners ringing the street sagged with moisture.

"The riders will be zipped up today," Carlin continued briskly, "trying to stay dry as they trek across California's wine country." He attempted to evoke a silver lining. "It's sure to be a scenic stage even with this bit of weather that's moved in."

Spigot turned grimly from the window. "You have to marvel at California's advertising genius," he said crankily. "They've got the whole world convinced it's nothing but blue skies and sunny beaches out here."

Carlin blushed uncomfortably as Spigot muttered under his breath. "I could have ordered up this slosh back home in England."

"Oh, and here's the starting line chap from yesterday," Carlin pointed out, eager to change the subject. He gestured to the television monitor providing live feed from the Davis starting line. The screen showed a tall, skinny man stripping off his rain jacket and marching confidently out of the hospitality tent. "They're going to let him have a second try at it today since the ceremony in Nevada City was, ah, hmm, interrupted."

Spigot leaned over the monitor, squinting his eyes at Monty's green cycling outfit. "That's a very distinctive outfit he's been wearing. I reckon he looks like a giant elf."

With a last steadying gulp of air, Monty strode in front of the wide ribbon stretched across the starting line. Photographers leaned in as he raised the ceremonial scissors . . .

FROM THE SIDELINES, Ivan Batrachos watched the fraternity pledges move through the crowd. Even amid a sea of raincoats and umbrellas, this group was easy to pick out. The bare, skinny legs poking out from beneath their trench coats left little doubt of their intentions.

Sure enough, as the riders congregated behind the starting line ribbon and the announcer ushered the Mayor's Assistant Life Coach out front with his ceremonial scissors, the trench coats made their move. The moment before the cameras began to flash, the pledge brothers dumped their coats and sprinted across the street. After standing, dumbstruck, in front of the severed starting line, Monty howled in indignation and charged after the masked men with his scissors.

Ivan allowed himself a rare chuckle of amusement as he moved beneath the dry eaves of a dormitory to study a road map of Northern California. Once he'd memorized his route, he folded the sheet of paper so that the portion depicting the city of Sonoma faced outward and slid it into the chest pocket of his leather jacket.

He fit a visored helmet over his closely shorn head, hopped on the motorcycle he'd stolen the previous morning from the National Hotel parking lot, and set off through the increasing downpour for the Sonoma Valley.

Chapter 38

INTO WINE COUNTRY

WHEN I FINALLY caught up to Monty, he was sitting on a curb next to one of the fraternity houses, wet and shivering. His nylon green shirt clung to his skin, making his torso look like a frozen pickle. His naturally curly hair had shrunk up into tight, shiny coils, each one sopping with moisture and dripping down onto his shoulders. His pale face looked gaunt, and his teeth were chattering loudly.

His physical discomfort, however, had done nothing to dampen his indignation.

Once again, his tormentors had reclothed, removed their distinctive rubber masks, and slipped away into the crowds. Monty had apparently come close to catching one of the streakers before he disappeared—or so I gathered from his monosyllabic reporting.

"Nearly," he sputtered, holding his hands out in front of his chest with about a foot's distance between them. ". . . had him . . ." His arms collapsed to his sides, his fists clenched in frustration.

I helped Monty up from the curb and draped his raincoat over his shoulders.

"Criminal ch-ch-charges," he spit out as I steered him in the direction of the van, where the cats were waiting in their carriers.

MONTY WRAPPED HIMSELF up in a cat towel—I refused to offer him my sleeping bag—and collapsed into the front passenger seat. He began to defrost under the full blast of the heater as the van motored out of town toward the interstate.

I was still trying to figure out how I might convince him to make a pit stop in Sonoma. Unfortunately, I couldn't use the race route as an excuse. I'd picked up a pamphlet at one of the hospitality tents detailing the course for Stage Two. While the riders would be cutting through the center of Napa Valley, their path would miss Sonoma by about fifteen miles to the north.

The heater and the cat blanket apparently combined to sooth Monty's despondent state and offended feelings. By the time the first signs giving notice of the Sonoma turnoff began to appear, a pinkish glow had returned to his thin cheekbones, and his nylon shirt was almost dry—albeit now covered in a thick coating of white cat hair. I raised my eyebrows expectantly as he cleared his throat.

I couldn't have been more surprised by the first complete sentence he'd uttered since I'd picked him up from the curb.

"Do you mind if we stop off in Sonoma on our way back?"

THE ROUTE LEADING into wine country, one of Northern California's major tourism draws, was well marked from all directions. The state had installed ample signage to ensure potential wine purchasers didn't get lost along the way. I, of course, had Isabella's backseat navigational support to help me. She had an uncanny ability to spot and call out relevant road signs, even if she couldn't actually read them.

Rupert, on the other hand, was far more interested in the contortions Monty was performing in the cargo area, where he was trying to change from his green cycling outfit into a suit and tie. It turned out his motivation for the spontaneous stop in Sonoma was an impromptu meeting with the Mayor's Life Coach that he had arranged while waiting in the hospitality tent earlier that morning.

"Not as much room back here as I thought," Monty said as he bonked his head on the metal roof.

I kept my eyes focused on the road, trying to ignore the nervous intuition gnawing at my gut. I couldn't help but feel wary of yet another coincidence facilitating my progress along the trail marked out by the toy bears' flags. I was starting to suspect that I was following a path laid far more recently than my uncle's death a year ago. With each bear I collected, I could be stepping further into a trap.

I shook my head and took in a deep breath. The Bear Flag Memorial was on the corner of Sonoma Plaza, a large green park situated around City Hall. What harm could possibly come to me in such an open public location?

As Monty's struggle with his clothing continued to produce strange sounds in the back of the van, I reached into my coat pocket and twisted my fingers around the toothpick handle held by the most recent toy bear. Given my history with Frank Napis, I didn't want to think too hard about that question.

THE ROAD BECAME rural as soon as we exited the interstate. Rolling green hills dotted with grazing cows presented a picture postcard of bucolic bliss. Even in the morning's gray drizzle, the serene landscape helped lull my anxiety.

Before long, the cows were bumped for a far more valuable commodity. Never-ending trellis lines combed across the rolling countryside, the supporting structure for thousands upon thousands of grape vines. Each individual plant had been painstakingly pruned and manicured down to a round clump of leaves perched atop a long, slender trunk. From the rain-streaked blur of the van's front windshield, I had the impression we were passing fields of fluffy green flamingos preening their leafy feathers in the wet, billowing breeze.

We caught a few glimpses of the area's famous wineries as the van chugged along Napa Valley's southern tip. Immense stone castles with elaborate archways provoked a fairy-tale mystique. Designed to enhance the wine-tasting experience, these glamorous structures provided a visual palate to match that aspired to by the wine.

As we passed from one valley to the next, the castles disappeared, and the narrow country road transitioned into a far more traditional farmland scene. Just as prominent in the local wine industry as its flashy neighbor, Sonoma was more discreet in displaying the fruits of its success. Parked along the roadside next to these vineyards, you were just as likely to see a tractor as a Mercedes.

Perhaps Sonoma's graceful handling of the recent years' wine celebrity had something to do with its mature age. The town's historical roots ran deep into California history. Over a hundred and fifty years ago, Sonoma was the Mexican Territory's northernmost military post, the last stop on the Mission Trail that connected twenty-odd churches and a small handful of presidios.

When the Mexican government disbanded the

mission system in the 1830s, the church-related infrastructure built up along the trail fell into disuse. By the time of the Bear Flag Rebellion in 1846, Sonoma's ramshackle mission and all-but-abandoned presidio were left guarded by the one-man army of Mariano Vallejo. He held a lonely post, the only notable Mexican military figure north of General Castro's encampment outside of Monterey.

An even-tempered administrator and an enthusiastic host, Vallejo was well-liked in the sparsely populated region between Sutter's Fort and Yerba Buena. He considered himself more Californian than Mexican and was openly amenable to the prospect of U.S. annexation—a future which he saw as inevitable. Vallejo no doubt participated in many lively separatist conversations with guests to his modest adobe.

As the van circled the perimeter of Sonoma Plaza, we passed the crumbling remains of Vallejo's Bear Flag–era home, attached to the still-intact Sonoma Barracks. The buildings were located across the street from the Bear Flag Memorial I had come here to visit.

Despite my concerns about Frank Napis, I felt a growing sense of anticipation as I drove by the monument, which stood in a clearing at the edge of the plaza. This was the site of the famous Bear Flag Revolt, the central topic of Clem's lectures, and the focal point, I suspected, of the trail of toy bears I'd been following. Perhaps here, I thought hopefully, I would finally figure out the nature of Oscar's Bear Flag–related treasure.

Monty was still straightening his tie in the rearview mirror when I picked out a parking space on the plaza's west side—closest to the restaurant that would host his lunch date, farthest from the corner with the Bear Flag Memorial.

I had determined that this was my best strategic line of attack—I could approach the next designated location from a safe Napis-surveying distance and keep Monty as far away as possible from my investigations. So far, he had been too wrapped up in his streaker drama to pay much attention to what I was doing, but eventually, I knew, his curiosity would kick in. I planned to keep him in the dark for as long as possible.

"Okay, well, enjoy your lunch," I said briskly as Monty helped me pull the stroller out of the van.

"You're sure you don't want to join us?" he asked as he attached a waterproof nylon cover to the stroller's main handle. The optional implement was designed to provide additional shielding protection to the occupants in the carriage. The weather had temporarily let up, but the dark clouds above us promised there was more to come. "The cats will be fine in the stroller, but you might get a little wet walking around."

"No worries," I replied quickly, eager to set off

on the hunt for my next Bear Flag clue. I pointed to the jacket I'd just pulled on over my shoulders. "I won't melt."

I reached into the van to retrieve the first cat. Rupert was apparently unconvinced of the rain-repellant properties of the nylon cover, but after a brief struggle, I managed to stuff him into the carriage compartment. Focused on the search for the next clue, Isabella was far more accommodating. She leapt inside and immediately took her seat.

"Mrao," she chirped up at me, indicating she was ready to go.

Monty bent down to check his appearance in one of the van's side mirrors as I started off down a sidewalk. Fifteen feet along the path, I passed a newspaper kiosk that had recently been filled with its afternoon edition. I could guess the contents of the lead story without reading the glaring headline.

Plastered across the paper's front page was a photo of a long-legged man in green cycling gear chasing after a group of streakers in rubber masks. The angle of the shot focused on Monty's apoplectic expression, strategically cutting out the unprintable body parts.

"Let's get going before he sees this," I said with a giggle, increasing the speed of the stroller. I had just turned into the plaza's park area when Monty's anguished screams rang out behind us.

$$\bullet \quad \bullet \quad \bullet$$

ON THE OPPOSITE side of the plaza, a man with a shorn head and a thin scar running down his left cheek slunk around the edge of the Bear Flag Memorial. In a small crevice on the monument's boulderlike base, Ivan Batrachos quickly found what he was looking for. He wrapped his hand around a dingy brown package whose outer surface had a slick waterproof coating. He paused for a moment, sizing up the small bundle. It was just the right size to hold a toy bear holding a tiny paper flag.

After a brief glance across the park, Ivan slipped the package into a pocket in his leather jacket and turned away from the memorial. He scurried over to the curb where he'd parked his motorcycle, mounted it, and sped off down the wet streets of Sonoma.

Chapter 39

THROUGH THE DELTA

INSIDE THE SANTA Rosa broadcast booth, Will Spigot and Harry Carlin bent over a television screen showing shaky motorcycle footage of a group of riders crossing the flat delta outside of Davis.

The area lay in an active floodplain, so, despite the nearby population densities of both

Sacramento and the Bay Area, the land was generally devoid of housing. Instead, fruit orchards dominated the landscape. Mimicking the exacting lines of the vineyard trellises to the west, rows of evenly spaced trees sank their roots into the delta's damp, sandy soil.

After several hours of rain, the orchards had taken on more than a foot of water. The cyclists splashed along the puddle-strewn road surface, dodging ruts and dips filled with a dark, gritty soup, their once-colorful racing outfits blackened by the plumes of muddy brown spray that sloshed up from their tires.

Carlin turned to look sympathetically into the camera. "The rain is causing some difficulties for today's broadcast. At present, our helicopters are grounded. We're getting occasional video feed from the motorcycles, but, as you can imagine, they're having a tough time keeping their lenses dry."

Spigot's mood had only soured as the rain intensified. "We think there's a breakaway of eight or nine riders, but we'd be hard pressed to tell you who exactly is in that lead group."

Carlin's face contorted as he turned back to the video screen. "If you squint just right, you might be able to make out one or two of the riders there on our screen."

The blurry video shot jumped as the motor-cycle's camera was suddenly knocked sideways, tossed through the air, and spun across the tarmac. It came to a stop focused on a soggy piece of furniture that had been discarded by the side of the road.

"Oh, look, there's a couch," Carlin said cheerfully. "It's got a nice floral pattern on it. Suit's your taste, doesn't it, Will?"

"Hmm, yes," Spigot said, feigning interest. "I quite like tulips."

The corners of his mouth turned downward as he tilted his head, assessing the chair. "They could have left it turned upright for me."

Chapter 40

SONOMA PLAZA

THE RAIN WAS still coming down as I began pushing the cat-filled stroller across Sonoma's central plaza. A block's width on each side, the plaza was the focal point of the downtown area. A network of sidewalks crisscrossed the square, meeting in the center at City Hall's rock-faced building. The park's perimeter was ringed by a collection of locally owned businesses, including a wine shop, a couple of furniture boutiques, several eating establishments, and an all-purpose mercantile store. The homey small-town feel meshed with the unseen but ever-present influence of the surrounding wine country wealth to create a Mayberry-meets-Beverly-Hills atmosphere.

On a typical Monday, the innocuous downtown area would have been busy with shoppers and tourists, but the morning's wet weather had chased everyone inside, leaving the place with an empty, forbidding air. Heavy sheets of clouds laycred the sky, blocking out the sun's warming light. Shivering, I turned the stroller onto one of the diagonal paths at the bottom southeast corner of the plaza and headed toward the Bear Flag Memorial on the opposite side.

The spreading foliage of the park's tall oak trees blocked out a good portion of the rain, so I stopped to dry my glasses on the tail of my T-shirt. With the help of raindrop-free magnification, I read a bold-lettered sign affixed to the side of a nearby trash canister. Dogs, it stated, were not allowed in the plaza.

"No mention of cats," I reported down to the stroller. "For once, we're not breaking the rules."

A few yards past the trash bin, we encountered the probablc rationale for the canine prohibition. A narrower side trail branched off from the main path to a series of small ponds. Clumps of tall grass edged the water, providing protective cover for visiting waterfowl.

Not more than twenty feet from the stroller, I spied a formidable-looking mother duck. She had heaped her brood of goslings into a downy pile, the single black offspring standing out amid the clutch of his bright yellow siblings. The mother bird eyed my stroller suspiciously before brusquely rousting her sleeping youngsters and ushering them away from the path. She, for one, was not fooled by the cats' stroller disguise.

After watching the duck's departure, I turned my head to survey the surrounding forest and suddenly realized the folly of my approach. The park's numerous thick tree trunks were plenty wide enough for someone to hide behind. Walking along this secluded sidewalk, I was an easy target.

"Maybe this wasn't such a good idea," I said nervously to my charges in the stroller.

Rupert grumbled sleepily beneath the nylon cover, as if he'd already tried to communicate that message when I pulled him out of the van. With constant glances over my shoulder, I increased the pace of the stroller. It would be best if I reached the Bear Flag Memorial—and whatever clue Oscar might have left there—as quickly as possible.

BACK AT THE Santa Rosa broadcast booth, Harry Carlin stared into the video monitor, trying to decipher the foggy motorcycle footage coming in from the field. Every so often, he turned his attention to the handheld computer in his lap and fiddled with its keys—to no avail. The riders were in a temporary media blackout. The television network had dropped its live coverage of the race, switching over to third-party infomercials until there was something of substance to report.

The only action in the broadcast booth involved an intense game of chess. Will Spigot and the producer sat on opposite sides of the board, fiercely concentrating on the small plastic figures spread out between them as the rain poured down on the street outside.

I APPROACHED THE Bear Flag Memorial from the rear, warily searching the trees that surrounded its small clearing for any suspicious characters. Although I couldn't shake the eerie sensation that I was being watched, the coast appeared to be clear as I stepped out from under the protection of the overhanging canopy of branches and pushed the stroller around the memorial's massive boulder base.

An iron gray statue mounted on top of the boulder faced outward from the plaza, overlooking the street, the Sonoma Barracks, and, beyond, the restored mission. The statue depicted a youthful, clean-shaven settler carrying the pole of an enormous flag. The billowing stone cloth furled against his shoulders, evoking a dramatic patriotic image.

Beneath the feet of the flag-bearing statue, the front of the boulder featured a large bronze plaque. The top half of the rectangular tablet contained a relief carving of a grizzly bear, fiercely guarding the state shield of California. The creature menaced me with an openmouthed growl and stood, I noted, on all four of its large padded feet.

I wiped a layer of mist from my glasses and began to search the memorial for some hint to the next piece of Oscar's puzzle. There was a small crevice on the side of the monument's boulder base, but after examining its cache thoroughly, I found nothing inside. There had to be another toy bear—likely a wet one—somewhere nearby.

Having checked every available inch of the portion of the memorial I could access from the ground, I expanded my hunt to a few surrounding benches and a nearby cupola, but no toy bears were propped up against trees or tucked beneath bushes. Hands on my hips, I returned to the front of the monument and looked up at the statue.

I thought back to Clem's presentation. I still hadn't caught the last part of his act, but I had read enough from Oscar's history books to fill in the next section of the story on my own.

"When we last left our Pathfinder," I could imagine Clem saying in his light Southern drawl. "He had departed Monterey and was reluctantly headed north. With every step he took closer to Oregon, he got colder and wetter . . . and his socks got soggier . . . and the wounds to his precious ego grew more and more aggrieved."

My holographic, ghostlike Clem popped open a long-handled umbrella and walked up to the boulder that formed the base of the monument. His wrinkled linen suit fluttered in the wet breeze.

"About a hundred miles north of Sutter's Fort, Frémont's snail-like march came to a full and complete stop. He could go no farther. He'd found the path to Oregon was absolutely blockaded by"— the imaginary Clem paused to pump his eyebrows at me—"a slight freeze and a light dusting of snow."

My glasses smeared again as raindrops began to streak down my lenses. I slipped them off and tucked them into my coat pocket. If Frémont had been so opposed to the rain in Oregon, I mused, he couldn't have been altogether pleased with spring weather here in the Bay Area.

"It was as he reached this moment of apparent impasse," my self-created Clem continued with a twirl of his umbrella, "that a military courier named Gillespie caught up to our stagnated Pathfinder.

"About five months earlier, Gillespie had set out from Washington carrying correspondence for several West Coast dignitaries. Gillespie fancied himself something of an espionage specialist. He tried to slip across northern Mexico disguised— rather conspicuously—as a traveling salesman."

Clem sighed disparagingly. "The costume didn't fool any of the Mexicans Gillespie came across. Fearing capture, he decided to eat the paper the letters were written on to prevent them from falling into the wrong hands. Of course, before beginning this high-fiber meal, he diligently committed their contents to memory."

Clem gummed his lips distastefully. "Now, you might wonder what valuable secrets were contained in these precious communiqués . . . so conscientiously carried across hostile enemy territory."

He shrugged his shoulders. "Seeing as most of these letters were not preserved for posterity" —he paused to make another sour contorted facial expression—"we'll just have to speculate."

Clearing his throat, Clem continued, "Gillespie delivered his first messages to the U.S. Navy's Commodore Sloat, who picked him up at Mazatlan on Mexico's southwest coast. Nothing in the regurgitated contents of Gillespie's stomach appear to have altered Sloat's standing orders, which were to maintain a conciliatory stance vis-à-vis the California Territory until he received clear information of a U.S. declaration of war with Mexico.

"Next," Clem said, stroking his mustache, "Gillespie proceeded to Monterey and Yerba Buena to convey messages to Larkin and Leidesdorff. Once again, there is no evidence to indicate the Polk administration had changed its strategic stance on California. If anything, by the time Gillespie reached the Bay Area, the situation in Texas had become even more delicate. The two nations were approaching the brink of war. As a last-ditch effort to avoid a formal military conflict, the White House had sent a special envoy to the Mexican capital to make a final offer to purchase the land north of the Rio Grande."

My Clem apparition strode back and forth in front of the boulder, stroking his chin thoughtfully. "I reckon the White House's message to Larkin and Leidesdorff went something like this: Stay the course, keep a lid on the pot, and for goodness' sake, don't start anything out there before we're good and ready for it back here."

Clem scratched his head of thinning hair with his free hand. "Frémont was Gillespie's last courier stop in Northern California. The delivery of Frémont's letters was more of a courtesy, really, to the powerful Senator Benton and his lovely daughter, Jessie.

"Only Frémont and Gillespie know the precise words that were conveyed that cold, wet Oregon night, but it seems unlikely Frémont's wife or father-in-law had written to urge him to instigate an uprising in Northern California that would instantly destabilize the territory."

Clem blew out a loud guffaw. "The Pathfinder, however, worked his own interpretation of the information he received from Gillespie. He was reading between the lines, so to speak—an interesting prospect when the words are floating around in someone else's stomach."

Glancing up at the statue, Clem shook his head. "Frémont was likely far more interested in pumping Gillespie for information about his travels through Mexico than the messages he brought from home. Regardless, after spending one night around his campfire with the, ahem, traveling salesman, Frémont immediately abandoned his Oregon mapmaking mission and reversed course to Sutter's Fort. There was no need for further deliberation. Frémont knew exactly what he must do next."

Clem returned his gaze back down to me. "His return to the Sacramento Valley would only serve to aggravate an already tense situation. It was a move that was calculated to do so."

I sighed as my mental vision of Clem disappeared into the pattering raindrops. Sucking in my lower lip, my face puckered in frustration. Was there nothing more? Had I come to the end of the trail and found nothing?

With Clem gone, I was left staring at the grizzly bear on the plaque beneath the statue. Leaning forward, I peered into the bear's bronze face and ran my fingers over the ridges of its feet.

If there were no further clues, all I had left to go on was the strange repositioning of the bear from the original flag and Oscar's handwritten note in the DeVoto book:

Local Indians, passing through Sonoma after the revolt, ridiculed the animal on the flag, calling it a pig or a stoat.

Stoat, stoat, stoat, I pondered as water ran down my forehead and formed a rivulet off the tip of my nose. Without the help of my glasses, the world around me was a blurry wet haze. My thoughts turned inward to the crudely drawn image from my sketchbook.

I closed my eyes, picturing the upright bear and its long, thumping tail as the details of the Bear Flag story filtered through my head. Catching my breath, I suddenly recalled an image that had drifted into my dreams the previous evening.

My eyes popped open as the bear morphed into—a kangaroo.

Chapter 41

THE OSOS

THE STATUE'S IRON face gazed down at the wet woman standing on the sidewalk below him. He read her puzzled thoughts as her head tilted, eyes closed, toward the gray sky.

I know a thing or two about this Bear Flag story, he thought proudly, feeling the furl of the stone flag across the back of his shoulders.

"When Captain John Frémont, the illustrious

Pathfinder, returned to Sutter's Fort, he learned that the Mexican Army had requisitioned a large herd of horses from Sonoma and were moving them south to Santa Clara. Frémont told us this was a clear sign that Castro was preparing to gather his troops and round up the American settlers in the Sacramento Valley. Coming from a man of such standing and experience, we took his assessment seriously. Frémont had been warning us for some time that Castro was up to no good, so when he gave the word, we were ready for action, ready to defend our homes and families—ready to declare our independence from Mexico.

"On June 10, 1846, under orders from Captain Frémont, a group of us rode out from Sutter's Fort, tracked down the herd of horses, and ambushed the Mexican Lieutenant supervising their transfer."

The statue's brow furrowed as he listened to the woman's internal commentary.

"Horse thieves? I should think not," he huffed indignantly. "Really, whose side are you on?" He cleared his mental throat.

"We brought the horses straight back to Sutter's," he said defensively. "Captain Frémont declared them the property of the United States government, and it was only as a show of gratitude for our services that the members of our regiment received a few head a piece to take home to our farms."

The statue straightened his already-stiff shoulders in affront. "Well no, *I* wasn't actually there when all this happened. This is well-established folklore—stop interrupting me."

With a last harrumph, the statue continued his tale.

"Now that we had begun our path to independence, we looked to Frémont to guide us on our next course of action. He suggested Sonoma as the best place to stake our territorial claim. That sounded like a good plan to us. Mariano Vallejo wouldn't hurt a fly, and it had been several years since he'd had troops in his barracks. What's more, we knew he was secretly on our side. He would not take up arms against us."

The statue looked out across the rainy intersection as it replayed the historic events of the day. "All night, we rode through the back hills and valleys, picking up more and more men at each stop along the way. We decided our group needed a name—something fierce, fearful . . ." The statue's face took on a dreamy expression of reminiscence. "Something that would capture the essence of our fearless leader. After much discussion, we settled on *the Osos*, the grizzly bears."

The woman on the ground below jerked as if she'd been startled by a sudden realization. The statue snorted at the image that flashed into her head.

"Kangaroos? Are you absolutely mad, woman? Why would brave patriotic men such as ourselves pick such a ridiculous animal to represent us?"

The woman sighed thoughtfully. As she bent toward the stroller to check on the occupants hidden beneath its nylon cover, there was a loud squawk from the opposite side of the park. The woman rose back up, pushed her wet hair away from her face, and looked out across the plaza.

Seeing nothing of concern, she wrapped her hands around the stroller's handle and swung the buggy resolutely toward the interior of the plaza's green square. Before she could set off down the path, however, the statue offered one last piece of information.

"If you're interested in the Bear Flag, you really should check in at the barracks across the street. They've got one on display in there that goes back almost to the time of the revolt."

Chapter 42

A DISTURBED DUCK

I BENT DOWN in front of the Bear Flag Memorial to check that the cats were still dry beneath the cover of the stroller. Isabella glared up at me, more perturbed by her reduced visibility than the moisture that had begun to collect on the surface of the cover. Rupert rolled over, exposing his stomach, hopeful that I would reach in and rub his tummy.

"Wran," Isabella called out sharply. She reached up to paw at the netting over her head.

"Don't worry," I said soothingly. "We're headed back to the van."

Just then, there was a loud squawk from the opposite side of the park, and I was again struck by the impression that someone, somewhere in the trees, was watching me. Anxiously, I craned my head to look around the edge of the monument, but the plaza's park was just as rain-soaked and empty of pedestrian traffic as before.

As I gripped the handle of the stroller and angled it in the direction of the van, I glanced up at the statue. It's fiercely proud expression looked out toward the street corner and, beyond, a collection of historical buildings. I twisted around to follow the eyes of the statue, staring first at the Sonoma Mission and then at the barracks next door. Squinting through the downpour, I saw what appeared to be lights on inside the barracks.

"Just one more stop," I murmured down to Isabella as I turned the stroller toward the nearest street corner.

"Wrao," she replied, sounding pleased.

HAROLD WOMBLER'S PICKUP rolled slowly through the rainy streets of Sonoma, its cracked— and leaking—windshield a watery portal to the outside world. His windshield wipers wagged back and forth ineffectually. At this state of wear, they were more for show than function.

Harold clamped down on his dentures as his wrinkled hands gripped the steering wheel, trying to guide his balding tires across the slick road. He needed to find a parking place soon. The truck wasn't really safe to drive in these conditions.

He glanced down at his amphibian passengers. The frogs gazed happily at the water droplets streaking across the windshield. "You two can't get enough of this weather," he said with a chuckle.

Harold circled his dilapidated truck around the exterior of the plaza until he found a large white van parked across from a small bistro. He swung the pickup into a slot next to the van and let the engine idle as he craned his neck to look out through the truck's back window.

Beneath the restaurant's waterlogged awning, Harold's eyes honed in on the curly hair of a patron seated at a table near the front window. The man's long, stringy arms flailed about as his head bobbed and swayed. Monty was presumably relaying his experience at the starting line earlier that day to the gentleman seated across the table.

Harold grimaced to himself as he shifted his gaze to Monty's dining companion.

"So that's what a life coach looks like," he mused to his frog companions.

Harold untwisted his torso and reached for the gearshift. As his face turned toward the plaza, he saw a woman with long brown hair pushing a cat stroller along a sidewalk. She was headed toward the opposite side of the park—to the Bear Flag Memorial, he presumed.

"Something doesn't feel right about this," Harold muttered uneasily as he cut the engine and engaged the parking brake.

"You two stay in here," he said, slipping a few crickets into the frogs' terrarium. All this rain, Harold thought with a painful wince as he locked the cab of the truck and hobbled off across the plaza, was not good for his arthritis.

The woman reached the memorial and circled around to its front side. She appeared to be focusing all of her attention on the statue and the plaque on the boulder beneath it, but Harold stayed off the main path, just in case, to avoid being seen. He sneaked around the edge of a pond, gimping from tree to tree as quickly as he could.

"She's taking an awfully long time to find this one," he grumbled under his breath. "Come on," he said impatiently. "It's not *that* well hidden."

Harold didn't see the mother duck and her brood of goslings until it was too late. He was concentrating so keenly on the woman standing in front of the monument that he nearly stepped on the feathery pile of young fowl. The mother duck squawked loudly and flapped her wings as if she were about to charge him. He dove face first into the wet grass, silently cursing the bird.

"I'll stuff a pillow with you and your lot . . ." Harold muttered threateningly.

After a long minute, he slowly lifted his head. The mother duck was still eying him fiercely, but the woman had turned away from the Bear Flag Memorial and was crossing the street for the historic Sonoma Barracks.

"What's she headed over there for?" he asked, his concern mounting.

Harold's gaze traveled across to the barracks' breezeway entrance. He issued a troubled grunt at the sight of a rotund man with enormous side-whiskers standing inside beneath the eaves.

Chapter 43

THE SONOMA BARRACKS

THE SONOMA BARRACKS sat low and nondescript across from the northeast corner of the Sonoma Plaza. It was a two-story adobe-style building with a red tile roof, creamy white stucco, and a rickety wooden balcony that ran along the exterior of the second floor. A breezeway cut through the center of the building, forming the main entrance.

By the time of the Bear Flag Revolt in 1846, the barracks had been vacant for several years. Vallejo was left alone to guard the town's makeshift presidio and crumbling mission. It was here, in his attached living quarters, that the Bear Flaggers found the General, still in his pajamas, at sunrise on the morning of June 14.

As I walked under the building's broad eaves, I reflected on what I had read about Mariano Vallejo from Oscar's history books.

By most accounts, Vallejo was an open advocate of American annexation, particularly for this portion of Northern California. Despite his posting with the Mexican Army, he saw the U.S.'s western expansion as the territory's inevitable future.

One of Oscar's reference texts had contained Vallejo's black-and-white portrait. He'd been a full-figured man with a soft fleshy face and kind un-affronting eyes. He wore his facial hair curiously styled in the shape of broad swooping side-whiskers. The poufs of thick bristly growth formed watermelon-shaped slices on either cheek, giving him the whimsical appearance of a humanized walrus. Above, below, and in between the side-whiskers, he kept his skin immaculately groomed in a close shave, leaving his nose and mouth clipped free.

It was exactly this figure that the cats and I met as we entered the shadowed corridor of the barracks' breezeway.

Isabella saw him first. *"Mreo,"* she murmured

quietly as my eyes adjusted to the darker interior light.

I was only momentarily thrown off by his presence. There was a familiarity about him, a certain *je ne sais Clem* in his eyes. My Sonoma search wasn't so fruitless after all, I thought with relief. I pushed the stroller forward, smiling timidly.

After watching Clem's performances in Nevada City and Sutter's Fort, I felt, somehow, as if I knew him. Subconsciously, I kept thinking of how much he reminded me of my Uncle Oscar.

"Ah, hello there," he greeted us warmly. "*Welkome* to the Sonoma Barracks." He bowed, spreading his arms wide. "*Comandante* General Mariano Vallejo at your service. I'll be your *person-nal* guide here this afternoon."

The suit that covered his portly figure conveyed the cut of an earlier era. Its wide lapels rested smoothly across his round barrel chest. The raised collar of his starched white shirt rose to meet the dimpled roll of a double chin.

The man before me seemed slightly taller than the Twain-impersonating Clem. Perhaps, I reasoned, it was simply a matter of the elevated heel on his knee-high boots.

His voice, too, had an oddly different tenor. But I chalked that up to the artificial Spanish accent he was using, heavily trilling his *R*s and over-emphasizing each syllable of every word. His command of Twain's dialect, I thought ruefully, had been better than his command of the General's.

Vallejo's stubby finger pointed in a swirl down to the stroller's wet nylon cover. I grimaced guiltily as he tilted it up to inspect the cats beneath.

"Hmm," he mused, releasing the cover. He turned to read an official state park sign near the entrance that listed the site's rules and regulations.

"No doggies allowed," he read slowly, before pursing his thick lips contemplatively. "But . . . no men-*shon* of the feline species . . . so . . ." He clapped his hands together. ". . . you are in the clear." He leaned forward to look down once more into the stroller. "I *can-nut* say that anyone has ever tried to bring cats in here before," he said good-naturedly.

Isabella's nose twitched as she stared up at him. The orange tip of her tail thumped warily against the floor of the carriage. Yawning himself awake, Rupert blinked sleepily up at the General, his blue eyes crossing as they caught sight of his distinctive side-whiskers.

Rolling the stroller over the concrete floor, I followed obediently after our guide, who stepped further into the breezeway, past a roped-off display of a small canon with spindly wooden wheels. He paused briefly to allow me to peek into

275

the first interior room, located across from the canon.

Glancing through the open doorway, I saw that the space had been furnished to simulate the barracks during its earlier operational years, when soldiers populated the living quarters. Wooden-framed beds lined the walls on either side of the room. A chest lay neatly at the foot of each one, and samples of each sleeper's clothing hung on designated pegs behind the headboards. Stiff wool blankets were mounded on top of each bed frame, exposing enough of the space beneath to reveal a mattress-less netting of corded wires.

With a flourish, General Vallejo grandly motioned us down the breezeway toward a second room, on the right side of the hall, that had been set up as a more traditional museum display. Poster dividers crisscrossed the room to separate numerous exhibits.

I felt only the slightest tingle of apprehension as he smoothly waved his hands at the doorway and invited us inside. "After you."

Chapter 44

THE BEAR FLAG REVOLT

VALLEJO'S ROUND FIGURE strolled across the dusty concrete floor, swishing past displays of an oxen yoke, a Western saddle, and a trio of three-foot-tall dolls dressed as celebrating Bear Flaggers.

"I think you will find our most *een*-teresting *eggs-zhibit* at the back of the room," he said suggestively.

The building's rock walls absorbed the sounds from the street, leaving the interior with the ambient noise of the water rushing through the gutters that ran along the rim of the roof.

The room had a damp, clammy feeling; it was only duskily lit. The wooden shutters that framed each of the wide exterior windows were bolted shut, blocking any natural light. It had been over a hundred and fifty years since this building was last occupied by Mexican soldiers, but the Sonoma Barracks still gave the appearance—from the inside, at least—of a formidable bunker.

I pushed the stroller after the General, leaning forward over the handlebar as I listened to his in-character commentary.

"It's a *drra*-matic story, that of the Bea*rr* Flag *Rr*evolt," he said, stroking his bushy side-whiskers. "One that I *un-for-tu-netly* experienced firsthand." He cleared his throat and straightened his wide lapel.

"You can *eee-ma-gene* my surprise. The morning of June 14, 1846, I was lying in bed, *pace*-fully watching the sun rise, when I heard someone kicking down my *frr*ont door." He nodded his head toward the center breezeway. "My bed*rr*oom was just around the corner there."

Vallejo shook his head, as if remembering. "On my *frr*ont stoop, I found a group of *buck-skeen band-deets*, armed to the teeth and *rr*eeking of spirits. They said they were here to decla*rr*e Sonoma an independent *rr*epublic. Let me assure you, it was a quite *un-see-vilized* way to start the day."

The General stroked his side-whiskers indignantly before continuing.

"Now, I was *nut* opposed to switching my allegiances," he said, touching his chest to emphasize his sincerity. "T*rr*uth be known, I had a *fut* in each camp." He spread his legs wide and tapped each booted toe against the concrete.

"I had *dis-kussed* the future of Califo*rr*nia at length with Tomas La*rr*kin, the American Consul in Monterey, and William Leidesdo*rr*ff, his associate in Yerba Buena. I thought we were all of a similar mind on the matter. There would be no stopping the Americans' Westward *ex-pan-shon*. Better, then, to join them and profit from it." He winked at me conspiratorially. "Leidesdo*rr*ff was particularly enthusiastic about the idea."

There he was again—William Leidesdorff. The man I associated with the tulip-printed wallpaper that had started this whole treasure hunt kept sneaking into Bear Flag conversations. My brow furrowed as Vallejo continued.

"But no one had said *any-ting* about this *rr*ough lot showing up on my doorstep," Vallejo said, shrugging his shoulders in confusion. "The Sonoma ga*rr*ison had been unmanned for *say-ver-al* years, leaving my wife and family unprotected."

He held his hands up, as if surrendering. "There was nothing I could do. I invited the leaders—or at least the most *rray-son-able* looking of the crew—into my hacienda for a glass of b*rr*andy. I hoped that would calm them down a bit." He smiled ruefully. "We went through *say-ver-al* bottles of b*rr*andy that day."

The General rubbed his temple, as if remembering the voluminous alcohol consumption.

"As the aftcrnoon wore on, we began to *rr*each the end of my b*rr*andy supply. I was so *shure* the *Americanos* were behind all this. I kept expecting one of my *al-lies* to arrive to help *fas-cili-tate* my situation. So, you can see, I was *ray-leeved* when the Osos finally told me they were under orders to take me to *Cap-i-tan Frray-mont*."

Vallejo leaned back with an expression of

279

exaggerated relief. "*Herre*, I thought, is the American presence I had been *wait-ing* for. G*rr*aciously, I permitted myself to be taken *pri-son-ner*. I was *nut* concerned; I considered it a mere formality. It was *nut* until they b*rr*ought me to Sutter's Fort that I *rray-al-lized* what that scoundrel *Frray-mont* was up to."

Vallejo shook his head back and forth. Then he blew out a gust of frustrated air, fluttering his lips as if he'd tasted something unpleasant.

"He was *nut* an hono*rr*able man, in my opinion—that so called *Path-finderr*. He was *rr*uthless and blood-thi*rr*sty. I suppose I should consider myself lucky that I only had to with-stand the *in-dig-nity* of being locked up for six weeks before La*rr*kin could a*rr*ange my freedom. Others who crossed *Frray-mont's* path fared a fa*rr* worse fate."

He sighed sadly. "When I finally *rray*-turned to my home in Sonoma, I was a b*rr*oken man, my body sick and diseased. All of my cattle and horses had been stolen, my crops destroyed."

Vallejo bridled indignantly. His side-whiskers puffed out as his cheeks reddened. "*Frray-mont* later tried to deny that he had been the one *puppet-teer-ing* the Osos, but I had no *dowt* who was *rray-sponsible*."

I watched, impressed by how seriously Clem was taking his role as General Vallejo. He seemed to be channeling inner emotions—as if he were projecting a personal modern-day grudge onto the egotistical explorer's historical figure.

He tugged once more at the wide lapels of his jacket, puckered up his lips, and spat at the floor. "*Frray-mont*," he said bitterly. "That is what I think of him."

Chapter 45

A FLOWERY FABRIC

HAROLD WOMBLER GIMPED through the plaza's wet grass as the woman with the long brown hair left the Bear Flag Memorial, crossed the intersection, and entered the breezeway of the Sonoma Barracks.

He paused for a moment, considering. Then he backtracked about a hundred yards into the park, keeping his cover by lurching from tree to tree, until, cautiously, he approached the street. Peering up and down the damp avenue, he hobbled across to the opposite curb. After a quick glance at the front cntrance of the breezeway, he circled around to the back side of the building.

Past the rubbled remains of Vallejo's hacienda, Harold turned right into an overgrown alley. Less than a hundred feet down the passage, he hefted himself over a rickety rock wall and dropped into a muddy courtyard. Several inches of water had pooled in the center of the rectangular half-acre, forming a barrier of thick gooey muck between his location and the back entrance to the barracks' breezeway.

Harold grimaced as rain ran across the green brim of his baseball cap and dripped down the front of his face. After studying the growing pond in the middle of the courtyard, he started off around the perimeter, his worn-out construction boots sliding across the slick surface.

He had to slosh through a stream of water gushing from one of the gutter's downspouts, but he eventually reached the barracks' back wall. As he approached the breezeway entrance, cold mud began to ooze through the holes in his boots. The accumulating grit quickly packed in around his toes. Grumbling irritably, he nudged his nose around the corner.

The breezeway was empty, but Harold could hear a man's voice coming from one of the interior rooms. His face scrunched up in disgust as he listened to the General's exaggerated accent. That's horrendous, he thought, rolling his eyes. Vallejo wasn't *French*.

Harold's muddy construction boots tiptoed across the concrete floor of the breezeway until he reached the exhibit room's open doorway. Holding his breath, he leaned around the opening to get a better visual of the Vallejo impersonator. Then he backed his way out to the courtyard.

Taking cover beneath the building's eaves, he fished through his pockets until he found a small cell phone. He gave the device a look of intense loathing before he flipped it open and began fumbling with its controls.

"How'm I s'pposed to . . ." he muttered under his breath. After several failed attempts during which time he nearly slammed the phone against the wall of the barracks, he finally managed to place his call.

A female voice answered on the other end.

"I don't like the look of this," he grumbled tersely. "She's inside the Sonoma Barracks with a rogue Vallejo."

The voice twittered worriedly out of the receiver.

"I can't go in there," he snapped back. "She'd pick me out immediately."

He held the phone up against his right ear, his already unhappy expression growing more and more affronted as he listened to the woman's instructions.

Harold made several uninterpretable sounds of disbelief before he managed to spit out a coherent sentence.

"You want me to do what?"

TEN MINUTES LATER, Harold propped himself against the side of his pickup, panting despite the cool rain trickling down his neck. His knees ached from the sprint across the park, but he had no time to waste. Sure enough, in the bottom right-hand side of the metal locker in the bed of the truck, he found a brown paper bag, just as Dilla had described.

His grim expression soured further as he lifted the bag out and peeked at the garment folded neatly inside.

"Tulips," he groaned. "Perfect."

Chapter 46

THE REPLICA

I STOOD WATCHING the Clemlike Vallejo as he finished his Frémont rant, waiting to see what else he had to say about the Bear Flag Revolt. But as his face lifted from where he'd spat on the floor, his gaze shifted to the front of the room, and his lips curved downward into a strangely discordant frown.

"I am afraid," he said in a flat tone, suddenly dropping his fake Spanish accent, "that you will have to excuse me. An old acquaintance of mine has just arrived."

I watched as the General strolled toward the front of the room, where a dumpy woman in a flower-print dress stood examining the saddle display. Her back was partially turned to me, and a headscarf of matching flowered material obscured the small portion of her face that I might otherwise have been able to see.

With a shrug, I focused my attention on the display the General had alluded to at the beginning of his speech. Here on the back wall of the Sonoma Barracks, mounted on a board inside an airtight Plexiglas case, was a replica of the original Bear Flag.

Made for the fifty-year commemoration of the revolt, it was this 1896 replica flag whose picture I had seen in my guidebooks and in the exhibit at Sutter's Fort.

I crouched down to read the handwriting on the flag's bottom left-hand corner. The ink had bled through the fabric, blurring some of the letters, but after several minutes of close examination, I was able to make out the signatures of the two surviving Bear Flaggers who had assembled the flag, Ben Dewell and Henry Reason.

The flag retained the made-in-the-moment improvisation of the original. The star and bear appeared to have been either glued or stamped onto the fabric. Not a great rendition of a bear, I thought to myself, but certainly not something that would have been confused with a stoat. The creature stood on all four of its feet, not upright, as the original bear emblem had been described.

I pulled out my notebook from the pocket in the back side of the stroller and flipped it to my attempted sketch of the original flag, pondering.

For some reason, Dewell and Reason had changed the positioning of the bear figure in this replacement flag. Was it an oversight or done intentionally? Perhaps they simply preferred the four-feet-on-the-ground stance.

More importantly, I wondered as I reflected on the notation my uncle had left in the margin by the description of the original flag, why had the change been significant to Oscar?

I reached beneath the stroller and pulled out the DeVoto book, which I had stashed into a lower zippered compartment beneath the carriage. As I flipped through the thick book to the section on the Bear Flag, a yellowed piece of paper tucked into the pages fell out and dropped to the floor.

The paper unfolded as it floated through the air, revealing a sheet of typewritten stationery. I reached down to pick it up, immediately focusing on the bold monogram next to the professionally printed header. This appeared to be official correspondence from the now-defunct Jackson Square Board, the organization which had been responsible for the historical preservation of the Jackson Square neighborhood.

The paper suddenly felt toxic in my hands. My eyes jumped to the signature line at the bottom, and I almost dropped the sheet as I read the identity of the author. The letter was written by Gordon Bosco, a onetime alter ego of Frank

Napis, in response to a query he'd apparently received from my Uncle Oscar.

Gulping nervously, I focused in on the main text. Water stains blurred much of the first paragraph, but from the portion of writing that remained legible, Napis appeared to be responding to Oscar's request for a valuation estimate on the original Bear Flag raised by the Osos in 1846. Presumably, Oscar had targeted the Board's President as someone with expertise in antiquities from the era.

I looked up from the letter, my thoughts racing as I stared at the Plexiglas surface of the display case holding the replica flag. If the original Bear Flag had been destroyed in San Francisco's 1906 earthquake, as DeVoto and every other source I'd read had reported, why had Oscar sought an estimate of its current worth?

Napis had raised this same issue in his response. After a few sarcastic remarks about the difficulties of assessing the value of an item that did not exist, he had provided a potential dollar range based on recent sales of items of similar age and historic significance.

The fingers of my free hand wrapped tightly around the handle to the stroller as I read the eye-catching amount.

ISABELLA POINTED HER nose into the air, trying to get a better angle on the figure in the flowered dress on the opposite side of the room. He was engaged in a glowering standoff with the side-whiskered man in the wide-lapelled coat. Her blue eyes scanned down past the hem of the lumpy flowered dress to the bony knees, hairy shins, and mud-splattered construction boots.

Hmm, she thought curiously as the man in the flowered dress stiffly followed General Vallejo out into the breezeway.

I wonder what happened to Harold's overalls.

Chapter 47

THE LIFE COACH

TWENTY MINUTES LATER, the cats and I exited the barracks. I hadn't located a toy bear pointing to the next stop on the hunt, but now, at least, I had a better hint of what kind of hidden treasure Oscar might have left for me to find. Somehow, I suspected, the original Bear Flag had escaped its widely reported destruction in the 1906 earthquake.

I began to retrace my steps across the plaza's park to the van. The rain had finally abated, and the slightest hint of blue was beginning to creep into the sky—but my head was still clouded with thoughts of the Bear Flag trail.

Isabella was apparently pondering her own theories. A light singsong of feline commentary floated up from the carrier compartment of the stroller. I rolled up the rain cover so I could look down through the mesh screen. Rupert was stretched out across the blankets in a deep snoring snooze, but Isabella sat alertly upright, her head tilted slightly to the left, her expression conferring the impression of focused deliberation.

"You let me know when you've got it figured out," I said with laugh.

As we neared the opposite side of the park, Isabella's musing chatter sharpened into an instruction-sending chirp. She leaned forward in the stroller, her eyes honing in on the restaurant across the street from the parked van.

I felt my forehead crinkle as I followed her gaze. Monty stood next to a table littered with a pile of used plates, silverware, and glasses. He stepped out into the aisle, turning toward us. With a brisk, efficient motion, he brushed his hands over the front of his suit and smoothed out the dark fabric. Then he leaned forward to shake hands with the man who had been seated across the table.

Monty's metal cufflink flickered in the afternoon's growing sunlight as his slender hand met the stubby-fingered grip of his lunch companion—a man in a wrinkled linen suit and tattered black bow tie with a bristly white mustache.

My mouth fell open as I recognized Clem's Mark Twain costume, and I whipped around toward the barracks. If Clem had been sitting at lunch with Monty for the past hour, who had been playing the role of General Vallejo?

The shadowed breezeway past the dripping eaves was vacant. The General, I felt certain, was long gone.

I pursed my lips for a long moment, a feeling of terror amplifying along my spine. I had one guess who had been entertaining me in the exhibit room. For the second time in as many days, I had the sudden intuition that I had come into contact with Frank Napis—and lived to tell about it.

As I struggled to calm my racing pulse, I tried to reassure myself that this was a good sign, an indication that I was on the track of Oscar's treasure.

There had to be something more for me to uncover, I thought, feeling a fresh wave of optimism. It was time to head back to the Green Vase.

Chapter 48

SNEAK ATTACK

A BRIGHT SUN hit the finish line's wet pavement outside Spigot and Carlin's Santa Rosa broadcast booth. Crowds of spectators were beginning to line the race route to watch the riders come in. Despite the day's soggy start, it looked like the fans would be treated to a thrilling finale for the race's second stage.

As yet, the commentators had little information about just who would be coming into town at the front of the peloton. The helicopters were scrambling to return to the skies, but the race would be nearly over before any overhead shots were available. Scattered radio reports indicated that the original breakaway group of ten riders had been whittled down to a much smaller posse, but the number of riders and the size of their lead over the peloton remained a mystery.

It had been a long rainy slog through the wine country hills for the waterlogged cyclists, a particularly dismal stage for the sprinters. The World's Fastest Man, who had thoroughly enjoyed the hot, flat finish into Sacramento the day before, now trailed in a straggler group at the back of the race. His only goal for this stage was to ensure he finished close enough to the main pack to avoid being eliminated from the overall competition. The yellow jersey would change hands at the end of the day, but who would be wearing it remained an open question.

Harry Carlin fiddled with the console of his computer, tapping keys and twisting dials as more and more data came in from the field. Suddenly, he pushed away from the counter and pressed his hands against the earphones he wore over his head.

"Oh, this could be interesting," he said eagerly as he listened to the static-laden voice coming through his headset. "We're starting to get some more concrete details."

Will Spigot looked up from the chessboard and cocked an intrigued eyebrow at Carlin.

"There are three riders remaining in the breakaway," Carlin reported to Spigot. "They've got an eight minute lead, and—your little friend from yesterday is leading the bunch."

"The one who got blown out at the Sacramento finish line?" Spigot asked, his interest piqued. He leaned back in his chair, considering. "Eight minutes is a good lead, but the peloton might still have time to reel them back in. What does the computer think?" he asked, an edge of excitement creeping into his voice for the first time that day. "Will they be caught?"

Carlin's face pinched with concentration as he returned to the keyboard and began frantically punching keys. "The computer is struggling to process all the new data coming in. It isn't sure what to think at this particular time," he reported, his voice perplexed.

The television monitor that had been pushed to the side of the booth suddenly burst into color with a shot of three muddy riders. The chessboard fell clattering to the floor as Spigot leapt across the broadcast booth to swoop in on the screen.

"That's him," he yelled, enthusiastically

pointing at the video picture. "Harry," he demanded, spinning around to face Carlin. "How far out are they?"

Carlin was now pounding the keys to his computer. "I believe they're about fifteen kilometers from the finish line," he replied.

"And the computer can't tell you whether they'll be caught?" Spigot asked again.

Carlin threw his hands up in exasperation, "The computer appears to be completely befuddled by the situation."

"We're back in action!" Spigot called out. He jumped into his broadcast chair and whirled it around to face the cameraman, who had just resumed filming. With a wink, he confided, "And not a minute too soon. I was about to lose that chess game."

THAT AFTERNOON IN San Francisco, a small group gathered behind the locked doors of Wang's flower shop. An impromptu meeting of the Vigilance Committee had been called to address the unexpected events that had taken place in Sonoma earlier that afternoon.

Dilla Eckles paced back and forth beside the makeshift lab table, nervously wringing her hands. Behind her, the cages stacked up against the back wall were busy with activity from the ninety-nine bald creatures spinning and scurrying inside.

"Well, that's it, then," Dilla said, throwing her hands up in the air. "Frank's stolen the last Bear Flag clue. She won't know where to go. We'll have to call the whole thing off."

Wang sat calmly in his wheelchair, his fingers twiddling with his oxygen tubes, his thoughts silently turning.

Harold Wombler looked uncomfortable as he surveyed the scene. He reached up to his green baseball cap and smoothed his fingers over the gold-threaded stitching of the cycling bear. Finally, he cleared his throat. "I understand there's another clue."

Hands on her hips, Dilla squared up in front of him, the fierce expression on her face demanding further explanation.

Harold's shoulders slumped forward as he dug his hands into the frayed pockets of his overalls. His thin lips squiggled uneasily. When he finally spoke, his scratching voice was the only sound in the flower shop.

"It's in the apartment above the Green Vase."

"In the kitchen?" Wang asked softly from his chair.

Harold nodded somberly as Dilla's head whirled around to look at her husband. A stern look on her face, she slowly returned her gaze to Harold.

"Where did you get this information?" Dilla demanded.

Harold stared down at his mud-crusted

construction boots, avoiding Dilla's stare. After a deep gulp, he finally answered.

"From the man who hid it there."

A figure appeared on the sidewalk outside the flower shop and knocked on the window. Dilla strode purposefully around the front rack of flowers, twisted the lock, and swung open the door.

A man in a wide-lapelled suit and walrus-inspired side-whiskers stood on the opposite side.

"Hello, Dilla."

Chapter 49

THE SLIVER OF THE MOON

AS MONDAY'S DAYLIGHT dimmed on a damp San Francisco, the sun made a brief appearance, casting up and down shadows across the hilly metropolis. The Embarcadero filled with a dense scurrying of antlike activity as the approaching sunset threw a flickering flash against the mural of rain-soaked windows, masking the city in a collage of dusky pastel colors before it sank into the western horizon beyond the blue of the bay.

The moon arrived early at its post, crawling stealthily over the Golden Gate Bridge, whose fiery steel burned red against the pale gray sky. On this night, its size was reduced to a thin sliver of illumination; the knife-edge of its curve sliced across the landscape.

With the cloaking cover of darkness falling in around its sharp shoulders, the moon sped along the city sidewalks, cutting a direct and deliberate path toward Jackson Square. It stopped in front of a familiar red brick building with crenulated iron columns and focused a pointed prick of light at a front windowpane, honing in on a tinted vase shape embedded in the glass. The image glowed an eerie green of resistance before allowing the moon's light to pour through.

Once inside, the flow of photons zoomed across the wooden floorboards to the stairs at the back of the showroom and then surged up the staircase to the second floor kitchen.

Two white cats with orange-tipped ears and tails played hide-and-seek on a floor full of shredded wallpaper. The curling scraps bore the printed images of purple tulips in various sizes and arrangements.

A woman with a metal scraper tackled the last bit of paper that remained pinned to the wall. She wore an oversized pair of orange plastic coveralls that crinkled as she walked, but she had long since removed her face mask and goggles. As the scraper dislodged the final piece of paper covering, she leaned in toward the framing with a broad-beamed flashlight and anxiously searched the wall's interior.

Thirty minutes later, after a lengthy but fruitless examination of the framing of all four kitchen walls, the woman sat down on a chair by the kitchen table, temporarily defeated, but not dejected. She tapped her chin with the handle of the scraper as she watched the cats pounce on each other in the piles of discarded wallpaper.

The moon had been waiting, somewhat impatiently, for just this moment. Carefully, it slid a finger of light across the tile floor to the dishwasher mounted next to the sink. The dormant appliance had not been operated in over a year. A mysterious plug in its plumbing had rendered it useless to the woman now living in the apartment above the Green Vase.

With the lightest touch, the moon planted a shimmering kiss of light on the rusted chrome handle.

As if a lightbulb had turned on inside the woman's head, her eyes traveled to the glinting metal handle. She stood up, crossed the room to the dishwasher, and cranked open its door to look inside.

Chapter 50

THE BOWELS OF THE BEAST

TWO CURIOUS CATS joined me as I pulled out the dishwasher's lower rolling rack and crawled into its square tub. It was a procedure I'd performed many times before, searching for the source of the blockage that caused the machine to cough up a soapy tidal wave every time I turned it on. After several forays into the bowels of the beast and a couple weeks' worth of emergency mopping sessions, I had given up and resorted to hand-washing my dishes.

It had been almost a year since my last futile attempt to troubleshoot this cranky appliance. During that time, the dishwasher had sat pushed against the wall next to the sink, its only useful contribution being the additional counter space provided by its top surface.

I puffed out a frustrated sigh, temporarily blowing a strand of stray hair off my grimy forehead as I peered into the tub area. There were, at first glance, no new approaches to the problem—but after having removed all the wallpaper from the kitchen walls, I had somehow got it into my head that *this* was the next logical place to check for a potential Bear Flag clue. Perhaps, I thought hopefully, the item causing the dishwasher's plug had been intentionally lodged in its hiding place by the previous inhabitant of this kitchen, my Uncle Oscar.

I reached out and spun the metal spider mounted onto the tub's base. It moved freely under my touch, and the drain below it appeared unobstructed. Craning my head upward, I checked the spigots where water entered from the washer's roof. They were clear and clean. There was still no obvious explanation for the plug.

I closed the washer door, pulled the locking lever into place, and turned the dial to start. Isabella clicked out a vocal warning as a rushing whoosh of water entered the machine. Blue eyes bulging, Rupert backed up several feet into the kitchen.

"Wra wrao ra ra rum." Isabella called out a warning as she retreated to a safer position on top of the kitchen table.

Sure enough, two minutes into the cycle, the first gurgling bubbles began to burp up and over the top seam. Quickly, I swung back the lever and cracked open the door.

A blast of hot air fogged my glasses. Blinking, I whipped the frames from my face and leaned into the steamy interior. Soapy water swirled in the bottom of the tub, and the sides were moist with splatter—but in the condensation pattern on the roof, I noticed a suspicious aberration. In a small square area on the ceiling's left side, the water droplets were dramatically smaller. Something above the plastic roof was affecting its heat transfer.

Padded feet crept up behind me as I twisted my head to stare at the top of the dishwasher's interior. Rupert's loud snuffling whistled in my left ear as he put his front paws over my shoulders. Then, I heard the distinctive sound of hungry smacking lips.

"Hmmm," I said, glancing back at his eager expression, which was focused on the top left corner of the dishwasher. He gulped as if anticipating a treat.

I leaned back into the washer and thumped the molded plastic of the ceiling with the tip of my thumb. A hollow empty sound echoed back into the kitchen.

I moved my hand an inch to the left. *Thunk.* Still hollow.

My hand slid over another inch, near the spot where the condensed water droplets changed in size. This time my thump returned a thick leaded *thud*.

"Aha!" I exclaimed as Rupert became even more urgent with his sniffles. Behind me, Isabella's feet dropped lightly onto the tile floor as she abandoned her perch on the kitchen table. A moment later, she circled around to my right side, ears perked, tail stretched inquisitively in the air.

Gently, I began pressing against the plastic roof

of the dishwasher with my fingers, trying to rock it loose.

"There's definitely something . . . in here," I said as two cats closed in on my work space.

Suddenly, the large piece of plastic that formed the roof of the tub slipped forward, releasing a burst of hot water. Rupert scooted sideways as I fell back on my rear. Isabella hissed at the dishwasher, her hackles rising in challenge.

Blowing on my singed fingertips, I righted myself and leaned forward once more into the washer's interior. Lying on the open door where it had fallen from the hole in the roof was a small metal box.

I used a pair of oven mitts to pick it up and, with effort, pried open the lid to study the contents sealed inside. The wad of fried-chicken-infused cash was likely what had drawn Rupert's interest. Relieved as I was to have found the money, I was far more interested in the item tucked next to it: a toy bear holding a California Bear Flag.

Slipping off the oven mitts, I lifted the bear from the container and carefully turned its paw, rotating the toothpick it held in its grasp. The gold-lettered writing on the back of the flag read: LARKIN HOUSE, MONTEREY, CALIFORNIA.

DOWN THE STAIRS from the kitchen, below the creaky wood flooring of the Green Vase showroom, an opening appeared along one of the basement's crumbling brick walls. Three men emerged from the entrance to the tunnel that ran beneath the streets of San Francisco, connecting the Green Vase's basement to the flower shop around the corner on Montgomery Street.

John Wang, limping along in his bathrobe, pajamas, and house slippers, was the first to step into the basement. He was immediately followed by Harold Wombler, muttering under his breath about stiffening joints. The last man in the group exited the tunnel wearing a costume meant to emulate the historical figure of General Mariano Vallejo.

The trio moved slowly, picking their way through the piles of boxes and crates until they reached a spot beneath the closed hatch in the basement ceiling.

A tiny mouse poked its head out of the Vallejo character's jacket pocket as Mr. Wang pulled a pencil-sized flashlight from his robe pocket and shone it at the glass eyes of the stuffed kangaroo standing silently in the corner. Then, slowly, the tiny point of light moved from the creature's face down to its large bulging stomach.

Chapter 51

A LONE MISSION

TUESDAY MORNING, I opened my eyes to find the cats sprawled across the covers, both of them clearly pleased to be back in the familiar environs of the Jackson Square apartment.

Isabella claimed the real estate at the foot of the bed while Rupert sprawled across the middle, leaving only a narrow wedge on the right-hand side for me. The orange tip of Rupert's fluffy tail thumped against my stomach, as if to suggest that it was I who was cramping him and not the other way around. Grumbling sleepily, I scooped him up and rotated him ninety degrees so that I could shift to a more comfortable position.

I plumped the pillow under my head and stared up at the ceiling . . . my uncle's ceiling . . . in my uncle's apartment . . . above my uncle's antique store. A year's worth of living here hadn't changed my perspective on who really owned the place.

I had often wondered, in the nights since Oscar's death, what he had thought about on his last night lying in this bed. Considering all his cryptic messages, hidden treasures, and secret packets of money—had he simply been preparing for a long life's inevitable end, or had my uncle foreseen what lay waiting for him that dreadful morning?

Rupert flopped over, deliberately turning his body back into a sideways alignment. I felt the pads of his feet pushing against my hip. One thing I could be sure of, I thought wearily as I once more readjusted the persistent furry heap lying next to me, Oscar's last night of sleep above the Green Vase showroom hadn't been disturbed by a bed-hogging cat.

TWENTY MINUTES LATER, I gave up the battle with Rupert and roused myself to prepare for the day's journey. This trip would be much shorter than my previous outing; this one I would take entirely on my own.

By the time I'd slipped into a clean T-shirt and jeans, Rupert had vacated his prominent position on the covers. The center of the bed wasn't as appealing, it seemed, if you weren't pushing someone else away from it.

Isabella circled around me, supervising as I tied the laces on my tennis shoes; then, tail pointed at the ceiling, she led the way downstairs.

After a stale bagel and a quick cup of coffee, I snapped up a pair of car keys from a basket on the kitchen counter.

"I'll be back this afternoon," I said briskly, topping off the water dish as I left the cats to their breakfast. "You should be fine here until then."

The munching sounds coming from the food bowls didn't register any objections. The cats had had enough travel for the time being.

A few minutes later, I stepped onto the sidewalk outside the Green Vase showroom to find Jackson Square lost in a quiet morning haze. The rainstorms that had swept through the Bay Area the previous day had left behind a thick dewy fog.

Past the empty glass-fronted shop next door to the Green Vase, I turned right down a narrow curving alley. Steep brick walls closed in on either side of me, forming an eerie, damp corridor, but no amount of spectral gloom could shake the purposefulness of my step. I refused to let my nagging anxiety about Frank Napis disrupt my next stop on Oscar's Bear Flag trail. The location written on the clue I'd found in the dishwasher, I assured myself, would be Frank-free. There was no way he could know where I was headed—or so I thought.

About a hundred yards later, the alley opened up into a one-lane side street that angled behind the Green Vase. The road wasn't wide enough for regular street traffic and remained basically unused, but there was enough extra space behind my building to park a modest four-door vehicle.

The car sometimes sat here for months. There was a grocery store a few blocks away, and it was easier to walk there than to try to find parking. I should have sold the car, I suppose, but on those few occasions where I needed to leave the city, it sure did come in handy.

I reached under the hem of the car's sheet cover. Gripping the fabric's edge with both hands, I whipped it up into the air to reveal the machine beneath.

The hood yawned sleepily as I cranked it open, a metal interior spring stretching into a long squeak. I reconnected the battery to its leads, generating a welcoming blink from the engine. After a few more minor vehicle checks, my trusty gray Corolla was ready for action.

I climbed into the driver's seat and plugged the key into the ignition. As the engine warmed to a gentle purr, I opened my road atlas to the page for Northern California and studied the route south to Monterey. The Larkin House was in the central downtown area, not far from the wharf. It shouldn't be too hard to find.

I backed out of the alley and circled around to the front of the Green Vase. Two furry faces watched from the upstairs window as the Corolla hummed past on Jackson Street and headed out of town.

Chapter 52

THE KITCHEN RADIO

RUPERT YAWNED SLEEPILY as he watched the Corolla drive off down Jackson Street. The duffel bag remained safely in its niche on the closet's top shelf, so he had no concerns about being left behind on today's trip.

Plus, he thought with a wide yawn, after two days on the road, he was feeling rather exhausted. He had a lot of sleep to catch up on.

It didn't help that he'd been up half the night trying to push his person over to her side of the bed. He let out a weary sigh. After only two nights away from the apartment, she was going to have to be completely retrained on their sleeping arrangements.

There was one more reason he was not eager to get himself loaded up into the Corolla, he thought as he stepped down from the windowsill and padded across the bedroom. It was a small and efficient car—perfect for the occasional drive around Northern California—but it had limited features. He had no delusions about *its* fried-chicken-cooking capabilities.

Mmm, chicken, he mused hungrily as he skipped back down the stairs to the kitchen. He needed another bite of breakfast before he tucked in for his morning nap.

The kitchen floor had been swept clean of the piles of discarded wallpaper that had littered the room the night before, but his person had not had time to affix anything to the stripped-down walls.

That was just fine with Rupert. He gazed approvingly at a section of bare two-by-four studs. There was no way that weird-looking mouse could sneak up on him now, he thought reassuringly.

Turning from the wall, he stretched his front legs toward the kitchen table. His chest brushed against the ground as his front toes splayed out, each individual claw extending to its full curving arc. His rump poked up into the air so that his fluffy tail plumed like the comb of a rooster.

This feels good, he thought as he reached the full extension of his armpits. My person has a name for this pose. What does she call it? Oh, that's right. The Funky Chicken. Mmm, chicken—hey, there's my food bowl.

The soles of Rupert's feet squished against the tile floor as he completed the distance to the feeding station.

Pad, pad, pad, pad.

Swooooosh.

Oh, bother, Rupert sighed as he froze, mid-step, bracing for his sister's incoming pounce.

Her slender white body hurtled through the air, expertly taking him out in a single tackle. The two of them rolled across the floor in a spitting, swatting ball of fur until they crashed against the side of the dishwasher.

Rupert scrambled to his feet and took off across the kitchen. Isabella chased playfully after him as he hopped onto the seat of a wooden chair, spun around, and issued a mighty roar from his chest.

"Werrrao!" You have woken the lion, he thought, his nostrils flaring for full intimidating effect. Prepare to be re-pounced.

Isabella scooted to the side as Rupert launched into the air. Back across to the dishwasher they raced. At the opposite side of the kitchen, Isabella leapt onto the counter by the sink, her brother tracking close behind. Scampering along the ledge, Isabella stepped nimbly over a small transistor radio before jumping back down to the floor. The bottom of Rupert's feet grazed the radio's control buttons as he bounced over it and landed with a wheezing grunt on the tiles next to his sister.

There was a second of static; then the local AM station's broadcast filled the room. Both cats sat on the floor, looking curiously up at the noisy black box.

HARRY CARLIN SMILED into the camera as the producer counted down from the end of a commercial break. A dizzy collection of roller coasters, merry-go-rounds, and other spinning, whirling amusement park rides provided the backdrop for the broadcast booth as the producer pulled his last finger into his fist, signaling the restart of the live transmission.

"Welcome back, folks," Carlin said pleasantly. "We're here just outside the Santa Cruz boardwalk at the finishing line for Stage Three of the Tour of California. The weather has improved dramatically from yesterday. Here in Santa Cruz it's downright balmy."

Will Spigot leaned into the camera shot, a wide grin on his pointed face. "This is more like it! I've even broken out my sunscreen."

Carlin chuckled politely. "We had quite a thrilling end to yesterday's stage in Santa Rosa. The breakaway managed to pull the wool over the eyes of the peloton and crossed the finish line well ahead of the main pack. Thanks to that time advantage, one of those riders will be exchanging his team jersey for yellow today."

Spigot propped his elbows on the counter of the broadcast booth. "Yes, my little friend from Sacramento has taken home a prize after all," he said affably. He cocked his left eyebrow knowingly. "He'd better enjoy this moment of glory though, because I don't think any of us fancy he'll be wearing it by the day's end."

Carlin cleared his throat. "Ahem. Well, today's course takes us from San Francisco down the coast here to Santa Cruz. The riders will be following Highway One most of the way . . ."

"I say, I'm feeling a bit hungry," Spigot cut in. He lifted his head into the air, sniffing loudly.

"Your breakfast isn't holding, then?" Carlin asked worriedly. His broadcasting partner tended to get cranky when he was hungry.

"Oh, I had a fine breakfast," Spigot replied as a man in a furry brown kangaroo suit walked past the broadcast booth. "Fancy eggs and bacon. But I just caught a whiff of something in the air. One of the vendor stands has cooked up what smells like an absolutely delectable dish. I believe it's fried chicken . . ."

Chapter 53

AMPHIBIANS ON WHEELS

A BROAD-SHOULDERED MAN with reddish orange hair whistled merrily as he parked a large white van in the basement level loading dock on the side of San Francisco's City Hall. It was a busy Tuesday morning, and the security guards manning the building's main entrance glanced only briefly at the video screen feeding images from the outside entrances. They had their hands full with a far more pressing issue on the first floor: One of the members of the Board of Supervisors was protesting the search of his briefcase.

Sam stroked the name tag sewn into the chest of

his faded gray-striped coveralls. His face was covered with a rough reddish stubble, and his thick hair had the dull sheen of accumulated grease—the result of a few days' abstinence from showering and shaving. It was almost a year since he'd relinquished his janitorial job at City Hall, but, he thought proudly, he could still play the part convincingly. That, combined with the updated security badge clipped to the front of his coveralls, should be enough to get him inside the building.

He had enjoyed his years working at City Hall, but he had to admit he was far happier in his current employment. Instead of passing his time watching all the interesting people that visited the building's famous rotunda, he now devoted his observational energies to his beloved frogs. He still worked a few hours a month at the Castro Street card shop, but he spent most days with his little green friends.

This last week, he'd been out in the field gathering data for some scientists from UC Davis who were studying a rare amphibian species they'd identified in the Sacramento Delta. He would have been tromping through the wetlands that very morning if he hadn't received an urgent message requesting his services here in San Francisco.

Still positioned in the driver's seat, Sam took in a few analyzing sniffs of the van's interior.

Despite his own rank, sweaty smell, he thought he detected a peculiar animal scent inside the van. He noticed a light dusting of white hairs on the dashboard. Feline, he surmised as he wrinkled his nose.

He preferred more of a citrus fragrance himself. He patted the front pocket of his coveralls. He would install one of his extra-strength orange air fresheners once he had completed this little errand. Mr. Carmichael, Sam felt certain, would appreciate the improved aroma.

Monty, Sam mused with a wry grin. That fellow only grew curiouser and curiouser over time. The outfit he was wearing today had really taken the cake. Sam had been sneaking peeks at those shiny green leggings all the way to Golden Gate Park—that was where Monty had got out and handed him the van's keys.

Shaking his head, Sam turned toward the glass-sided terrarium resting on the front passenger seat.

"Green leggings," he said to the two frogs with feathery orange mustaches sitting inside. "What could be sillier than that?"

Sam tapped the security badge on his chest once more. "Are you ready for your tour of City Hall?" he asked the frogs as he picked up the terrarium by its rooftop handle and clambered out onto the pavement. Confidently, he walked up to the loading dock door and waved his badge in front of the scanner. There was a slight click as the lock disengaged.

City Hall's basement level was quiet and empty. Most of the building's activity at this hour, he knew from experience, was taking place on the main floor above him.

Carrying the frogs, Sam crept silently down a side corridor and slipped through an unmarked door to a narrow staircase that would take him up past the street level to the second floor. He whispered chattily to the frogs as he made the ascent, recounting several interesting tidbits about the building's long history as well as his memories of San Francisco's Previous Mayor, of whom he was still quite fond.

"Now, then, the Current Mayor," Sam said as they reached the landing at the top of the stairs, "the one you're about to meet—I haven't got much to say about him."

But he went on to tell the frogs several minutes' worth of details anyway. They politely nodded along throughout this entire dialogue as if they appreciated his informative insights and commentary.

Sam pulled up the sleeve of his coveralls to check his watch. Any minute now, the Mayor's receptionist would leave her desk and walk down the hall for her second cup of coffee.

"Every morning at precisely eight forty-five . . ." Sam murmured down to the frogs as he stepped cautiously into the recess behind a wide marble column.

Just then, the door to the Mayor's office popped open, and a stern woman in a gray wool skirt and solid practical-looking pumps stepped briskly outside. Sam scooted across the polished floor to catch the edge of the door with his fingers as the woman clipped smartly down the hallway.

Inside the Mayor's office suite, the plush red carpeting muffled Sam's footsteps. Noiselessly, he crossed the reception area and entered a small meeting room adjoining the Mayor's inner office.

After softly pulling the door shut behind him, Sam stepped around a table and chairs to reach the floor-to-ceiling windows that looked out over the wide balcony the room shared with the Mayor's adjoining office. He sat the terrarium on the floor and pushed open the bottommost pane.

"Wait here," he whispered to his inquisitive green friends.

The frogs watched as Sam squeezed himself through the opening in the glass and crawled across the balcony to peek into the room next door. The tip of Sam's freckled nose grazed the bottom rim of the windowpane as he watched a man in a black suit, narrow blue tie, and swept-back, gel-coated hair enter from the reception area.

The Mayor strolled across the plush red carpet

to a leather recliner positioned behind an enormous wooden desk. He folded his newspaper and placed it neatly on the desk's polished surface next to his half-drunk paper cup of coffee. Then he turned in his chair to stare at a large oval mirror affixed to the nearest wall.

Sliding backwards across the balcony on his stomach, Sam returned to the meeting room. Carefully, he lifted the frogs out of their tank. He petted each one gently on the head and brushed his fingers through the feathery orange hair of their mustaches before he set them outside on the balcony.

Then, he reached into a side pocket of his coveralls and pulled out a pair of tiny gold-rimmed tricycles.

THE MAYOR BREEZED into City Hall that morning, a man of recently regained poise and confidence. There would be no more hiding from the press. No more ducking cameras. No more sneaking up the back stairs to his office. Today was a new day, he vowed, and he would attack it with gusto.

He had nodded to the security guards as he stepped through their scanners. He'd waved at the group of tourists standing next to the visitor's information kiosk. He'd even smiled at the President of the Board of Supervisors on his way up the central marble staircase.

The light streamed through the enormous arched windows below the rotunda's soaring dome as the Mayor marched purposefully down the second floor hallway toward his office suite. Near-perfect weather was in the forecast for the afternoon. The rain from the previous day had moved inland, and the trailing fog was scheduled to clear the city by mid-morning—which was fortunate because he had several public appearances planned, the first being the San Francisco starting line for Stage Three of the Tour of California that would take place in just a few hours' time.

The Mayor brushed a hand over the top of his carefully styled hair. Everything, it seemed, was falling into place. His secretary had even convinced the race organizers that, due to other pressing engagements immediately following the race send-off, he would be unable to don a cycling outfit—or a hair-crimping bike helmet. Yes, he thought with a deep bolstering sigh, a fabulous day awaited him.

He strode purposefully into his office, stepped behind his large wooden desk, and eased comfortably into the leather chair behind it. After neatly arranging his folded newspaper and coffee cup on the wide polished surface, he prepared to begin his important morning ritual. It was one he had practiced several times with his Life Coach. He'd felt a bit self-conscious about it at first, and he dared not let anyone see him talking to himself in this manner, but he'd found it actually did make a difference.

And so, the Mayor straightened his tie and turned to face his image in a mirror he'd hung on the nearest wall.

"I am the Mayor," he said slowly and distinctly. "I'm good enough. I'm smart enough. And doggone it. People like me."

Then he smiled. The same broad steady grin he'd given to the President of the Board of Supervisors just minutes before.

The Mayor was about to repeat the mantra when he noticed a slight movement reflected in the bottom corner of the mirror.

"What the—?" he exclaimed, startled as he swiveled around in his chair toward the wall of windows that looked out over the balcony.

Timidly, he stood up from his desk and walked over toward the windows. Halfway across the room, he was seized with a feeling of complete and utter terror. His slender hands trembled. The recently tanned skin on his face paled to an icy blue.

It couldn't be. He blinked rapidly and squeezed his eyes shut for a long moment before reopening them—but the horrifying image had not disappeared. It was still there, outside on the balcony.

Two small frogs in feathery orange mustaches

were riding tiny tricycles across the stone floor on the opposite side of the windows.

The Mayor scampered back across the room, pulled out his leather recliner, and crawled beneath his desk. With a shaking hand, he reached up to grab the receiver of the phone. The tip of his finger fumbled along the base of the unit until it found the bright red call button that connected to his receptionist.

"Yes, sir?" her crisp efficient voice answered immediately.

"Mabel," he said, sounding feeble and hoarse. "Something's come up. Please cancel all my appointments for today."

"Sir?" she replied, sounding concerned.

"And Mabel," he added sheepishly.

"Yes?"

"Call the Life Coach. Tell him I need him here immediately." The Mayor cringed as he thought of the scene on his balcony. "Tell him it's an emergency."

Chapter 54

HAROLD'S ENTOURAGE

MONTGOMERY CARMICHAEL BUSTLED down a sidewalk near the west end of Golden Gate Park, pushing his bicycle along beside him. His plastic helmet swung from the handlebars as the metal soles of his bike shoes clacked against the pavement. He was heading, as planned, to the San Francisco starting line for the next stage of the Tour of California.

It had been a somewhat shady move, he conceded—sabotaging the Mayor—but he'd discussed it at length with his trusted mentor, the Life Coach, during their lunch in Sonoma, and they'd both agreed he had no other choice.

As it turned out, the Life Coach was the one who had brought up the idea in the first place. Testing the Mayor with a surprise frog appearance on the balcony outside his office, he had assured Monty, was an excellent way to measure how far the Mayor had progressed with his therapy sessions. The Life Coach had hoped that an unexpected frog sighting might actually boost the man's shaky confidence.

Lucky for me, Monty thought smugly, the Mayor still has a ways to go on that front.

Monty quickened his step, his mind set on righting the wrongs of the two previous starting-line ceremonies. This was his last chance to get a race-themed photo for his political portfolio, an album that would be used to develop the advertising strategy for his upcoming mayoral campaign.

The Life Coach had helped Monty with the logistics of sneaking the frogs into City Hall. He'd called in a few favors to get an extra security badge and had tracked down Sam from his fieldwork in the delta.

Monty had been in charge of obtaining the actual frogs. That had been the most delicate aspect of the operation, but Harold had begrudgingly agreed to let Sam borrow them.

Apparently, the frogs had put on quite a show on the Mayor's balcony. Minutes ago, Monty had received an urgent phone call from the Mayor's receptionist. She had apologized for the last-minute notice, but could he, possibly, step in for the Mayor at this morning's race festivities?

"Could he step in for the Mayor?" he asked himself rhetorically, puffing his chest out proudly. In his mind, he practically *was* the Mayor—that's what the Life Coach was always telling him.

When the Mayor eventually departed for the Lieutenant Governor's position in Sacramento, Monty planned to run as his replacement. San Francisco, in his modest opinion, could do no better than a Mayor Carmichael.

If you looked on the bright side of things, as he was wont to do, it was actually advantageous that the first two starting line events had been disrupted. Now, the photo would be taken with a San Francisco backdrop, a much more appropriate setting.

Monty glanced down at his cycling shirt, smoothing his hands across the shiny green and purple argyle print that covered his chest. This was a focus group–tested outfit. According to the Life Coach, it had scored exceptionally well with San Francisco's outdoorsy, environmentally conscious voters. It would provide an excellent contrast to more serious shots of him in his dark businesslike suit.

Traffic barriers were being moved into position as Monty approached the outer edge of Golden Gate Park. The starting line would be set up on the road next to the beach, about a half mile south of the Cliff House. A typical morning fog blanketed the area, but the rain that had tormented the riders the previous day was on its way east to dump snow in the Sierras.

Monty pulled to a stop a hundred yards away from the ring of hospitality tents as a group of muscular, blue-suited individuals gathered around him. They were members of a private security team he had hired to police the crowds surrounding the starting line for anyone wearing suspicious-looking trench coats or carrying rubber masks.

"All right, men. You know what to do," he said firmly. "Take no prisoners—or rather, take all prisoners."

Several of the security officers looked at him skeptically. Monty straightened his shoulders and clarified his instructions. "Don't let any naked people run in front of my picture!"

Monty's face firmed in resolution as he

dramatically crammed his helmet down over his head and tightened the chinstrap—a knight in shining spandex, he marched confidently into the main hospitality tent.

MONTY HAD BECOME so consumed with his vengeance for the streakers, so obsessed with his quest to become Mayor, that he had readily accepted the Life Coach's explanation for the unusual outfit he'd been wearing during their previous day's lunch meeting in Sonoma.

The Life Coach had claimed that he'd been at a dress rehearsal for a local theater group of which he was a member. He had not had time to change out of the wrinkled linen suit, fake mustache, and wild flyaway eyebrows that were all part of the costume for the role he was preparing to play as Mark Twain.

He looked pretty convincing, Monty thought as he followed the race organizer out of the hospitality tent to the starting line. I'll have to see if I can get tickets to the show.

HAROLD WOMBLER STOOD at the back of a group of racing fans, waiting for the starting line ceremony to begin.

A woman in a scarlet red suit and matching three-inch heels stepped into an open spot beside him. A similar red color painted her lips and her long polished fingernails. Miranda Richards drew several appreciative looks from the crowd; Oscar's attorney hadn't lost any of her curves in the year since his death.

"Nice of you to join us," Harold said sarcastically. "I haven't seen you around lately."

"I've been following your progress in the papers," Miranda replied blithely. "Your antics have been getting lots of press coverage." With a deprecating sigh, she crossed her arms over her chest. "Don't you think you've gone a bit overboard with the show you're putting on today?"

Harold's grin stretched unnaturally from ear to ear. "That's the only reason I signed on to this gig. This morning's exhibition is my best work yet. Carmichael's going to flip his lid."

Miranda's mouth curled sarcastically. "Not to mention what it's going to do to the Mayor," she replied caustically. "The *real* Mayor, that is."

Harold grunted his lack of his concern. "I never voted for the man. You know that."

The race organizer wrung his hands nervously as Monty stepped up to the starting line and raised the ceremonial scissors. The riders crowded in behind the ribbon, a colorful backdrop of nylon shirts, plastic helmets, and metal bikes. The cameramen leaned in for the shot. Monty beamed triumphantly as a voice called out, "Hey, there's the Mayor."

Monty's thin face tensed as the cameramen spun

around to pan the sea of spectators. A man who looked very much like the Mayor was moving through the throngs surrounding the race route— and he was not wearing a plastic mask. He had the same swept-back hairstyle, the same pale clean-shaven face. Startled onlookers jumped out of the way as the figure approached the starting line, parting the crowds like a ripple in a pond. Hushed murmurs of shock and confusion escalated in volume as the man emerged shirtless . . .

WILL SPIGOT AND Harry Carlin sat in their Santa Cruz broadcast booth, positioned at the finish line for Day Three of the race. A television screen showed live feed of the scene in San Francisco where the racers were preparing to depart.

Suddenly, Spigot pointed at the video monitor.

"Isn't that the Mayor?" Spigot asked, his voice incredulous. "I heard they did things differently there in San Francisco, but I have to say, this is a new one on me."

Carlin sputtered, nearly speechless as the camera panned the crowd. "Wait, wait," he gasped. "There's another one."

Spigot whipped his head to look at Carlin; then he quickly returned his gaze to the screen. "Another what? Another Mayor?"

"There's a whole group of them . . ." Carlin took in a deep breath and attempted to describe the scene in his most serious broadcasting voice. "It appears that the starting line has been taken over by an entourage of naked Mayors."

"What is this madness?" Spigot replied with an incredulous frown.

Carlin's voice cracked as he struggled to maintain his composure. "Actors, I'd have to guess."

A howl of anguish broke through the video as the image shifted to a tall spindly man in green leggings waving an oversized pair of scissors in the air.

Spigot leaned back in his chair. "Well, this'll rack up another delay getting the stage started, but I must say, it's quite entertaining watching him chase after those buggers."

Chapter 55

MONTEREY

I DECIDED TO take the scenic route down to Monterey, avoiding the commuter traffic that clogged the main southbound interstate. Just outside of San Francisco, the Corolla veered west onto the exit for Highway One.

The road quickly joined the coast, curving in dramatic *S*-turns as it parted a seam between the cliffs and the sea. I rolled down the windows, let the ocean breeze whip through my hair, and listened to the foaming waves crash against the beach below.

Cut off from the Bay Area's main transportation arteries, the coastline was remarkably remote and, for the most part, I had the road to myself. The only exception was a man in a black leather jacket who zoomed past on a motorcycle, his face anonymous behind his helmet's tinted visor.

It would take about four hours, five tops, I figured, to drive down to Monterey, check out the Larkin House, and get back to the Green Vase. By the time I returned that afternoon, I hoped to have uncovered the location of Oscar's hidden Bear Flag.

I should have known it would turn out to be far more complicated than that.

IVAN BATRACHOS PARKED his stolen motorcycle in an open slot near the wharf in downtown Monterey. He pulled off his helmet, hung it on one end of the handlebars, and left the keys in the ignition. This was the motorcycle's drop-off point. The police, he expected, would eventually reunite the bike with its original owner.

Ivan stretched his legs, enjoying the picturesque harbor view. The Larkin House was a short walk on foot from this location, and he had plenty of time for a cheap breakfast at one of the seafood places on the pier. He unzipped his jacket and conscientiously tapped his fingers against the silver flask tucked into the inside pocket. A little food on his stomach would probably help him down the floral liquid inside.

A SHORT HOUR'S drive down the coast, the cliffs gave way to rolling dunes and low-lying vistas filled with strawberry and artichoke fields. Highway One swung a long curve around the inner rim of Monterey Bay, taking me ever closer to my destination, the former adobe of the American Consul, Thomas Larkin.

At the time of the Bear Flag Revolt, Monterey was the largest settlement in Northern California, the seat of what limited power the Mexican government could muster. Nowadays, the town sat sandwiched between Santa Cruz's surfer hangout and Carmel's glitzy multimillionaire retreat. The Monterey of the twentieth century was predominantly known as a family tourist destination, featuring a world-class aquarium, Steinbeck's Cannery Row, and some of California's best-preserved historical landmarks.

I parked the Corolla down the street from the Customs House and set out on a wide pedestrian walkway overlooking the harbor. Hundreds of sailboats were packed in along the water's edge, their un-sheeted masts forming a dense thicket across the blue horizon. Sea lions belched and barked from every available inch of rocky beach, wallowing about on the pebbly sand, showcasing their buoyant blubber as well as their exceptional side-whiskers.

Staring at the upturned face of a nearby sea lion, I couldn't help but reflect on my Sonoma Barracks encounter with General Vallejo. It was still hard for me to believe it had been Frank Napis beneath that costume. After all my encounters with the man, how could I have been fooled by his disguise? I had been so certain it was Clem behind that bushy facial hair.

As I approached the front porch of the Customs House, I once more resolved to dismiss my concerns about Napis. Turning my thoughts instead to the Bear Flag story, I picked up the tale where the man impersonating General Vallejo had left off the previous day.

The Bear Flaggers' capture of Sonoma triggered a chain reaction up and down the California coast. Larkin frantically passed the news on to U.S. Navy Commodore Sloat, who was berthed on the *Savannah* near the mouth of the Monterey Bay.

Sloat puzzled over the development. Frémont had absented himself from the Osos' daylong booze fest at Vallejo's hacienda, remaining behind at Sutter's Fort, but everyone in Northern California knew he was the one responsible for their actions. By Sloat's estimation, Frémont had directly violated the President's orders to wait for confirmation of a formal declaration of war before initiating any hostilities. Perhaps, Sloat reasoned, Frémont had received new information from the Texas front—or from his influential father-in-law. In any case, the Commodore found himself in a decidedly uncomfortable position.

Finally, after much discussion with the hand-wringing Larkin, Sloat decided to send a group of men ashore to take Monterey. Castro and his soldiers were several miles away at San Juan Bautista, so Sloat's crew met little resistance. On July 7, the American flag was raised on the pole outside the Customs House where I now stood.

Two days later, a similar action took place in Yerba Buena. Under orders from Sloat, an equally befuddled Captain John B. Montgomery sent men to land from his rig, the *Portsmouth*. William Leidesdorff supervised the raising of the American flag; then a group of soldiers, led by the grandson of Paul Revere, rode inland to Sonoma to replace the Bear Flag with the Stars and Stripes.

Young Revere found the Bear Flaggers now under Frémont's direct command. Wary of the political ramifications of being seen as the instigator of the Sonoma initiative, Frémont had waited until the Osos sent word that they had successfully taken Sonoma before overtly taking charge. Sensing that the initial threat of a Mexican military response had passed, Frémont stepped up to declare himself "Military Commander of the U.S. Forces in California" and quickly renamed the group the more official-sounding "California Battalion." Frémont then led his roughneck cavalry to Monterey to rendezvous with the increasingly anxious Commodore Sloat.

It was here, I mused as I turned away from the harbor onto the quiet Calle Principal, where Frémont's fortunes began to fade.

Unbeknownst to anyone in Northern California, the U.S. had formally declared war with Mexico a few days after the Bear Flag Revolt, but it would take several weeks for that information to reach the West Coast. In the meantime, Sloat began interrogating Frémont— what authority had he relied upon for this preemptive seizing of the California Territory? Headstrong, egotistical, and easily affronted, Frémont did not respond well to Sloat's questioning of his motives and rationale.

In the months following the Bear Flag Revolt, Frémont's patriotic reputation would be subsumed in the military scramble to ensure the U.S. kept hold of the territory whose capture he had so rashly precipitated. Once the new state of California was safely secured, Senator Benton would use up much of his political capital defending his ill-begotten son-in-law.

Many of Frémont's former associates would also come to rue their affiliation with the impetuous explorer. In order to distance themselves from the fallout of Frémont's shenanigans, they would begrudgingly agree to help mask his pivotal role at Sonoma, repainting the revolt as a spontaneous uprising—instead of one masterminded by the Pathfinder.

· · ·

ON A QUIET Monterey street around the corner from the Larkin House, the Mayor's Life Coach pulled a large white van into a shaded parking space. Sam had conveniently handed over the keys to the vehicle after he and the frogs finished their task at the Mayor's office that morning.

The Life Coach glanced in the rearview mirror at his bristly white mustache and scraggly eyebrows, ensuring that his false hairpieces were still firmly attached to his face. As he exited the van, he smoothed his hands over his rumpled linen suit. Then, he locked the door and slipped the key into one of his pockets.

The morning's bright sunshine cast a warm glow on the sidewalk as the Life Coach strolled around the corner to the Larkin House. My son, he thought as a slight facial tick tweaked his upper lip, has proved useful once again.

The Life Coach strode briskly up the porch steps and gazed at his full reflection in the adobe's front windows. Clem's Mark Twain outfit had been a simple enough disguise to copy. It had easily fooled that silly accountant who had seen him sitting across the table from Monty at the Sonoma restaurant—he had seen the surprised look on her face through the window.

Now, he was ready to give her an up-close viewing.

"Clem," he muttered under his breath as he

stepped from the end of the porch through a gate to a side courtyard. "I know who you really are."

A dark chuckle rumbled in his chest as he fed a key into the lock of the door to the main house.

"Oscar, you're no match for the likes of Frank Napis."

Chapter 56

THE LARKIN HOUSE

AFTER A SHORT walk down Calle Principal, I stood in front of the two-story structure of Consul Larkin's former residence, unaware of the danger that lurked within. A cream-painted composite of adobe and brick with a fir green trim, the building fit in seamlessly with the surrounding neighborhood, a quiet mix of residential and discreetly commercial buildings.

At first glance, the house didn't have the look of a hundred-and-fifty-year-old building, but as I took in the details, I began to see evidence of its longevity. A wide balcony stretched around the circumference of the house, reminiscent of the architectural style of the Sonoma Barracks I'd visited the day before. I climbed a short flight of steps to a front porch whose flooring was paved with smooth timeworn bricks.

At the end of the porch stood a green-painted gate marked "Entrance." Pushing it open, I found a courtyard that spanned the adjoining half-acre lot. The area was filled with redwood trees whose tops soared hundreds of feet above the roof of the house.

Beneath the sky-high canopy, the yard looked as if it could use a good pruning. Several overgrown bushes and shrubs crowded in among the tree trunks. Toward the opposite side of the courtyard, I could just make out the edge of a large stone shed.

Immediately to my right, a door led into the main house. A sign hanging over the knob indicated that the curator had stepped out and would return within the hour. Inching up onto my tiptoes, I tried to look through the dusty panes of glass to the interior.

As my forehead touched the surface of the door, it swung inward, creaking open a few inches. The lock hadn't engaged properly, it seemed, when the curator left the premises for his break.

I leaned back from the doorway and checked through the courtyard gate to see if anyone was approaching from the street, but it was empty. There was no telling how long the curator would be gone. Slowly, my head swiveled back toward the entrance of the house.

The door squeaked on its hinges as I pushed it fully open and crossed the threshold to a small parlor. Family photos and several midsized paintings hung from walls painted a dull off-white color. A pair of mismatched love seats lined the longer sides of the rectangular-shaped room; a fireplace occupied the wall at the far end.

The sign hanging over the outside knob fluttered slightly as I pushed the door shut behind me. Catching a breeze, the sign flapped upward and flipped back against the glass, revealing a small plaque affixed to the door's exterior framing. The printing on the plaque listed the regular hours for the museum—which was closed on Tuesdays.

ALTHOUGH IT HAD been extensively renovated over the years, the Larkin House still retained the same basic floor plan as the original adobe. What had once been a breezeway running through the center of the first floor was now a fully enclosed hallway that connected the front and back portions of the house.

Standing in this central hallway, just behind the entrance to the front parlor, Frank Napis stroked his fake mustache as he heard the front door creak open, tentatively at first, then, after a long moment, with a second squeaking shove that indicated a fully committed entrance. Tentative footsteps trod across the ancient wooden floorboards as someone stepped inside and began to look around.

Through the reflection of a mirror posted at the front end of the hall, Napis watched as Oscar's niece began her search of the sitting room.

I MADE MY way slowly around the parlor, carefully studying the details, my eyes peeled for any reference to the Bear Flag Revolt.

The room was tastefully done, if a bit ragged around the edges. A couple of frumpy lamps, a few tottering end tables, and several worn throw rugs furnished the space. Outlets on the wall indicated the house had been wired for electricity. Several generations of Larkins, I suspected, had lived in the adobe, each one layering on its own renovations and personalizations.

I scanned the room, honing in on the pictures hanging from the walls, which seemed the most likely to have a connection to the 1846 time frame. My eyes swept from frame to frame, finally stopping at a small, dusty portrait propped up against a window seat near the front of the room.

The boyish face hiding behind the wild curly nest of an unkempt beard was instantly familiar. I'd stared at another version of the same man in the display area at Sutter's Fort. I bent over to look more closely at the picture of Captain John C. Frémont.

The sunlight streamed in through the window, causing a glare on the picture's protective glass covering, so I picked it up to get a better view. As I brought the frame closer to my face, my fingers pressed against its loose cardboard backing, and the brackets holding it together began to slip. I had to juggle the frame to keep the glass cover from dropping to the floor. Gathering the pieces on my lap, I sat on the window seat to fit them back together.

"My luck, this is when the curator will walk in," I murmured to myself.

Just then, there was a creaking shift of the floorboards, followed by a jarringly familiar voice. "I see you've taken an interest in Captain Frémont."

I looked up to find a man standing in the doorway leading from the parlor to the interior of the house. He wore a familiar linen suit, rumpled black bow tie, and ankle-high lace-up boots.

"Oh, ah, hello," I stuttered, my cheeks blushing at the disassembled picture frame in my lap. "I hope you don't mind, but I let myself in."

I set the pieces of the picture on the window seat, stood up, and took a step toward him. "We haven't formally met," I said, holding my hand out. "My name is—"

"Haven't we?" he cut in. There was an odd gleam in his eyes.

The man's upper lip twitched, causing his mustache to vibrate. Something in the movement struck a panicked chord in my memory. I hadn't picked up on it during his stage performances, but now, standing face to face, I was starting to feel a wary premonition creeping up my spine . . .

"Clement Samuels," he said, gripping my hand as he cleared his voice. The thin lips behind the mustache formed a disconcerting smile. "I've seen you in my audiences, haven't I? Weren't you at the Nevada Theatre?"

Chapter 57

A MUCH-NEEDED BUCKET OF FRIED CHICKEN

MONTY PUSHED HIS bike along Columbus Avenue, tired, weary, and dejected. After a long wait by the side of the road at the east entrance to Golden Gate Park, he'd given up hope that Sam was coming back to pick him up.

It had been a long ride home for the aspiring mayor of San Francisco. Several steep hills had impeded his progress, and the chain had fallen off his gear shaft, complicating his navigations through the city's heavy traffic. What's more, he couldn't stop worrying about where that crazy ex-janitor had run off with his precious van.

Monty stopped at a curb to wipe a layer of sweat from his forehead. He looked down at what had been his last clean cycling shirt. It was now smeared with grease from his attempts to fix the chain. Finally, he had to confess, he was ready to give up on the cycling-themed photo op. It was time to admit defeat and move on. He'd sit down with the Life Coach later in the week to plot out another approach.

But first, he thought as a luscious fried chicken scent wafted out of a newly opened North Beach bistro, it was time to get some nourishment.

AN HOUR LATER, Monty arrived at the doorstep to his Jackson Square studio, still uncomfortably grimy and sweaty, but feeling much more optimistic about life after having eaten nearly half a bucket of fried chicken. He paused, licked his fingers, and glanced across the street at the Green Vase storefront.

Aha, he thought with a flash of inspiration. *There* was an audience who would listen to his woes.

He crossed the street, leaned his bike against the red brick edifice, and peeked through the showroom windows.

"Halloo!" he called out, cupping his hands against the glass. As his voice echoed through the building, the racing patter of padded footsteps thundered across the second floor kitchen, thumped rapidly down the steps at the back of the building, and skidded at top speed across the showroom floor. A moment later, Rupert threw himself against the front door's glass panels, wheezing and huffing with his highest level of sniffing power. Every fiber of his being squealed with delight at the smell emanating from Monty's paper bucket.

Grinning, Monty fished a key out of a small pocket in his bike shorts and slid it into the lock. Isabella crossed the showroom in a far more dignified fashion and watched with disapproval as he opened the front door.

"If she didn't want me in here, she'd change the locks," Monty replied defensively to Isabella's accusing glare. He peeled off a chunk of chicken for Rupert, who was bouncing up and down, vainly trying to reach the bottom of the bucket. "Here you go, mate."

Isabella leapt onto the cashier counter, her tail swishing testily back and forth.

"Peace offering?" Monty suggested, holding out a piece of chicken. Isabella sniffed disdainfully, but edged her nose toward his hand.

Monty left the morsel on the counter for Isabella; then he swaggered across the showroom to the dental recliner. After dropping onto its worn leather cushions, he pulled the recline lever and extended the footrest.

"That's much better," he said with a sigh. Rupert hopped on his lap and immediately stuck his head into the bucket of chicken.

"Hey, hey," Monty protested. "That's not all for you!" He reached over to the display case and picked up the handles of the tooth extractor. Playfully, he aimed the pinchers at the back end of the furry white body snorkeling inside the bucket.

"And what do we have here?" he asked, dropping the pinchers onto the floor as he noticed the trapdoor to the basement lying open. "Is your person down there?"

He glanced at Rupert, whose head was still firmly planted inside the bucket. Then he looked questioningly at Isabella.

"Wa-ow wa-ow," she replied, her voice garbled by a mouthful of chicken.

Monty eased off the recliner, leaving Rupert to the bucket, and bent down to look into the hatch.

"Hall-oo," he called out again, this time aiming his voice at the dark hole, but there was no response.

"Hmnh," he mused. He started down the steps, the soles of his cycling shoes clapping loudly on the loose slats.

When he reached the basement's concrete floor, he tugged a gray moth-eaten string to turn on the single bare lightbulb mounted to the ceiling. The bulb provided little additional lighting, but it was sufficient to illuminate the wide empty place behind the stairs. A sweeping pattern in the otherwise dust-covered floor indicated that a large object had been pushed to the foot of the stairs and, presumably, carried up to the showroom.

After staring at the bare spot on the floor, Monty called up to the cats in the showroom, "Hey, what happened to the kangaroo?"

Chapter 58

THE LEIDESDORFF CONNECTION

THE MAN IN the rumpled linen suit dropped my trembling hand.

"Yes, I'm sure I remember you from my previous performances," he said slowly as I stared at his white mustache and flyaway eyebrows.

Despite his matching costume, I was beginning to doubt this was the same Clem I had seen in Nevada City and at Sutter's Fort.

He raised a stubby finger into the air near my face. "But—I think you're still missing the last act. Please, let me finish the story for you."

Gulping nervously, I glanced sideways at the door to the courtyard, several feet to my left. The linen-clad man hovered a mere arm's length to my right.

"After his role in the Bear Flag Revolt," he said dismissively, "Captain Frémont becomes far less interesting—to you and me anyway."

"Less interesting?" I repeated tensely as I tried to ease toward the door. "Why do you say that?"

The Clem impersonator let out an indifferent *sfit* of air. "A few months after taking command of the Osos in Sonoma, Frémont found himself caught in a political tug-of-war between the U.S. Army's General Kearney and the U.S.

Navy's Commodore Stockton. It would take Washington several months to catch up with the events on the ground in California. In the absence of a clear chain of command, the first two American military leaders on the scene fought with each other as much as with the Mexican resurgence in the south. In the end, Frémont managed to get himself court-martialed for disobeying orders. Despite a subsequent presidential pardon, his reputation and motives—particularly regarding his role in precipitating the Bear Flag Revolt—would be forever questioned."

The man paused and stroked his hands across the front of his chest. "But, as I said before, that aspect of the story is of little interest to us." He leaned toward me, his mustache twitching unnaturally. "Frémont's fate wasn't the focus of *your uncle's* investigations."

I felt myself freeze with the confirmation of my suspicions. This was not the Clem who had been parading around as Mark Twain in Nevada City and Sutter's Fort. This was . . . Frank Napis.

"No," he continued smoothly, as if he hadn't noticed my tightening expression. "Oscar couldn't have cared less about Frémont's later political implosion. It was the Bear Flag your uncle was after."

Napis paused and licked his lips. "The flag that was destroyed in the 1906 earthquake wasn't the original flag. It was a replacement. In the weeks immediately following the Sonoma revolt, someone made a switch."

I felt a bead of perspiration break out across my forehead as Napis pumped his fake eyebrows at me.

"Let's review, shall we? Paul Revere's grandson rode out to Sonoma to fetch the rebels' flag and replace it with Old Glory. When he returned to Yerba Buena with the Bear Flag, Captain Montgomery noticed something odd about the design. The flag's emblem had been modified; it no longer resembled a bear. Yes, the creature was brown and standing upright on its hindquarters. But stretching out from its posterior was a long ground-sweeping attachment—a tail."

I thought back to the sketch in my notebook and Oscar's notation next to the DeVoto text:

Local Indians, passing through Sonoma after the revolt, ridiculed the animal on the flag, calling it a pig or a stoat.

And suddenly it became clear to me. The creature on the flag that the local Indians had laughed at and tried to describe as an upright pig or weasel had instead been a . . .

"That's right," Napis said as if reading my mind. "A kangaroo."

I shook my head, curious despite my growing fear of being trapped in a room with my uncle's arch nemesis. I was still missing the last piece of the puzzle.

"But, the Bear Flag, the state flag of California . . . it's clearly a *bear*."

Napis's dark eyes flickered. "The Osos began to have misgivings about Frémont when he showed up at their Sonoma camp, denied any responsibility for instigating their revolt, and assumed leadership of their group."

The coarse hairs of Napis's mustache again twitched from the influence of an involuntary facial tic. "One of the Osos modified the flag's bear—a little nineteenth-century graffiti, if you will. It was a silent statement of rebuttal.

"When the flag arrived in Yerba Buena, someone there realized the significance of the kangaroo image and what it might mean for the other American officials in Northern California if Frémont's flagrant violation of the White House's orders were discovered. The Vice-Consul had been powerless to stop Frémont from starting the revolt, but he and Larkin feared they would be seen as complicit."

I found myself filling the name in almost automatically. "William Leidesdorff. He stole the original flag? But . . . why?"

Napis stepped behind me and scooped up the picture frame from the window seat.

"Look on the back of Frémont's picture," he said softly as he handed me the frame so that the already-loose cardboard backing faced upward.

My hands shaking, I lifted the backing to reveal the backside of the picture inside. With a halting voice, I began to read the charcoal pencil handwriting that creased the delicate paper.

"He bounces from one camp to the next, without plan or predictability, oblivious to the destruction he leaves in his wake, like the long thick appendage of his namesake. Sutter was the first to coin the nickname, but we all use it now. Pathfinder? That doesn't do the troublesome scamp justice. No, those of us who have come to know Captain Frémont call him by another name. We call him . . ."

Hesitating, I bit down on my lip.

Napis finished the caption for me. "They called him 'the Kangaroo.' "

And in that moment, I knew what Frank Napis was after. I knew where my uncle had hidden the original Bear Flag.

"I've got to go," I murmured under my breath as I dropped the Frémont picture on the window seat.

Still staring at Napis, I began to shuffle backwards. My hand reached behind my back for the door. As my fingers closed in around the handle, I pulled it open, anticipating the squeal of the hinges.

Napis didn't move to stop me. His face bore a strangely satisfied smile.

I never saw the man crouched outside in the

courtyard. By the time I heard the creak of wood from his step across the threshold, it was too late.

A light *thunk,* expertly delivered, pounded against the back of my head. As the floor rushed up to meet me, everything went black.

Chapter 59

THE STUFFED KANGAROO

I AWOKE TO a throbbing pain at the base of my skull and a cloth tied around my head, gagging my mouth. Blinking, I tried to take in my surroundings.

I was seated on a wooden chair with my hands bound behind me, my upper torso strapped to the seat back. I tried to wiggle my shoulders, but the rope was securely fastened.

From my limited vantage point, I appeared to be surrounded by an open room with walls constructed of the same stone composite as the fence that had bordered the courtyard outside the Larkin House. I was now located, I suspected, inside the stone shed I'd seen earlier on the opposite side of the property.

The front door to the building opened and the perpetrators of my current predicament entered carrying a large furry brown object. I watched as Frank Napis, still dressed as Clem, held the beast's shoulders, while Ivan Batrachos, his head shaved bald, hefted the feet. From the snippets of conversation floating in my direction, I gathered they'd brought the stuffed creature in from a vehicle parked around the corner.

"Nothing like a van to haul everything you need," Napis commented as Ivan righted the kangaroo on the floor about five feet in front of my chair.

I hadn't seen Ivan since he'd been apprehended and sent back to prison. His bald head was a shock, and he appeared to be a bit wobbly on his feet. He reached out for the kangaroo's shoulder as if to steady himself.

He noticed my open eyes. *"Luck whooze back wid us,"* he said, his speech noticeably slurred.

Napis glanced testily at Ivan and then turned to me. "I think you'll recognize this item," he said smarmily.

The stuffed kangaroo looked just like the one I'd found in the Green Vase not long after my uncle's death. The beast had been located inside a shipping crate lodged over the trapdoor to the basement. The kangaroo's pouch and mouth cavity had contained clues related to the Leidesdorff spider toxin and tulip extract antidote.

After all the inspection the kangaroo had received during that caper, I found it hard to believe the dead critter had still more secrets to reveal. But, as I reflected on my earlier conversation with Napis inside the Larkin House, I had to conclude that all clues pointed directly to the kangaroo.

"Your uncle found the original Bear Flag," Napis said, rubbing his hands together like a child waiting to open a present. "I know because he sent a letter to the Jackson Square Board asking me to provide an estimate of its value." Napis clenched his hands into fists. "He was taunting me—he knew I'd been looking for the same treasure for years."

I focused my attention on the kangaroo, trying to mentally block out both Napis's voice and the apparently inebriated Ivan, who was staggering circles around my chair.

After the ignominious ride to Monterey in the back of the van, the kangaroo's brown fur looked even more tamped down and mottled than before. Its right arm was crooked out, unnaturally, so that its paw rested on its hip—but it must have been bumped during transport. The arm didn't appear to have the same curvature I remembered.

"Given the frog episode last summer"—Napis paused for an exaggerated cough—"I felt the need to reinvent myself before returning to Jackson Square."

The kangaroo's black lifeless eyes looked out into the room, the dull gloss of the plastic surface reflecting the fading afternoon light from a window somewhere behind my chair. My gaze traveled down the beast's face to its mouth and the stitching that held its thick rubbery lips in place—the lips that I had sewn back together almost a year ago after I'd retrieved the package that had been stored inside . . .

Napis unclenched his hands and drummed his fingers against his chest. "When the Mayor arrived in Hawaii for his extended vacation, I arranged to make his acquaintance. It was only a matter of time before he took me on as his Life Coach. He graciously allowed me the privilege of hiring an assistant. My *apprentice* has been an invaluable resource. A free flow of information." Napis's lips flattened into a grimace. "Too much information, to be honest."

I stared at the kangaroo, trying to be sure of my observation. I had used a thick black thread to sew up the mouth of Oscar's kangaroo, but this creature's lips were secured with a clear vinyl cord.

"With Mr. Carmichael keeping me apprised of the situation at the Green Vase, I just had to bide my time, waiting for the right moment"—Napis paused and, with a deprecating sigh, nodded toward Ivan, who appeared to be growing more and more incapacitated by the minute—"waiting for my associate here to be released from prison."

As if acknowledging Napis's reference, Ivan pulled a small silver flask from the pocket of his leather jacket, unscrewed the lid, and swallowed a gulp of the liquid inside.

"A *leettle* celebration of my release," Ivan said tipsily.

"You couldn't wait another hour to start in on that?" Napis snapped.

"She looks *thersty*," Ivan mumbled. "Care if I offer her a sip?" he asked, tilting the flask in my direction.

Napis looked perturbed by this interruption, but he shrugged his shoulders dismissively. "If you must," he replied.

Ivan stepped toward my chair, bent down, and loosened the gag tied over my mouth. "You *wanna* celebrate with me, don't you? After all, you're the reason they sent me back to *preeson*."

I looked up at him incredulously. The last time Ivan had offered me a drink, it had been laced with the delusion-inducing spider toxin. I had no intention of voluntarily repeating the experience.

"Trust me," he whispered silently, his speech suddenly unimpeded as Napis paced an impatient circle around the kangaroo. Then, he took another slug from the container himself.

Ivan waved the flask in front of my face, and a dense floral scent accosted my nose. I glanced once more at the kangaroo and reluctantly opened my mouth. As Ivan tipped the flask to my lips, a cool flowery liquid trickled down my throat.

Napis stamped his foot irritably, indicating he'd been delayed long enough. "Ivan," he said crisply. "The shearers, please."

Chapter 60

A DARK NIGHT

THE MOON ROSE stealthily into the early evening sky, the bulk of its globe masked in darkness, a tiny illuminated sliver the only indication of its presence.

Not wasting any time, it quickly found its way to Jackson Square, sneaked up the street to the Green Vase antiques shop, and burgled through the keyhole of its iron-framed door.

Once inside, the moon paused to stroke a shadowy hand along the curving sides of a green vase positioned on the cashier counter before crossing the room to a stroller parked near the stairs at the rear of the store. A brief check beneath the unzipped net cover confirmed the carriage compartment was empty.

The moon heard a slight murmuring sound emanating from the second floor, so it crept up the staircase to the kitchen. From the top of the stairwell, it observed the following scene:

An elderly woman with curly gray hair sat at a worn wooden table in the center of the room, gently rubbing the distended stomach of a large male cat curled up in her lap. A grimy-faced man in a dirty green cycling outfit lay sprawled across the floor beneath the table, a droning snore buzzing from his gaping mouth. Perched on a second chair pulled up next to the table, a slender female cat listened attentively as Dilla Eckles read a story from a book with a shiny green cover written by a man named Samuel Clemens.

Every so often, Dilla looked up from the text and glanced at a furry figure standing in the corner of the kitchen. Intrigued, the moon slunk silently over to inspect the stuffed kangaroo.

The creature's dull glassy eyes looked vacantly out into the room. Its fur was dusty, mottled, and contained the slight scent of cedar chips. One of its arms kinked out so that its paw rested on its hip.

As the moon drew closer to the furry face, it saw that the critter's lips were sewn together with a distinctive thick black thread.

THE MOON PONDERED the scene from the kitchen as it rolled down the coast to the quiet streets of downtown Monterey. After a short hike along Calle Principal, it located the unlit exterior of the Larkin House.

Stepping cautiously through the front gate, the moon skulked around several overgrown bushes until it reached a rock-walled building on the opposite side of the courtyard. Crouched in the shadows outside the building's largest window, three figures cautiously monitored the proceedings inside: an elderly Asian man with a long spindly beard, a wrinkled old geezer in shredded overalls, and a cartoonish-looking character clad in a kangaroo costume.

Mr. Wang's chest wheezed for oxygen as he whispered into a walkie-talkie, issuing instructions to a squadron of police cars en route to the property. His free hand clutched the head of a cane, the top handle of which wobbled back and forth as he leaned his weight against it.

Harold Wombler stood next to Mr. Wang, grumbling under his breath as a light evening breeze ruffled through his loose-fitting overalls, exposing the red knit fabric of the long johns beneath. He pulled a silver flask from one of his many pockets, unscrewed the lid, and downed a mouthful of the container's clear liquid. Smacking his lips together, he handed the flask of tulip extract antidote to the last member of the group.

The man in the kangaroo suit unsnapped the fastenings to his headpiece and tilted it up to take a sip from the flask. The face beneath the headpiece was vaguely reminiscent of a man who had once run an antiques shop in San Francisco's historic Jackson Square neighborhood.

Sitting on the man's left shoulder was a hairless mouse in a furry green jacket. Several large purple petals appeared to have been stuffed into the front of the mouse's jacket. The petals' upper fringes formed a purple ruffle against the mouse's tiny chin.

The moon tilted its rays into the window of the stone building. Inside, a man in a rumpled linen suit crouched next to the bulging belly of a stuffed kangaroo. Frank Napis's thin lips curled beneath his false white mustache as he flicked on an electronic device and aimed it at the dead animal's bulging stomach.

A bald, brawny ex-con in a black leather jacket paced back and forth behind Napis and the kangaroo. The skin on Ivan Batrachos's shaved head crinkled apprehensively as he took a swig from his own silver flask. Then, wiping his lips, he bent down next to a brown-haired woman bound to a wooden chair and offered her a drink. With a grimace, she took a reluctant gulp—just as the whirring sound of an electronic razor filled the night air.

Chapter 61

THE HAIRLESS MOUSE

A FEW MINUTES later, Frank Napis bent over the now-bald stomach of the stuffed kangaroo.

"Aha!" he exclaimed, running his fingers over the beast's shaved belly, just above the opening to its pouch. "I knew it. You can see the outline of the package inside."

He pulled a small pocketknife from the coat of his linen suit and carefully traced it over the rough surface of the de-furred skin.

"Right about here should do it," he said, aiming the knife at a seam along the bulge.

Even though the animal had been dead for years, I still couldn't bear to watch. Wincing, I turned my head away from both Napis and the kangaroo. Out of the corner of my eye, I caught a glimpse of Ivan's face. For some reason, he appeared to be holding his breath. Instinctively, I did the same.

The next thing I heard was a loud *pop,* followed by a hissing release of aerosolized air. I whipped my face forward to see a reddish-brown plume rising from the kangaroo's punctured stomach. A dense, powdery mist began to fill the room.

Frank Napis spun around, his puffy face filled with rage. His entire upper torso was covered in a rust-colored ash. His hands reached out, as if to throttle me. He took one staggering step forward—before collapsing into a gasping heap at the kangaroo's feet.

Ivan coughed out a hoarse "sorry" before taking another pull from his flask and ducking out the front door.

"Hey!" I called out in frustration. "Don't leave me in here!" I nearly choked on the involuntary breath that followed. The ropes binding me to the back of the chair seemed only to tighten as I struggled against them.

Ivan had left the door slightly ajar. Through the half-inch opening, a trickling stream of water began to enter the room. The fluid quickly spread across the floor, soaking the kangaroo's feet along with Napis's linen suit.

I tried to convince myself the water was nothing

but the delusional side effect of the toxin that had just been released, but it was no use. An overwhelming sense of panic began to wash over me. I pulled my tennis shoes up to the rim of my chair, fearful of the drowning powers of the water that had begun to pool below.

Just then, a tiny hairless mouse wearing a furry green jacket poked his nose through the crack in the doorway. I watched, awestruck, as he began paddling across the room. His scurrying strokes were somewhat hampered by a packet of tulip petals stuffed into the front of his jacket, but he gradually made his way to my chair.

Nimbly, the mouse scaled the chair leg, scampered across my lap, and climbed up my left arm to my shoulder. He bent his chin down toward his chest and, with a flash of his tiny incisors, pulled a tulip petal out of his jacket. Gripping the oval-shaped disc in his front paws, he made a chittering mouse sound; then he rushed toward my face and pushed it through my protesting lips. The water on the floor began to recede as the tulip's flowery texture coated the inside of my mouth.

I had just started chewing on the mouse's last petal when the front door swung fully open. Harold Wombler appeared in the entrance, flapping his green baseball cap as if to help push the toxic dust from the room. Policemen in gas masks swarmed past him. The officers tromped loudly over to Napis's comatose form, rolled him onto a stretcher, and carried him outside to a waiting ambulance.

As the brown fog began to clear, I realized that a man in a kangaroo suit had knelt to the floor near my chair. Without hesitation, the mouse hopped onto the man's outstretched hand. After gently tucking the mouse into a pocket hidden in his furry chest, he unsnapped the head portion of the costume and lifted it up.

I found myself face to face with the man I'd last seen in the Sonoma Barracks posing as General Vallejo—minus the walrusy side-whiskers.

I managed one last word before passing out. "Oscar . . ."

Chapter 62

HOW TO MOON A CAT

A WEEK LATER, I pushed a cat-filled stroller down Jackson Street, heading toward the financial district. After the stroller outings in Sacramento and Nevada City, it seemed quite natural to be walking around San Francisco with my feline cargo.

Isabella now enjoyed being rolled around to visit and investigate new places—so long as her human driver obeyed her constant flow of navigational instructions. She hopped inside the carriage whenever she saw me preparing to go out. Rupert wasn't nearly as keen about the idea, but he refused to be left behind.

Of course, there were many places where it wasn't practical to bring the cats, but I had been assured they had a standing invitation to today's destination—which was more than I could say for myself. While my cats were welcome at Wang's flower shop, I was starting to get the distinct impression that I was persona non grata.

Mr. Wang had postponed meeting with me several times since I returned home from Monterey. It had taken a great deal of persistence on my part, but at last I had wrangled his agreement to see me that afternoon. Despite all of his stalling tactics, I was determined to get some answers about the events that had taken place in the Larkin House courtyard—and, most importantly, about my uncle.

However, as I rounded the curve of Columbus and crossed over into the financial district, I nearly turned back for the Green Vase. Monty stood on a street corner outside the Transamerica Pyramid building, cheerfully waving at passing vehicles and pedestrians. A small crowd had formed on the sidewalk in front of him; several cars honked their support.

Monty was milking his newfound celebrity status for all it was worth. State and local news media had covered each of his streaker-chasing episodes during the bike race, and the story had spread with each occurrence. His face was now instantly recognizable throughout Northern California, particularly in downtown San Francisco.

Meanwhile, the Mayor's Life Coach had disappeared, leaving the embattled politician without much-needed emotional guidance for his paralyzing frog phobia. Monty had already been promoted to fill the vacancy. His star, it appeared, would continue to rise.

Despite the throng of onlookers blocking Monty's view, I was unable to slip past unnoticed—the bright green cat stroller didn't help me blend in to the surrounding foot traffic. Grimacing, I returned a weak wave from the opposite side of the street and powered ahead at maximum speed.

Down the next block, I found the flower-filled facade of Wang's flower shop. Lilly greeted me at the entrance and ushered me inside. She glanced curiously at the cats inside the carriage as I guided the stroller's swiveling wheels around the front rack of flowers to the open area at the back of the store.

Wang sat in his wheelchair, waiting with a wan smile on his face. "Please come in," he said as I took a seat on a chair beside him.

After a brief exchange of pleasantries with the cats, he got right down to business. "I've just spoken with my former colleagues in law enforcement. Let me give you an update on Frank Napis."

Once he'd recovered from the paralyzing dose of spider toxin he'd received from the punctured stomach of the kangaroo, Napis had been transferred to a high security prison cell at San Quentin. This time, Wang assured me, Frank Napis had been put away for good. It would be a long time—if ever—before I would have to worry about the likes of him again.

The news brought a welcome sense of relief, but it wasn't the main topic I'd come to discuss with Wang.

"That's all well and good," I replied politely, "but I wanted to talk to you about—"

"Ivan Batrachos?" Wang cut in with a mischievous grin. "I understand he's very happy to be out of prison."

Despite abandoning me in the toxin-clogged shed in the Larkin House courtyard, Ivan had received special accommodations from the prosecuting authorities for his assistance in Napis's arrest. He had agreed to work with Wang and his police colleagues as part of a deal that gained him early release from his latest prison stint.

Wang had been hesitant about the arrangement at first and had worried about Ivan's true allegiances throughout the operation. But with Harold vouching for his former employee, Wang had reluctantly agreed to go along with the plan.

In the end, it turned out Ivan's motivations were based primarily on revenge. He had blamed Napis for triggering the parole violation that led to his last year of incarceration and had been more than willing to return the favor.

"Okay," I said, rubbing the back of my head in remembrance of the thunk I'd received from Ivan. He still hadn't redeemed himself in my book. "But what about—"

"The Bear Flag?" Wang broke in again.

"I gather that's not what was in the kangaroo?" I said with a frustrated sigh.

Mr. Wang's gray eyes flickered as he stroked his long wispy beard. "Now, why did you think the Bear Flag had anything to do with the stuffed kangaroo?"

"Well, there was the stoat reference in Oscar's DeVoto book," I offered. "And the writing on the back of the Frémont picture in the Larkin House . . ."

I stopped as Wang wheezed out a chuckle. He leaned over so that he could pull a piece of paper out of his pants pocket; then he handed it to me. I unfolded the sheet and scanned the contents. Printed inside was a copy of an article written by a group of Bear Flag historians, the original source of the writing Oscar had referenced. I read the familiar passage:

> Local Indians, passing through Sonoma after the revolt, ridiculed the animal on the flag, calling it a pig or a shoat.

"Shoat?" I sputtered. "What's a *shoat?*"

Wang nodded. "A shoat is a little suckling pig. When your uncle copied the text, he substituted a *t* for the *h*. He flagged the page in DeVoto and left the book out where Napis would be sure to see it. He knew Napis wouldn't be able to resist a clue to a treasure of such historical significance —especially since his interest had already been piqued by Oscar's letter to the Board."

"And the writing on the back of the Frémont photo?" I asked, feeling more and more deflated. "Calling him a kangaroo?"

Wang shrugged dismissively. "Consul Larkin's observations of Frémont's character certainly helped with the ruse."

I was growing rather exasperated by this conversation. "All right," I said briskly. "Enough beating around the bush. I came here to talk to you about my uncle."

Mr. Wang cleared his throat uncomfortably. His fingers fiddled with the wisp of his beard as he looked up at the ceiling. "Well, you see . . ."

Just then, the front door swung open and Monty paraded inside. "Greetings, friends and neighbors!"

NOT FAR AWAY from Wang's flower shop, in a narrow North Beach alley around the corner from Jackson Square, a man in a rumpled linen suit pulled a red bicycle to a stop behind a newly opened restaurant. Succulent smells floated out of the kitchen, the hallmark of the proprietor's signature dish, crispy fried chicken.

Whistling contentedly, Clem parked the bike

inside a small shed, which contained, in addition to a wide array of cycling equipment, a number of curiously shaped boxes and crates. After securing the lock on the door to the shed, he walked around to the front of the restaurant where an eager crowd of joggers had gathered.

A man in a dirty green baseball cap and shredded overalls worked his way through the crowd, handing out rubber masks and explaining the rules of the contest. After completing the designated route and returning their masks, each of the runners would be treated to a full meal inside the restaurant.

WILL SPIGOT AND Harry Carlin stood near the center of the group, stretching their limbs in anticipation of the coming sprint.

Spigot turned to Carlin, a wry grin on his face. "You know what they say, Harry?"

"What's that, William?" Harry had an impish look about him, as if he were a small child about to do something he knew was prohibited. His ruddy face exuded the joy of a schoolboy anticipating a coming prank.

Spigot pointed up at the sign of an Italian bistro next door to the chicken restaurant. "When in Rome . . ."

MONTY'S INTERRUPTION HAD doomed my chances of getting anywhere with Wang about the man in the kangaroo costume. Any voicing of an Oscar-related question within Monty's earshot would have set off an avalanche of ridiculous theories that I was unprepared, at this time, to refute. Reluctantly, I had allowed myself to be corralled out of the flower shop without a discussion of the Oscar topic.

Silently, I pushed the cat stroller back toward Jackson Square. Monty chattered away, oblivious to my frustration.

"I've got an important meeting with the Mayor this afternoon," he said, clearing his throat importantly. "A life coaching session in his office at City Hall."

With a groan, I tilted my head skyward, praying for a diversion that would spare me from another one of Monty's life coaching seminars, but there wasn't a cloud to be seen. I accelerated the stroller to a near jogging pace. Unfortunately, Monty had no trouble keeping up.

We finally rounded the corner of Jackson Street, and I sighed with relief at the sight of the Green Vase. As we neared the entrance, I noticed a cylindrical package leaning up against the front door. Monty continued to babble on about his life coaching skills as I picked up the parcel and studied the label, which contained my name scrawled in an eerily familiar handwriting. After a gulp of hesitation, I twisted off the end cap and carefully tilted the container sideways. The frayed edge of a rolled-up fabric slid out the opening.

"I'm trying some new techniques with him." Monty continued on with his one-sided conversation. "He's making great progress. Should be ready to tackle a whole tankful of frogs in another couple of weeks . . ."

Carefully, I unfurled a large rectangular flag. The cloth was limp and ragged, as if its fibers were barely holding together. A red cotton strip had been sewn across the bottom rectangular length. On the canvas's upper-left side was a five-pointed red star. An upright grizzly bear stood at the center of the flag, looking up at the star. The bear's rear end had been modified with the addition of a thick kangaroo tail.

"Good grief, that's hideous," Monty said, peering over my shoulder.

Before I had a chance to respond, a loud boisterous noise rumbled in the distance.

"Hello, what's that?" Monty asked, craning his neck toward Columbus.

Suddenly, a large crowd of joggers rounded the corner and turned toward us. There were twenty, thirty, maybe forty members in the group. Each one wore a rubber Mayor-emulating mask over his head. Their feet were clad with a wide variety of running shoes. There was nothing in the way of clothing in between.

I turned to look at Monty, who was in a state of shock. Even after his three previous streaker experiences, he was unprepared for this surprise attack. His eyes bulged, his mouth fell open, and his cheeks puffed out as if filled with water—he looked like an engorged mosquito. Then, he spun around and sprinted off down the street, waving his arms wildly in the air and hollering at the top of his lungs.

As I watched Monty's fleeing form, the crowd of naked runners swarmed around the stroller and quickly swept past, a mobile mass of flashing skin, bobbing rubber masks, and flopping body parts.

A moment later, the street fell silent. I looked down into the stroller and shrugged my shoulders. Isabella yawned, as if unimpressed by the display. She had sat stolidly in the stroller throughout the event. Her brother, however, had a different reaction entirely.

Rupert had huddled in the carriage compartment, his eyes crossed in confusion, his whiskers trembling with uncertainty. Now that the runners had passed, he turned a tight circle on the pile of towels in the bed of the stroller and started digging a hole.

AT THE RESTAURANT around the corner in North Beach, Clem and Harold waited on the front steps for the racers to return. As the pack pulled up panting and began to re-clothe, they related the responses of the tall, stringy man, the woman with the long brown hair, and the animals inside the stroller.

Harold slapped Clem across the back of his shoulders. "See, now that's what I'm talking about. That's how you moon somebody," he said with a proud grin. Then, picturing Rupert's confused face, he added, "That's how to moon a cat."

Center Point Publishing
600 Brooks Road • PO Box 1
Thorndike ME 04986-0001 USA

(207) 568-3717

US & Canada:
1 800 929-9108
www.centerpointlargeprint.com